Elizabeth Swados

Leah and Lazar

A NOVEL

SUMMIT BOOKS
NEW YORK

Leah and Lazar

1

Her Addiction

Leah had a radio alarm clock. Often she would set it for three A.M. She liked to lie in bed and imagine what part of her town was awake. She knew the big Mack trucks on the thruway were moving—like animals with lighted eyes. She knew the airplanes were flying in the sky looking down at the town as if it were a dented Christmas tree. She knew the nurses in the hospitals were wheeling around their double-decker trays. Now and then she would hear a car pass on the street outside her front window. She knew the driver was alone.

Most important, Leah liked to put on her terry-cloth robe and shove her feet into her soft slippers. Her long blond hair went in all directions from restless sleep. She'd pull it away from her eyes, out of her mouth and try to shove it behind her ears. It never stayed because it was so thick, so she'd nervously stuff it into the top of her nightgown so as not to lose time. She'd go out into her completely black house and feel safe counting everyone's sleep. Because she was very small and thin no one ever heard her. She'd step down the carpeted stairs and peer into the unlighted living room. Once her eyes were adjusted to the dark she could see outlines. And there it was. A tiny red glow, the size of a thimble. It was coming from an easy chair. The back of the chair faced where Leah stood. The glow came from her mother's cigarette as she sat there silently late at night. It was a lamp to her. Sometimes when she was halfway down the stairs she would see the glow pass in front of her like a firefly. It was extraordinary—knowing its source, but not seeing it. She would hear some movement in the kitchen and then watch the glow fly slow motion back to its chair. This was her happiest time. She didn't wish to interrupt or let her know she was there. It was enough just to feel her. She knew all her other reasons for waking were lies.

This was her nourishment. She'd smile to herself in the dark, go back up to her room and ease her head onto her pillow. As if she'd seen a star, she was now equipped to deal with her most impossible nightmares.

2

The Cure

When Leah was young her mother became ill. The family lived in a small city in upstate New York near Canada where winters lasted until the end of April and the summers ended abruptly with frosts in September. Crops were always dying unexpectedly in the farmlands outside the city. The little baseball teams were always calling off their games. Leah heard this on her brother's transistor radio. Lazar said they lived in America's version of Siberia. He looked after their mother, along with a German maid, because their father was busy at work. Lazar was much older than Leah. He was fourteen and she was nine. They lived in a large Victorian-style house with long narrow hallways, steep stairs and French windows. Mother often sat in the front den, looking out the picture window at the park across the street. She wore two or three sweaters and covered herself in a blanket. The den was furnished with antiques Mother had purchased at auctions. There was a barometer made out of dark wood. Leah often peered into the barometer taking in its arrows and North, South, East and West signs. The arrows never moved.

"Don't bother with that," Mother said to Leah. "It won't change anything."

Once or twice Leah saw a notebook on her mother's lap. It was a loose-leaf Lazar had given her to write down her thoughts. But the pages remained empty and Mother sat staring, smoking her long cigarettes, coughing and sighing. Leah wanted to take the notebook and draw in it or write letters, but she didn't dare. Her mother's silence was forbidding and Lazar had warned her never to bother Mother unless he or Mother indicated it was the proper time to do so.

By the time Leah came home from school Mother was in bed. Lazar, with the maid's help, fixed trays full of steaming soups and coffee. Leah didn't know if her mother ate. Mother's room was down a long hall and Leah could not hear what went on. Leah stayed alone with her door closed, leaning on her windowsill looking at the cars as they went up and down the street. She knew her father's car was a Buick convertible, silver with a black hood. She waited for it to pull up the drive. She hoped he'd bring her a present. Some jewelry on an elastic band or a bottle of glitter. She enjoyed watching the tires of different cars make patterns in the slush and at night she liked the gleam of the headlights on the wet black streets. She waited for screeches and crashes because there were many car accidents on the curve near the house.

Once a man had come to the front door bleeding. His forehead was split open like an eyelid. Leah thought perhaps the man was being chased by a murderer. Mother told Lazar not to let the man in—that it might be a ruse—the blood might be ketchup. Leah watched the man go to the neighbor's house next door. She was disappointed. She'd hoped he was a foreign dignitary and that he would fall in love with her while waiting for the ambulance, and that he'd wait ten years and marry her.

Lazar came by once or twice a week to report on Mother's progress.

"You can't talk to her yet," he'd say. "But she is reading an Agatha Christie novel and enjoying it immensely. She wants me to check your ears, but that would be undignified. Just promise me you'll wash them."

Leah always assured her brother that she would. She tried to keep her wild, unruly head of hair organized for his inspection. She tried to get the sleep from out of the corners of her wide, gray eyes. Lazar told her she was as beautiful as a mad Polish princess. He himself was often grubby, with his white socks and their black toes. His fingernails were dirty and his neck had lines of black on it as if he'd rubbed himself with newsprint. He was tall and skinny with thick glasses and crossed eyes. He moved nervously as if always impatient. Yet he was handsome in a proud, furious way. He brought Leah books to read, suggested outfits for her, and now and then gave her a short hug and a smacking kiss.

"This is a sad life for a girl such as you," he said to her. "But maybe you'll grow up to be Emily Dickinson."

"When will Mother be well?" Leah asked her brother.

"Maybe never," answered Lazar. "Or maybe she is quite well as she is."

The German maid laid out Leah's clothes, fixed her meals and picked her up from school. But she was no friend. She was a young immigrant and Mother had given her strict instructions on the etiquette of household help. Leah remembered that her mother had insisted that the young woman shave her armpits. "They smell less that way," said Mother, "and this is no farm."

Father came home late at night. Leah could hear him yelling. He often came in slamming the front door and cursing in a loud grating voice. He explained to the empty house that things at his office were bad. Lazar told Leah that Father had telephones to every country in the world. That Father was going to become King of Siberia. Once Father had taken Leah to his office. It was a large complex of rooms near a city of smoking factories. Leah had met a switchboard operator, a secretary and an errand boy. Father took Leah into the storeroom and let her take as many pens, pencils and yellow pads as she wanted. But he was rarely home and she knew him best by his car and his booming voice late in the night.

Leah wondered why Father yelled so much at Mother if she was sick. She could hear her mother's murmuring voice and her father's shouting. She could hear Lazar pacing in his room next to hers. She could hear him walk to his door, open it a little, close it and go back to his bed. She heard Lazar put records on his hi-fi, turn them off, turn on the radio, turn it off.

Often she heard the rain or hail outside her window. She didn't like it when it snowed because the snow fell quietly. Her parents' dialogue was a continuous music through all of this and neither she nor Lazar slept until it stopped.

The winter Leah's mother was most sick many doctors came and went. Leah measured their sizes and tried to guess their specialties. There was a short stubby man with a bald head and a mustache who carried a doctor's black bag and greeted her with cheerful jokes. There was a tall skinny doctor with a large hooked nose, gray greasy hair and a slight hump on his back. He carried no black bag and smiled at Leah with pale thin lips, but said nothing. Once Mother was visited by a woman doctor who wore a fancy matching skirt and jacket and a silk blouse with a large bow around the collar. She had spiked heel shoes and painted fingernails. The woman tried to talk to Leah, ask her about school, her friends, her favorite TV shows, but Lazar stood at Leah's door, glaring, with his arms folded, and Leah felt Lazar was telling her that to talk to this woman would be a form of treachery. So Leah answered in yesses and nos and the woman went away. Lazar rewarded Leah with a photograph book called *The Family of Man* filled with pictures of people from all over the world and lines of poetry printed in italics.

The winter was one of the worst in the city's history. The snow came up to Leah's thighs and often she couldn't get to school. Lazar turned on his radio every morning to hear if the Board of Education had canceled school for the term. The airport was closed. Poor people couldn't get heat. Once Leah thought she heard the news reporter talking about old people getting frozen in their cars. She imagined a white world inhabited by gray-haired, blue-faced characters from a horror show in Madame Tussaud's wax museum. Leah looked out her window at the vast gray-white desert. Her father came home earlier, his brown hat covered with white, his dark mustache covered with ice. Leah thought of the phrase "King of Siberia."

Mother had begun running through the house at night. Leah could hear her footsteps. The wind was loud and sang in many notes. Leah heard Father running after Mother shouting at her to slow down. Leah heard Mother tell Father that she was checking the heat. Leah could feel Lazar leaning up against his door. "Foolishness," she heard him hiss. "Foolishness."

Once after Mother and Father had been racing for a long while, Leah heard strains of music coming from the living room. The notes were broken and fell unevenly like the icicles that surrounded the house. Leah sneaked down the long stairs and saw her father seated at the little blond piano in the wide dark living room. Mother was leaning up against it. She was singing in a low gravelly voice. "The autumn leaves . . . drift by my window . . . Mother was singing. Father was playing with his eyes closed. Leah felt Lazar's breath on her back. Lazar said nothing. He began to sway a bit and hum along. He put his arms around Leah's waist and pushed her gently back and forth. Then he turned her around and lifted her hand into his. They danced on the narrow stair while their parents sang. Lazar lifted Leah up and put her feet on his. He danced her up and down.

In the morning Lazar and Father greeted each other but did not speak. Leah, Lazar and Father heard Mother in the attic. She was checking for cracks where the wind could come through. Lazar said she was concerned about insulation.

The bad snow passed, but the winter went on. Mother did not leave her room at all. She did not even visit the den with the picture window and the barometer. Once Leah heard sobbing from Mother's room. Leah was compelled to go and see the picture that went with the sound. She stood at the door. She saw her mother on her knees on the plush blue rug. Her mother was in a nightie and she was pounding her fists on the floor. Lazar was kneeling beside her. He was in his pajamas, trying to hold her. Father was standing above them in a suit. His fists were clenched. Mother was screaming in a scratchy voice. Leah thought she sounded like a wildcat. Lazar was trying to hold her, but Mother pulled violently away and tried to claw him. Father lifted Mother up from under her arms. Mother kicked and Leah could see underneath her nightie. Leah closed her eyes and let out a gasp. She felt the three of them stop and look at her. She opened her eyes. They were frozen there. Then Father threw Mother on the bed, shoved Lazar out, and closed the door behind him.

Lazar walked quickly past Leah and Leah ran after him. She put her hand on Lazar's shoulder. He pushed it away and ran into his room. Leah went to hers. She went to the window and waited anxiously for an ambulance to arrive. But none came. Lazar knocked on her door. "It's the spring," he said to Leah, not entering the room. "It's never coming this year. It's like Scandinavia. The earth is going to close in on us. Soon there will be only one hour of sunlight per day and that will be obscured by the fog."

Leah looked at her brother's shaking body and his sweating face. She wasn't scared by what he said but by how he was behaving.

"I just thought you should know," said Lazar.

Leah and Lazar stood staring at each other. Music came from their parents' bedroom. Father had turned on the radio. Leah knew it was an FM station that played jazz. Father liked Benny Goodman. Leah and Lazar went toward the music. They got to their parents' door and heard muffled humming from inside. Lazar opened the door a crack. He peeked in and then abruptly closed the door again. The sweat was pouring down the sides of his face and ears.

"They're dancing," he said to Leah. "Don't look."

Lazar began to cry and ran down the stairs and out of the house. He was still in his pajamas. He had no shoes on. Leah went to the den window and saw her brother jumping through the melting snow farther and farther into the interior of the park. There was no sun. The trees were bare, wet and dark. She saw her brother's silhouette against the smoky background of the sky. Many cars were going by on the glistening street. It was late afternoon, but all their headlights were on. The bad weather made a traffic jam and the cars were honking their horns so Leah couldn't hear what Lazar was screaming.

The family was in the lounge waiting for their flight to Miami. Father's business was going well. He often talked at dinner about the "intellectual acrobatics" of dealing with factory workers, getting high productivity at low cost, selling his wares in a competitive market. Leah was still not sure what Father did. But he had bought Mother a blue evening dress made out of a shiny fabric. The dress had sequins covering its blouse and thousands of pleats in its skirt. Mother bought white satin high-heeled shoes and had them dyed to match. She also owned a mink coat. Now they were going on vacation.

The flight was delayed because it was late February and snowing heavily. The sky was blocked off with what looked like bags of black clouds. Mother bought a carton of Kents and several movie magazines, and sat silently reading, not looking out the wide frosted windows from which came the whining and squeaking of the airplanes. Leah stood with Lazar looking at the planes.

"They're veritable dinosaurs," said Lazar. "They may have engines, but God gave them minds of their own."

Leah had never flown before.

"Do you know the allotment theory?" asked her brother.

Leah replied that she didn't.

"God gives us each a number of plane flights which he has filed away in his heavenly index," said Lazar. "If we unknowingly go over our allotment we crash."

Leah was used to her brother's horror stories, but could not help looking anxiously at the sky.

"For instance," said Lazar, "I've flown once to Washington and once to Cleveland. Let's say God only put two allotments in my file. That means I shouldn't be getting on this plane."

Lazar didn't look at Leah, but continued.

"Or you. Say you're not meant to fly at all. That means there's no possibility of our surviving this trip."

Leah cringed. Lazar went on.

"The curse of the situation is that, on any given flight, any *one* passenger may have reached the end of his or her allotment. That means a hundred innocents with files stocked full of thousands or millions of possible airplane rides could perish because of a single person's fate." Lazar kissed Leah on the cheek. He was in a jubilant mood.

"Remember, sweetie," he said, "there are *no* accidents."

Leah was relieved to see Father coming out of the coffee shop. He was dressed strangely. Bright madras pants for Miami and a camel's hair winter coat for the cold.

"How many allotments do you think Daddy has?" she asked.

"Oh endless endless endless endless endless," Lazar replied bitterly.

Father had bought gifts for his family. He gave Lazar an oversized plastic comb, a foot long with a picture of an airplane on it. He gave Leah a stiff stuffed poodle with a rhinestone collar and yellow eyes. He'd bought Mother a necklace made from seashells and fake pearls. For himself he'd purchased a pipe that was carved in the face of an old man. Mother didn't look up. She continued reading.

Father was jaunty. "Ready for the voyage?" he asked. His voice was loud and Leah felt Lazar stiffen.

The storm did not appear to be letting up. But a voice came over the loudspeaker and announced that the flight to Miami was boarding. Mother looked up and glared at Father.

"Come on," said Father. "Five hours and we'll see palm trees."

Mother said nothing and walked solemnly toward the gate. Lazar held her hand. Leah walked behind them. Father walked behind her.

"Wait," Mother said, and all four stopped. She dipped her hand into the straw shoulder bag she was carrying and pulled out a metal flask. She unscrewed its top and tilted it to her mouth, closing her eyes. Leah smelled something strong and sweet.

"Oh Christ," said father.

The plane was dark, lit only by tiny little eyes of lights. The interior was cold. Leah thought it smelled funny. She could hear the snow turned to loud rain pelting against the box-shaped windows.

The captain's voice came over the loudspeaker. Leah liked his attitude. He sounded like William Holden when he played fighter pilots in World War II movies, full of confidence and jokes. He told the passengers that the takeoff would be a little choppy at first, but soon they'd be flying above the weather and they would see the sun. Leah was sitting next to Lazar and Mother and Father had the two seats in front.

"You *see?*" Leah heard Father say to Mother and then she saw him slap Mother's thigh.

"Pilots have allotments too," whispered Lazar.

The plane began to taxi to the runway. Leah watched the rain streak the windows. A stewardess was talking about oxygen and safety exits. Leah studiously found her proper exit, checked her seat belt, looked for the compartment from which the yellow mask would fall, and felt safe. Lazar was holding on to the armrests. He was so rigid that Leah could see the veins in his forehead. She heard Mother speaking rapidly in a low voice to Father. Father laughed a phony, hearty laugh at first and then Leah heard him growl.

"Impossible," he said to Mother. "This is altogether *too much."*

Mother kept chanting nonstop. She was murmuring directly into Father's ear. Lazar was in a trance, clutching the armrests and clenching his teeth.

The plane made its stop to wait for takeoff and Leah was shocked to see Father bolt out of his seat. He walked quickly and grimly to the rear of the plane where the stewardesses sat. Two stewardesses came forward and knelt in the aisle beside Mother and talked comfortingly to her. Mother was weeping into a Kleenex. Leah felt the seat in front of her shake with Mother's sobs. The other passengers in their area turned and looked at Mother and the kneeling stewardesses. It seemed to Leah that they were annoyed. One stewardess, a brunette wearing a little blue cap, walked toward the cockpit. Leah was grateful to see that she had no expression on her face. The plane was completely silent. Leah looked over at Lazar in the next seat. His head was still back and his eyes were closed, but his hands were relaxed. He seemed to be asleep. The pilot's cheerful William Holden voice came over the loudspeaker. He explained to the passengers that there was an ill passenger aboard and they had radioed to the tower to send a car. He assured everyone that the wait would not be a lengthy one. The passengers on the plane looked more sympathetically at Mother. They began talking among themselves. Leah felt grateful for the noise. She couldn't register that the pilot was speaking about Mother and imagined a man with a heart attack or a woman giving birth. She saw the spinning red light of an airport car pull up beside the plane and a white truck carrying stairs. Leah still didn't believe it was Mother who had caused the delay until she saw Father stand up and heard him quickly say, "Come on, children."

Father's face was ashen. His eyes were dark. He avoided the gaze of the other passengers. Mother had stopped crying and smiled sweetly at the stewardesses and thanked them at the plane's door. Lazar bowed into the aisle and shouted, "Have a bon voyage." Some of the passengers waved at Lazar and told him thank you.

"Look at this runway," Mother said. They were standing in the pouring rain waiting to get into the emergency car. "It's how I imagine the salt flats of Nevada to be. Or the Sahara Desert. It's so wide and open and desolate. Some big plane'll come pouring out of the sky and descend on us like a vulture. There's beauty in this."

Mother was weaving a bit. Lazar didn't dare answer Mother because Father was furious. But he nodded at her. His glasses were steamed from the cold, the wet and his own perspiration. Leah felt sleepy. Father sat in the front of the car next to the driver-mechanic. Father's head was in his hands. The driver-mechanic told stories about emergency landings and people sliding on tubes out of airplanes into white foam. They drove along the wide dark flat which was lit on and off by the flashing beams from the tower. Mother looked happily out the window. "Like the Sahara at night," she said. Mother put her arm around Lazar. Leah watched the fat plane bump off the far end of the runway and ascend into a pile of floating clouds. Then it was gone.

"Trains are sexual symbols," said Lazar. He was eating a piece of French toast and having difficulty trying to put a whole triangle into his mouth at once. The powdered sugar stayed on his lips and he looked like a clown. Leah and Lazar were seated at a small table in the dining car. They were on the third day of their journey. Leah watched the flat gray land whizz by and looked at the tiny brick houses, their string of television antennas and empty streets. She shivered. They'd passed through Rochester, Syracuse, Utica, Canajoharie, Troy, Albany, and Newburgh on the way to New York

City and south to Miami. Father said the trip would take about five days. He was in his sleeping compartment, reading. Mother was with Lazar and Leah in the dining car, but she was seated at another table reading a mystery novel. Now and then she looked up at the two of them and smiled.

"It's the motion of the train," Lazar continued. "The going forward but the moving back and forth." He wiped his mouth with a soggy napkin. "I read that somewhere. Or maybe I made it up."

Leah had a room all to herself. The bed pulled out of the wall like an ironing board, the toilet was in a closet and there was a small couch next to the window. A black porter came each morning to put Leah's bed back into the wall. He had a big smile and a bright red uniform. "You tell me each morning what day of the month it is," he said to her. "I forget, what with my traveling back and forth all the time." Leah made sure to be awake and dressed when the porter arrived. She sat primly in her window seat and watched him make her bed. Then she'd tell him the day of the month and slip one of the powdery one-dollar bills Mother had given her from the bottom of her change purse to "tip the help."

Father kept to his own room, smoking a pipe, reading and writing notes to himself on a yellow legal pad. He'd brought a lot of work for the trip. He joined them at dinner the first night and talked nonstop through the potato soup, roast beef and apple pie. He told Leah and Lazar about when FDR died and how they put his coffin on a train with red, white and blue flags. He said a band on the caboose played "Hail to the Chief." Father told how masses of men and women followed the slow-moving train through small towns weeping and crowding the tracks. Lazar tapped his fingers impatiently while Father talked on and on. He banged in rhythm with the train's chugging. Father glared at Lazar's fingers, but they didn't stop. Mother blinked her eyes slowly and constantly as if warding off a heavy sleep. Father fin-

ished his stories about FDR and growled at the apple pie
dessert as if it were his only companion, a boring, dissatis-
fying old woman he'd been assigned to. "I don't sleep well on
trains," he said. "It's the noise or the lights or something."

"Please excuse me," said Father and he left the dining car
for his room.

"I always do," said Mother.

Father took his meals alone in his room for the rest of the
train ride.

At breakfast Lazar ordered a second helping of French
toast. Mother was still at the table across the way, drinking
coffee and reading her mystery. Leah decided to go exploring.

"If you want to escape," her brother told her, "remember
to do a somersault when you land. And try to aim for a
cornfield. That way you won't break your neck." He
smoothed Leah's crumpled sweater (she had trouble dressing
in the cramped sleeper) and he gave her a wet kiss on her
cheek. "That's how Woody Guthrie did it," said Lazar. Leah
left the dining car self-consciously. "Don't forget to write,"
shouted Lazar. Mother did not look up.

Leah slipped sideways through the crowded coach-cars.
She held her breath when she crossed the metal divide between two cars. She heard the screeching of the wheels and
the grating of the tracks. She felt the wind from the motion.
The air was cold, but it felt good. She was stuffed up from
the muggy heat of her compartment and sleepy from lack of
exercise. She enjoyed making the daring cross from one car
to another and wanted to find the caboose Father had talked
about. Or at the very least she hoped to discover the baggage
car where Lazar said they kept puppies in cardboard boxes.
Leah was becoming brave enough to stay on the metal between the coaches and hold on to the railing. She looked out
over the dreary Southern towns and knew she could never
jump without breaking her neck. Standing there was enough
for her. The porter came through and scolded her. "It's

against regulations, miss, and I'd be to blame if something happened to you." Leah was sorry the porter was disturbed and quickly made her way through the coach to the next opening in between the cars. She was shocked to see two men leaning on the rail smoking cigarettes and drinking from a large bottle in a paper bag. One of the men was blond and balding with a bright red face and blue eyes. He had a large belly and his khaki pants hung below it. His eyes were bleary and bloodshot. The other man was small and lean and dark. He had stubble on his chin and gleaming black eyes. He wore blue jeans and a blue-jean jacket with the collar up. Leah thought he was handsome. And he was more cheerful than the blond man. The dark man smiled at Leah when she came on the platform.

Leah decided to go into the next coach lest the porter find her again.

"Stay, missy, stay," said the dark man. He had a Southern accent. Leah thought he was her father's age.

The blond man said nothing but cursed and spat on the ground outside the rail.

"You're as pretty as a girl can be," said the dark man. "What's your name anyway, sweetheart?" he asked.

Leah told him her name was Millicent.

"Millicent?" The dark man smiled (he had bad teeth under his strong lips). "Why I've a daughter name's Mary. Both M's, huh?"

Leah nodded. She'd never heard a Southern accent before. She liked the dark man.

"Want some gum, Millicent?" asked the dark man. He reached into his blue-jean pocket with one hand and pulled out a double pack of Wrigley's Spearmint. Leah saw that the man's hand was very dirty and covered with cuts and bruises. She tried not to stare. She said nothing.

"No poison in the gum, Millicent. Your mother tell you not to take candy from strangers?"

Leah nodded.

"Well you're a good girl. But take a piece anyway. It'll make a lonely daddy feel glad."

Leah reached for the gum.

"Cool it, Bob Roy," said the blond man. His voice was gruff and hoarse. The blond man looked scornfully at Leah. "Just the way a child gets herself in deep trouble," said the blond man. "Carrying on every which way on a dangerous stoop with strangers. Where's your mother?"

Leah saw suddenly that the dark man's other wrist had a large metal bracelet on it. And attached to the bracelet was a chain. The opposite end of the chain was hooked into the belt of the blond man. The blond man also was carrying a gun.

The dark man grinned sheepishly at Leah and shrugged. "I'm a convict, Millicent," he said. "This here man is takin' his puppy dog for a walk."

"Bob Roy's going to the penitentiary in Georgia," said the blond man. He was very Christian and stern. "He broke the law, little girl. You shouldn't be taking any kinda gum from him."

The dark man snarled at the blond man. "It's just gum," he yelled.

Leah couldn't take the gum but didn't want to leave. The dark man smiled quickly at Leah and said, "Maybe you could write me in the penitentiary. Lotsa fellas have pen pals."

The blond man snorted.

"Fuck you, Bob Roy. She don't look old enough to write."

"Sure she can write," said the dark man. "You can write, can't you, sweetheart?"

Leah nodded that she could.

The dark man sighed sadly. "I'll be there long enough," he said. He leaned in toward Leah and pulled a bit on the blond man's belt. Leah and the two men were being shaken around by the turns of the train. Leah was afraid she'd fall into the dark man.

"I broked the law, Millicent," he whispered to Leah. "And I regretted it the moment it was done." Tears came to the dark man's eyes.

"Don't start your sob story, Bob Roy," said the blond man.

"It was temporary insanity, Millicent," said the dark man. "But he don't believe me."

"Hah," said the blond man. He looked bored.

"God's my witness," said the dark man. "And there are two sides to every story. Take my address and I'll write you all about it." The dark man winked at Leah. "And I'll send you a slice of gum."

The dark man took a pencil from his back pocket, leaned against the shaky door of the train and scribbled his address on the inside of a matchbook.

"Sometimes they have visiting days. You can come on down to Georgia and meet my Mary."

He handed Leah the matchbook. She took it in her sweaty hand. The blond man got impatient.

"Child, you're enough to make a mother cry," he said. "Get outta here now or I'll pull this here emergency brake."

Leah yanked hard on the heavy metal door. When she got inside the coach she tucked the matchbook inside the top of her knee sock. She was terrified Mother or Father or Lazar would find out what she'd done. She was also afraid the dark man would find out where she lived and, if he escaped from the penitentiary, he'd come to get her. She worried that the officials in the penitentiary would learn about her from the blond man and report her to her local police. She knew if she could get rid of the matchbook, she'd be saved. She walked fast through the coach and out onto the next landing. She checked all around her. When she was sure she was alone, she threw the matchbook over the side and felt an immense relief. She didn't stop to watch it fall.

Leah found her way back to the dining car. Lazar and Mother were sitting together laughing and playing a game

of dots. The shaking train made it difficult for them to draw
their lines straight. Leah stood near them awhile, peering
over their shoulders and taking in the safety from their
smells and body heat. She realized not much time had
passed at all. The morning wasn't over yet. She took a seat at
Mother's old table and stared out the window. The Savan-
nah was coming into view. It was green and brown and full
of cargo boats. Leah hadn't seen a river before this trip. She
stared at it hard and said "river river" to herself as if she
were learning a language. She tried not to hear that the
wheels of the train sounded like chains.

Father had made reservations at the Diplomat Hotel in
Hollywood Beach, Florida. Leah liked the palm trees outside, the wide carpeted hallways inside, the elevators whose
buttons lit up, the gift shops, the restaurants and the miniature golf course. There were two swimming pools—a shallow
square one for children and a large curved one with blue and
white dividers and two diving boards. One of the diving
boards was as high as a tower and Leah spent much time
watching the boys with sun-bleached hair cannonball off it.
She didn't dare climb on it herself.

Leah was fair-skinned so Mother made her wear a T-shirt
over her bathing suit. The T-shirt got soaked when she went
into the children's pool and clung to her skin. She wanted to
take the T-shirt off, but Lazar said she would get bubbles on
her skin if she did. Lazar bought a pair of mirrored sunglasses and smeared his nose with white cream. He wore
flowered swimming trunks and a matching terry-cloth jacket.
He had rubber thongs on his feet and Leah saw that her
brother's toes were swollen as round as tulip bulbs. His big
toes were painted orange with Mercurochrome. "Ingrown
toenails," Lazar told her. "Makes it impossible to swim." For
that reason Lazar refused to go into the water. He stayed in
his hotel room till midafternoon ordering turkey club sandwiches from room service and he used the phone with the red

message light to make reservations for Youth Trips to Parrot Jungle and the Seaquarium. Leah didn't know if her brother went on these trips. He didn't seem to like the sun. She did know that he went to Arthur Murray dance classes in the late afternoon. His toes didn't seem to bother him then. Lazar read to her from the brochure—"Learn the dances from the islands," he said. "The fox-trot, mambo, merengue, samba and cha-cha. Glide around our ballroom floor with our own professional instructors. Enjoy our cocktail hour and appetizer buffet. Come alone or bring your mate." Lazar invited Leah to join him, but Father ordered Leah not to go.

"Get some breeze and air and salt, dammit," said Father. Father swam laps in the large pool and played golf near the hotel. Mother slept late in the mornings and lay on the terrace of her room in a one-piece bathing suit with no straps. Mother covered herself with a clear oil and put pink plastic spoons over her eyes. "She's baking," Lazar explained. Mother took her meals in her room and went for walks late at night on the golf course. "This is her cure," said Lazar.

One morning Father came to the children's pool and shouted for Leah to get out. "You'll never guess who teaches swimming here," said Father. "Buster Crabbe!" Father explained to Leah that Buster Crabbe was an actor who played Tarzan on TV and was an Olympic swimming champion. "I want you to learn how to dive off the high board."

Father proudly introduced Leah to the man with massive shoulders and strange white teeth. He had tan hairy arms and he wore a thick gold ID bracelet. His fingernails looked polished and his hair did not seem real. "Hello there, little sweetheart," said Buster Crabbe. Leah wondered why the swimming teacher was wearing flowered white underpants and not proper swimming trunks. His eyes were a glassy green. He lifted Leah in his big arms and began climbing the tower of the high diving board. Leah looked down and saw the top of Father's new straw golf hat. Mother and Lazar were nowhere to be seen.

Buster Crabbe coaxed Leah out onto the diving board. She crawled, lying down, pulling herself on her belly. The boys with sun-bleached hair were waiting impatiently to do their cannonballs. Leah felt embarrassed. She was also afraid she might flip over and fall flat on the water and crack. Buster Crabbe was wiggling his fingers at her for her to come farther and farther. It felt like a dream to Leah. She reached the end of the diving board and the big man lifted her up in his arms and held her out over the water. Leah closed her eyes. She smelled hairspray. "Pull up your knees," growled Buster Crabbe. Leah felt the man huffing as if she'd become too heavy for him. His ID bracelet was pressing on her back and it hurt. The next thing Leah knew she felt herself falling in the air and then the water hit her like a slap. She opened her eyes and saw her T-shirt filled with water like a white balloon. Her legs looked fuzzy and pale. She saw the sun reflecting on the greenish-blue surface and wondered if there was air on top if it. She'd never had her head underwater before. She opened her mouth and took in bitter-tasting liquid. She couldn't cough. She felt an enormous thump next to her and saw Buster Crabbe. He was moving in slow motion. Leah thought he was an enormous goldfish. He put one of his big fins around her and yanked her to the surface. Then he lifted her onto the edge of the pool.

Leah felt herself shaking. Her teeth were chattering. She worried they'd break on each other. Father was next to her and wrapped her in an immense Diplomat Hotel beach towel. "Bravo," he said gravely. Buster Crabbe applauded her from the water. His hair looked as though it had fallen sideways on his head. Leah vomited. Father called one of the poolside waiters to clean it up. He told Leah to go to her room and change into a dry bathing suit.

Leah felt as if her legs were out of control. She was kicking Father. She heard herself coughing and screeching. In the next moment she was waking up in her hotel room bed. She was in a cotton nightgown and her hair was damp. Music was coming from Lazar's room next door. Leah got out of bed, put on a dry bathing suit, remembered to take the big plastic key and followed the sounds of the music. It was loud because Lazar's door was open. A tune with horns and drums and piano was playing. Leah saw that Mother and Lazar were dancing. He was counting out loud. "One two, skip hop turn," he was saying. Lazar was dressed in a white suit. Mother wore her blue dress with the sequins and the matching dyed shoes. She had on lipstick and diamond earrings. She followed Lazar gracefully and laughed when he made a mistake. She had a cigarette in her hand that rested on Lazar's shoulder. She counted with Lazar and they dipped and turned together and moved their hips at the same time. Leah tried to stay behind the door out of sight, but Lazar saw her.

"Mother's much better," he said lightly. "She's helping me practice for the mambo contest."

"Lazar's the best in his class," said Mother.

The two of them kept practicing.

"I dove off the high diving board today," said Leah.

"How brave," said Mother in rhythm to the mambo.

"How very brave," answered Lazar in the same rhythm.

"When's the mambo contest?" asked Leah.

"At midnight tonight," answered Lazar. He was swiveling his hips and crossing one foot over the other. Leah had no idea that Lazar could move so well. He looked like a grown man on a television special. Mother was only a little taller than he. They were engrossed in each other's steps.

Leah didn't know what time it was. There was no clock in her room and she didn't own a watch. Lazar had explained that this was because the management didn't want the customers to stop buying drinks. "They're trying to create a vacation time zone," he said.

Leah went back to her room and pulled a large beach

towel off the bathroom rack. She went out to the pool. She knew it was late because no one was there. The pool was lit up, however, with colored floodlights and phony lanterns with glass flame bulbs inside. Leah took a beach chair near the high diving board. She lay back and stared at the tower a long time. Then she fell asleep. She dreamed she was climbing the tower in the pitch black of the night. She crawled out onto the diving board and there was a strong hot wind blowing. It nearly blew her off. She thought she felt someone behind her and turned and saw the criminal Bob Roy from the train. She dreamed it again and turned around and there was no one there. But she did not dare to climb back down because she was afraid she'd fall and crack on the concrete. Or she was sure Bob Roy was waiting for her. She looked down over the pool and saw a deep dark pit. She told herself not to, but she jumped off the diving board and began falling a long slow fall which had no end. She became too frightened so she adjusted her dream and landed in the water. She made no sound and felt nothing wet. The pool was black ink. She was under the surface and could see the colored lights. She swam toward the lights but could not get to the place where the water became air. She saw another figure under the water, but it wasn't Buster Crabbe. It was Mother in her blue dress. The sequins were glittering from the reflection of the light on the water. Mother's blue skirt billowed all around her like a sail, her wavy hair moved slowly in the water like golden weeds. Mother's legs were moving up and down. She looked as if she were dancing a mambo. Leah waited for Mother to come and save her but Mother was smiling and sinking beneath her. Mother was waving. Leah forced herself to wake up. The perimeters of the pool area were a blur. She thought she saw her mother's dress again walking away from the pool toward the golf course. She couldn't see the hair or face of the woman in the dress. The woman was weaving slightly and walking quite alone, but with a real destination in mind. Leah wanted to sit up, get onto her feet and follow, but she couldn't. She fell into a dreamless sleep. When she awoke she was startled to see a man in a white suit sitting on the edge of her beach chair. Then she realized it was Lazar. He was looking out in the direction of the golf course and tapping his knees nervously with his fingers.

"Did you win the mambo contest?" asked Leah.

"No," said Lazar. His voice was quiet and sad. "My partner was this middle-aged lady from Cleveland named Mrs. Freed. She wore a red satin dress and had platinum hair all teased up like a nest. She looked like a cocktail waitress. Mother and Father were there and they were watching. Mrs. Freed and I made it all the way to the finals, but she got drunk and began making certain kinds of remarks to her friends about my age. I tried to keep my end of it up but she lost her concentration. Some couple from Brooklyn won. They looked like a miniature orthodox rabbi and his wife. The emcee was the judge and he was a dishonest and misguided character. You know who he was?"

Leah shook her head.

"Buster Crabbe," said Lazar. "The hit man Father hired to try to drown you this afternoon."

Leah reached for her brother's hand but he was preoccupied and began biting his nails.

"When Buster Crabbe was presenting the silver cup and the champagne bottle I grabbed the microphone from him and stated that I wanted to lodge a protest on behalf of the younger generation. The people in the ballroom just laughed. They were all very drunk and big fans of has-been TV idols. I tried to expose the whole thing. I said I thought it was scandalous to make art competitive and to appoint figureheads with no background as our critics. I asked the crowd if they thought Buster Crabbe could mambo as well as me or Mrs. Freed for that matter. I asked the dancers in the ballroom to think about Buster Crabbe's reasons for

choosing who could mambo better than the next person. I
implored them to explore in themselves what they thought a
good mambo really was. I warned them that their vacations
were being poisoned with the very values they'd sought to escape. I prophesied a time when younger wilder versions of
the mambo would prevail and men like Buster Crabbe
would be delegated to the yellowed pages of antique *TV
Guides*."

Leah thought her brother was being an awfully bad sport.
She also knew he'd gone off. He always talked like Father
when he went off.

"What did Mother and Father do?" she asked.

Lazar closed his eyes. He was having a bad thought.

"Oh they left midway through my speech," he answered.
"And besides, some conspirator from the hotel management
turned off my microphone before I'd hardly begun. No one
heard me. They were dancing to the band and shaking
hands with the judge."

Lazar was fixed on the direction of the golf course.

"Let's go for a walk," he said to Leah. "If you feel well
enough."

Leah followed sleepily behind her brother. He seemed to
be in a hurry. They walked down the steps from the pool
area and on to the winding pathway toward the golf course.
The golf course was completely dark and stretched like a
long road into blackness.

"Doesn't this remind you of the runway back home?"
asked Lazar.

Leah didn't answer. Something had caught her eye. She
saw a flare of blue fabric in the distance moving back and
forth like a thin flag. The figure was sailing gracefully and
quickly like a sapphire ghost. Lazar saw it too and stood
with Leah absolutely still, watching it reverently. As the figure moved in and out of the trees and into the sand traps
and onto the green Lazar put his arm around Leah. The fig-

ure began circling around the marker near the putting hole. Leah moved closer to Lazar and tried to put her head on his chest.

"Don't celebrate," said Lazar. "This doesn't mean we're friends."

Leah watched the figure disappear down the next fairway.

The next morning Father knocked on Leah's door. It was very early, but he was dressed in his full uniform for golf. This day it was a bright yellow pair of cotton pants, a yellow and green striped T-shirt and a madras green, yellow and red cap. Leah didn't dare tell Father his cap didn't match. He already seemed angry. "Want a ride in the golf cart with me?" Father asked. He smiled, but his eyes were dark. "Come *on*," he said. "I'll let you drive." Leah dressed quickly. Father waited outside her door. She heard him shifting his weight from leg to leg, heard him sigh, felt his impatience. She pulled a T-shirt over her head and put on a pair of shorts with an elastic waist so she wouldn't take time in buttoning or zipping things. Her sneakers took more time. She tried to put them on with the laces tied, but the backs bent underneath her heels. She had to take them off, untie them, shove them on, tie them up again.

"Let's move along," said Father. "I want to get there before the crowds come."

Leah slipped her key in her waistband and joined Father.

Father walked several steps ahead of Leah and she followed him to the pro shop where the golf carts were parked.

She enjoyed pressing on the accelerator and brake and she and Father shared the little black steering wheel. They went along for several holes in the damp morning air without speaking. Leah didn't watch Father play; she spent her time memorizing which was the accelerator and which was the brake. She was afraid she'd get them confused. The golf course was long and flat and had several bridges which crossed over swampy creeks that were dug several feet down from the surface of the fairway. "I'll bet there are alligators down there," said Father. The golf carts weren't allowed to go over the bridges; paths had been paved that made narrow circles around them. After seveal more holes Father began to lecture Leah on the game of golf. He told her the rules, the object of the game, the difference between the woods and the irons, how to recognize the putter.

Leah tried to act interested, but she wanted to concentrate on her driving. She remained silent and kept saying to herself, "Left is the brake, right is the accelerator."

Father raised his voice. "You damn well ought to talk to me a little," he said. "When I get back to the wars, we won't have any time. Make a speech for me. Sing a song. Tell me your views on life." Leah remained silent. Father had taken his hand off the steering wheel and the responsibility of where to go was difficult for Leah. Father's face became red, his eyes cold. His voice got quiet. "Well we're all going home today," he said. "It's earlier than I thought, but your mother is homesick. We're going in shifts. Mother and Lazar are taking the train. I'm flying. Do you want to go with them or me?"

Leah didn't answer. She veered off the cart path and onto the main fairway. The golf cart was heading toward one of the creeks. Her hands were frozen on the steering wheel. She thought the cart was broken, that it couldn't turn. Father began to realize what was happening. *"Brake* damn it," he shouted. They were right at the edge of the creek when Father leaned over Leah and stomped on her left foot with his own, stopping the cart with a violent jerk. He turned the ignition key off. Father's face was pale. His cap was out of place. Some golf clubs had spilled off the back and onto the grass. Father took Leah firmly by the shoulders and made her look at him. "What was the purpose of *that?*" he asked her. Leah couldn't think of an answer.

The ride back to the pro shop was silent. Father drove. They passed by the outdoor restaurant near the pool.

Mother and Lazar were having breakfast. Father called out to them and waved. Leah had her head down and didn't look up. "I'll go with them on the train," she said to Father.

He stopped the golf cart abruptly. "Then get out and walk," he said. Leah did as she was told. Father drove quickly ahead into the parking lot full of empty carts. Leah avoided him for the rest of the day and stayed hidden until he'd left for the airport.

On the train home Lazar was friendly. He visited Leah frequently, brought her potato chips and chocolate milk. "You look sexy with a tan," he told her. Lazar looked better. His nose was red and peeling, but his eyes were clear and he had no dark circles underneath them. All the hours he didn't spend with Mother he passed with Leah. He was full of stories and songs. "Mother's much better," he said. "She says she's prepared for her season in hell. She can live like an ice queen now. She's rested. I think I'll make the honor roll this year and maybe I'll find an older European countess and go steady with her. I've kept a journal of our trip and I plan to get it published."

Lazar's visits were constant and animated. He tucked her in every night, brought her breakfast and took walks with her through the train. But Leah was wary. She didn't trust the change in her brother's mood. He seemed to be relieved to be going home. Finally she dared to ask the question that was haunting her. "Are we friends yet?" she asked Lazar.

Her brother smiled. "Comrades," he answered. "On one condition."

Leah asked what it was.

"You must swear to never tell anyone I lost the mambo contest. We both know that I *did* win it in the truest sense, but people get particular when it comes to details."

Leah swore she would never tell.

"Now we are truly friends," said Lazar.

The ride the rest of the way home went very quickly.

3

Lazar in Love

Leah knew Lazar was in love. He'd told her he was going to try it. And now he was in what he called "love training." He went to Arthur's Clothing Store and bought himself a velvet smoking jacket. His ritual hour in front of the bathroom mirror was full of medleys of songs, recipes of aftershave combinations, and rehearsals of different incantations of romantic voices. He stacked his records high, kept them turning on his little record player. His room was Off Limits. He wanted to sit very still and think of his beloved. His chosen sweetheart was a short, dark-haired cellist with the high school symphony orchestra. They'd met while rehearsing a variety show. Her name was Nancy-Lynn Weinstein. Whenever his father or mother tried to confront Lazar with chores such as cleaning his room or getting his homework done, Lazar was emphatic. "You must be gentle with me," he said. "My heart is a bread. It is rising. Don't jostle me; don't crush me." Father had no understanding for this kind of talk whatsoever. Mother laughed.

With Leah, Lazar became biblical. He took her for walks in the park. "Behold that flower," he said to Leah, pointing to almost anything. "The color is brighter than it has ever been before, and its fragrance is so strong. I am drunk from it. And the birds and the wind sing her name—Nancy-Lynn. Oh Nancy-Lynn Weinstein."

Lazar confided in his sister. "Do you know how we kiss?" he asked. "On the lips!" he answered himself. Lazar told Leah he'd show her if she promised not to tell. He kissed his sister hard on the mouth, pressing on her teeth and making little indentations on her lips with his braces. Leah tried to imagine this love which her brother was screeching about. Lazar was dancing in the park, singing "Take my haaand, I'm a stranger in paradise." She had mated some of her dolls—late at night shoving them together, a rabbit and a stuffed terrier; she'd had her Barbie doll sit on her Ken doll's lap; once she'd even embraced her best friend, Annie, during a sleep-over and said, "Let's play married," but Lazar was a fiend in a new world. She was impressed by him and a little frightened.

Lazar went out on dates dressed in bright silk bow ties; he bought flashing madras jackets and striped pants; he bought a pair of Western cowboy boots, white with bright red flowers all over them. Father said the bills were outrageous. Mother said to let Lazar be. He took the fat red Chevrolet every night and came back very late. Sometimes the shy, plump girl was with him. They'd stay downstairs in the living room. Leah could hear Lazar humming and reciting, she could hear the music coming from the hi-fi. In the morning the couch would be strewn with books: poetry, novels, classics from which Lazar would read to his love—there were also Lazar's own notebooks, filled with his writings to Nancy-Lynn.

"This is not just a feeling," Lazar said to his sister. "It is a calling. I was meant to be a great lover. A lover in pain and ecstasy. My whole day is dedicated to her."

Lazar's energy had never been higher. It seemed he didn't need to sleep. If Leah awoke early she would find her brother sitting in the breakfast room of their house staring out the window at the garden.

"The light is so beautiful as it comes up," said Lazar. "And the stars are tired when they leave the sky. The morning relieves the night of its duties. They both make worlds for the lover to contemplate. Yes," he would say excitedly chomping on his breakfast and scribbling in his notebook, "I will write that down exactly and leave it on Nancy-Lynn's doorstep this morning." Then he would dash out of the house, checking himself in a mirror as he went, and take the car, roar out of the driveway and head toward Nancy-Lynn's house.

Leah would have been much more jealous of her brother's distraction had he not included her in almost everything. One night he took Leah and Nancy-Lynn to a Chinese meal. He ordered egg rolls, spare ribs, sweet-and-sour pork and lobster Cantonese. He ate most of it himself, the food dribbling on his chin, showing a wide open mess as he talked and ate without stop. Nancy-Lynn sat quietly, her hands folded politely, with an amazed smile on her face. Leah couldn't believe this plump plain girl, with a mole on her chin and small brown eyes and tiny teeth with big gums, was Lazar's goddess. It seemed that Nancy-Lynn didn't believe it either because she was half asleep throughout most of the meal.

"We shall be married soon," announced Lazar. "You are the first to know. We shall be married before anyone else ever finds out. Before the rabbi who marries us, or Polynesians who entertain us on our honeymoon. In fact, we shall be married before *we* even know it. We shall just wake up married one day the way one wakes up with a fever or a song in his head."

Lazar was in a generous spirit. "And we'll adopt *you*, Leah. That way you won't have to be without me." Lazar sang "Love is a maany splendored thiing," until the waiter came over and told him to be quiet.

"We are engaged—the three of us," said Lazar. "Give us extra fortune cookies."

Lazar's exultation was limitless. He told Leah that Nancy-Lynn's house was a castle and her window a balcony. He bought a transistor radio, turned it to his favorite station, waited until an appropriate song came on and then turned up the volume and howled along with it beneath her balcony. Lazar bought a book on numerology, found the numbers that matched up with each letter of both their names and then called Nancy-Lynn every time the clock struck one of the "holy numbers." He sent musicians to perform at her door, and once hired a clown from a local kiddie park to lead an elephant with a heart painted on its side outside her window. Lazar stole money from Father's dressing bureau to cover his expenses. He had loud violent arguments with his father—Leah often heard Lazar shouting at his father, "You know nothing about Love. It is an art. You know nothing about it."

Lazar told Leah that Nancy-Lynn's parents, middle-class Jews in the retail clothing business, found him charming and thought he was a stimulating companion for their daughter. But after a while he reported to Leah that their attitude was changing. "They're threatened because they're not intellectuals," he said. They told their daughter they thought Lazar was unstable. They didn't mean to hurt her they said, but they didn't think Lazar was a good influence on her. Lazar said this was common in the age-old war of passion versus mediocrity. He said it only added fuel to his flame.

What Lazar didn't know was that the object of his love was unhappy. Nancy-Lynn's parents were surprised when their daughter burst into tears and begged them to protect her from Lazar, saying that she felt trapped by him and was fearful that if she tried to send him away he'd do something violent and unspeakable to her. She told them that he had bought a marriage manual and was reading the instructions out loud to her. She told them that Lazar had said he would come to her in the night—soul out of body—and enter her soul like a dybbuk and stay there forever. She said she couldn't practice the cello anymore because Lazar had written long rambling unrhyming poems to all her etudes and the words confused her concentration. Nancy-Lynn was in such a state that her father became enraged and called Lazar's father to tell him to keep his son away. He said that Lazar was a "psycho." Lazar's father apologized to Mr.

Weinstein for his son's behavior and promised to take care of it. He forbade Lazar to leave the house, except to go to school.

At first Lazar went around singing, "Just like Romeo and Juliet ba da da, just like Romeo and Juliet." He explained to Leah that the greatest lovers in the world went on in spite of incredible protest and controversy. "King Edward abdicated his throne," said Lazar. "And I'd do no less." But Nancy-Lynn began to ignore Lazar in school and would not answer his letters. Lazar's spirit went dark. "She's been poisoned," he said.

One day Leah was composing her own poem on the way home from school. She was staring down at the sidewalk and speaking to herself in a deep raspy voice. There had been a mass-murderer in her town, a teenage girl who drowned the children she baby sat for, and this had been in the papers and on Leah's mind. Often Lazar would jump out from behind corners and put his hands around Leah's neck, and Leah would scream. Father ordered Lazar to stop it. But Lazar called it "reality training." Her poem was a tribute to the baby-sitter and to Lazar. Although she didn't know the young woman or any of the children involved, she imagined what a killer's voice would be. She sang—

> "It's twelve o'clock
> You know the time
> In just five minutes
> they'll commit the crime.
> You hear a creak
> they open the door
> the next thing you know
> you're on the floor
> you feel a chill going
> down your back
> they throw you in a
> potato sack

you start to cry
you start to shiver
the next thing you know
you're in the river."

When Leah reached her house no cars were there. Not Mother's nor Father's. She rang the doorbell and Elana, the maid, came breathlessly to greet her.

"What a mess," said Elana. Leah did not know what Elana was talking about. Then she saw. All the kitchen was covered with shattered glass. And on the glass were domes and smears of blood—like finger painting.

"I ain't supposed to tell you," said Elana. "But your brother Lazar went whacko. It was like he was doing a boxing match with no partner. Smashing around in here screaming like a hyena. All over some girl—Nancy-Jean or Nancy-Ann—"

"Nancy-Lynn," said Leah quietly.

"Well Nancy-somebody," said Elana.

Leah went silently up to her room and felt a sadness come over her. The end of a wild time. Now Lazar would disappear. She didn't think about the violence. She went to sleep. A girl taking an afternoon nap.

She awoke when she heard Mother's car in the driveway. Soon Mother was at her door, then sitting next to her on the bed. She took deep drags from one of her long Kents and stared past Leah through the window.

"Lazar had a little accident," said her mother. "He tripped and his hand went through the back door. It isn't serious. Just so you should know." Her mother didn't smile. "Why don't you go in and give him a kiss?" said Mother. "Perhaps that would perk him up."

Leah was afraid. She approached her brother's door as if it were a locked room about which there had been rumors and warnings. She tapped on it lightly, half hoping her brother wouldn't hear.

"No entry," he said. "Absolutely no entry."

"It's Leah," whispered his sister. His voice made her want to look at him. She wanted to see what a madman looked like. She wanted to see what blood did. He was lying down very still on his bed. His hands were bandaged and they looked like paws. He had stitches under his chin as if he were a goat and the stitches were his scraggly beard. There was blood now caked brown on his nose. One of his eyes was black.

"No kisses," said Lazar. "Absolutely no touching and no kisses."

Leah obeyed and kept respectful.

"I would like to sing you a Sufi song," said Lazar. "Sit down." His voice was cold and his demand was frightening. Leah didn't know where to sit.

"You may sit at the very foot of my bed, but you are not to touch me or feel sorry for me. Do you understand?" Lazar's voice was quiet and Leah nodded her head, afraid that her voice would in some way touch him and he would become furious at the violation of his orders.

"The song goes as follows. You will listen to it and you will leave. And you will not speak to me again until I choose to speak to you." Lazar began singing. Leah didn't understand why Lazar blamed her for what had happened. He was always dealing out his friendship and then snatching it away in bits and pieces with rules and reasons that were entirely his own.

Lazar was singing—

> With Love comes sorrow
> and the heart's blood
> Love loves the difficult things
> Love loves the difficult things
> Love is a cruel pain
> Love's suffering
> Sometimes it tears the veil of the soul

Sometimes it draws it together
An atom of love
An atom of pain
Love is the very marrow of beings.

Lazar sang himself to sleep.

Leah left his room. It was silent in his room for many hours. Later that night, she heard her brother's voice again. It sounded animated and happy. Frank Sinatra's records were playing one after the other. Lazar was talking on the phone. He was talking to a long-distance operator.

"Yes, cutie," Lazar was saying, "I want to call Switzerland. Home of the Alps and long-horned cows. I must order a flower—a *kind* of flower. As far as I know it only grows in Switzerland on the tops of the highest mountains. Why are you giggling? You sound cute. What is your name? Janice? Well, Janice, the flower I'm talking about is edelweiss. It is delicate and fresh. No *I'm* not fresh. I want this flower. It is for a wrist corsage . . . for my senior prom. I want it sent special delivery—by tomorrow. I want the smell and the sun of the mountains still glowing on them when they arrive—yes, it is for my date. She *is* lucky. I want them to crate it in a damp little wooden box—the way they send leis from Hawaii. It's called edelweiss—edelweiss, edelweiss, every morning you greet me, soft and nice, clear as spice, every morning I greet thee— Call the ambassador to Switzerland or a Swiss florist!"

Lazar bubbled on until Leah drifted off back into her own sleep. She figured either Lazar had found a long-distance operator girl friend or there was no one on the other end of the telephone. Either way, he was happy again and this meant that she would be forgiven for whatever part he thought she'd had in Nancy-Lynn's desertion of him.

4

Algebra

Although he had vowed to make summa cum laude in high school, Lazar was only making C's in most courses and he was failing Algebra. Leah knew this because they'd spent a long afternoon with her pen-and-ink kit, construction paper and erasers trying to forge his report card. He'd been able to add, divide, multiply and subtract but his method of calculating was complicated-to-noisy. In his mind he still had to say "five times five is twenty-five—carry the two—two times five is ten—add the two—comes out to one hundred twenty-five." Leah often saw him moving his lips. The voices in his head were clear and deliberate, but not fast. And he accepted this, even took a little joy in his simple calculations until Algebra turned up in the ninth grade. Then he'd had to repeat it year after year until his whole graduation was threatened by it. "It's a religious litany," Lazar told Leah. "That means I chant it over and over again until I die." Algebra was metaphor to Lazar. It was a foreign language for which there was no dictionary. It was road signs he couldn't read. He was cut off from mathematics as if he'd been listening to two instruments play a duet when suddenly a third joined in and he'd lost the basic theme. Lazar told Leah that it was celestial proof that poets weren't meant to be electrical engineers. But she sensed he felt bewildered and betrayed. He told her that he sat in the classroom staring at the blackboard as if he'd been transported to Cape Canaveral and was about to be spun off in a capsule without having signed up. The parentheses and lines and dots; the

little numbers above the letters; all the materials of Algebra
seemed to require a dedication to science, the building of
bridges, the discovering of cures for fatal diseases. Lazar
was cursed and awestruck by Algebra. He was also totally
helpless. If his tests were multiple choice, he'd score in
the low thirties by guessing. He showed Leah how he would
look at the equation, look at the choice of answer A, B or C
and try to create the right answer either by making up a
story to go with the answer ($b + a = 5^2$) (bell + armor = an
army of 52); or he would close his eyes and try to pray the
right answer off the page—as if it were in braille or as if
he had extrasensory power. However, if the test had only
direct answers to specific problems—equations to be cal-
culated—Lazar always got zero. He would valiantly fill
in numbers and letters that looked visually beautiful to
him; he wrote them in different styles and shapes, but
Lazar was so wrong that his teacher wrote a letter to his
parents suggesting he either get tutored or not go on to
college.

Father decided to tutor Lazar. He'd close the two of them
off in the den with the Encyclopedia and the dark brown
leather chairs and his father would read Lazar the rules of
Algebra in a deep Shakespearean voice. Leah could hear Father's voice through the doors. The prose of the Algebra
textbook came alive with a military urgency. Lazar was
being read orders. He loved the sound—he didn't understand the words. Lazar's father read each rule with great
tenderness. Then he'd put down a simple equation for Lazar
to complete. This was when the harmony exploded. Leah
heard the concert reading change to shouting. The answer
was always wrong. Lazar's father thought he was being de-
liberately defied. Lazar felt jammed and bolted shut. He was
in pain. It was confusing to be deprived of the numbers of
the earth. He didn't know why he couldn't answer his father's questions. He never admitted this, but he'd emerge
from the den pale and trembling. "I'm being trained for spy

work," he told Leah. "I'm learning to withstand Oriental torture."

The tutorial sessions went on for two weeks, every evening when Father came home from work. An uneasy dinner always followed. The failures in the den made Father talk louder and more rapidly about his business and his ideas about Eisenhower, McCarthyism or sports. Lazar became irritable, snappy and more sarcastic. His food rimmed his plate like Saturn's rings. He chewed with his mouth hanging loose as if he were a marionette and his latches had become unwired. He winked at Leah, who sat directly opposite to him, as if they shared some private wisdom. Leah did not know the source of the winks. Mother looked intensely at all of them, but her spirit was, in truth, aloof and her heart was in some other melancholy distant space. She accepted Father's hour-long lectures as if they were arrows and she was a ghost through which they passed. She only interrupted him to ring the delicate silver bell for the next course.

Lazar was aware of creating a criminal atmosphere. He told Leah he was the biblical sacrifice for the family. "All our ancestral wrongdoings are wrapped up in my math scores," he said. "Including our great-uncle who was a Bolshevik." He didn't know how to stop it. He described to Leah his dreams of escape. On the way home from school he imagined rare blood diseases, violent hit-and-run accidents, a call to serve in a young man's army where he would be shot into a thousand pieces of dust. These or anything to prevent his Algebra tutorial. He resented not so much the assault on his own brain as the way it was prying at the family. "This isn't good for Mother," he said. He thought perhaps prayer could lead to understanding. He imagined all-night vigils under the stars in which their shapes and positions would reveal the mysteries of equations to him. All of this proved to be hopeless and he approached his dreaded six o'clock hour with Father as one going to confess a terrible dishonesty to a cruel and strict confessor.

Father was tireless in his pursuit of Algebra. He barely said hello to Leah when he came home in the evening. He went straight to the den and took new books he'd bought out of crisp paper bags. He began each session as if they had never begun before; he reacted to Lazar's failure with a shock that was so fresh he seemed to have lost any memory that it had been going on for days; his tirades, however, were filled with incriminating details against his son. He remembered every bag of garbage that had not been taken out, every evening Lazar's light had gone out later than midnight, every lamp that had been broken, every present and trip he had given his son. Leah heard the lists. She stood outside the den praying Lazar would succeed. She rooted for him as if the dusk sessions were sports matches. She clenched her fists and waited for Lazar's answers. When they were wrong, she stamped her foot. She kept a vigil, stood there every day as if her presence could help her brother. Lazar continued to leave his tutorials as if he had just visited his father on his deathbed. Leah heard Lazar in his room rehearsing maneuvers to try to win the man. He always failed. His father was a bawdy, innocent, proud, unmovable monster. On one occasion his father, exhausted from his work and saddened by his adult life, said quietly to Lazar, "We'll quit this now. There's no reason to do this to you or me. We'll transfer you out of your class." Lazar responded by ardently refusing to give up. He begged his father to keep being there. Lazar even managed to answer a problem. His father was tired and did not hear any firecrackers go off. Lazar looked depressed afterward. He told Leah he hadn't taken his chance to escape. Now he was trapped. He and Father were married by this Algebra. He saw it going on for eternity.

One evening, over something very small, a knife falling on the floor, or an elbow on the table, Lazar's father erupted into violence. Lazar's chin was covered with mashed potatoes. His father began with a napkin and tried to scrub the potatoes off, saying he was tired of living with a slob. Then

he grabbed Lazar by the neck of his shirt and began to shake
him as if to loosen his head from his body and jiggle it off.
Lazar began kicking back and tried punching Father in the
stomach, but Lazar was too scrawny and Father held him
off. Lazar began a narration of the events, trying to tell
Mother to look at the man she had married. But his squeaky
voice was interrupted by his own gasps and Mother sat very
still as if hypnotized. Leah did not want to look as Father
shook and shook her brother until she thought his bones
would turn to sawdust. She hid her face in her arms. She
peeked in and peeked out as if looking in a toy slide projector
filled with Disney animals. Finally Lazar mumbled something—it was too quiet for Leah to understand, but the tone
was unmistakable and mocking, and it was as if Father's
body were a ship and all the furnaces exploded into power,
the cannons lowered and the bombs were unleashed from its
hull. Lazar's father let a slap fly across Lazar's face whose vi-
brations caused the center ceiling lamp to swing and whose
sound echoed on the windows and in the glassware. Lazar's
glasses went speeding off and crashed somewhere. Blood
began to pour from his nose—not just a stream, but in
gushes and throbs. The power of the blood was enormous. It
spattered and rushed until tension was converted into injury.
Everyone was relieved. Even Lazar. Father held Lazar's
head back and pushed ice onto his son's nose. He did it with
the passion of a man singing a sad song. He walked Lazar
around like that for an hour. The two of them walked past
Leah as if she were someone in a crowd watching a parade of
noble mourners. Then it was dark outside. And everyone
went to his or her separate room.

The tutorials stopped after that. And Father went to
school and persuaded the dean to allow Lazar to take two
English courses to get enough credits for graduation. Father
was proud of his politics and repeated this conversation in
great detail several times in the following months. But Lazar
never thanked him.

5

A Grown-Up at a Cocktail Party

On the way home from school Leah found a perfectly shaped bright red oak leaf. She thought her mother would appreciate it and that Lazar would approve. He'd planned a party for the three of them at five P.M. He called it a "get acquainted Happy Hour." He told Leah to bring a gift. She went straight to her room, Scotch-taped the leaf onto a piece of yellow construction paper, and fell asleep. When she awoke it was five-thirty. Leah felt ashamed. She still fell into what Lazar called "puppy sleeps." She didn't dream or stir and sometimes she slept all day long. Lazar warned her that she might have contracted an African germ that swam through her blood and made it maple syrup. She was dizzy and foggy from these sleeps. Her pillow was wet with drool. She knew she had to comb her hair, change her clothes and go down the long hall to her mother's bedroom. She worried that she would have missed the party, that Lazar would become angry with her, and not speak to her for days. This worried Leah because Lazar told her that in a year he was going into the world and he was trying to prepare her for life without him. Leah was also worried that she might not get to see Mother. Mother was ill again and didn't leave her room. Often she had a dream that she and Mother were in Spain together to see the bullfights. In the dreams there was a long steep set of concrete stairs on the top of which was a tobacco store. Her mother told her to wait at the bottom of the stairs while she went to buy a pack of Kents. In the dream Leah waited and waited but Mother never returned. So Leah

50

went to the bullfight alone. It took place in a huge stadium like where Father took her to see the local baseball team. Mother was the matador in tight black pants with gold embroidery. Mother wore a hat with a wide brim and played a pair of maracas. In the dream the crowd cheered so loud her mother couldn't hear Leah calling her. Leah watched as the bull was released from his pen. He was as large as the buffalo she'd seen at the zoo and his horns were ivory and glinted in the sun. Always the bull gored her mother, but the crowd never stopped cheering. She could never get the dream to stop before the bull jabbed its horn into her mother's stomach and lifted her high into the sky. In the dream Leah always looked down onto the stretcher and always Mother was smiling as the handsome young Spanish picadors leaned over her bleeding body and held her beautiful perfectly manicured hands. Leah would run after the stretcher, but Mother had disappeared.

When Leah awoke from this dream she'd always do what she wasn't supposed to do. She'd go down the long hall to her mother's bedroom and open her mother's door. As soon as she tiptoed up to her mother's face, leaned over it, and felt her mother's breath on her cheek, she could go back to sleep. She told no one about her dream. Not even Lazar. It seemed treacherous.

When Leah got to her mother's room it was 5:45. Mother was propped up in bed with pillows covered with organdy. She had on a sheer beige nightgown which made Leah turn her eyes away. Mother looked healthy, but her manner was cold.

"I thought you were coming at five," said Mother.

Leah explained that she'd overslept. Then she remembered that she'd forgotten the oak leaf and knew she'd forgotten because she thought it was a stupid idea.

"Where's Lazar?" Leah asked Mother.

"He's gone to get me a drink," said Mother. "Pull up a chair, Leah. Your hair needs cutting."

Mother no longer looked at Leah. Mother was looking at
the dreary winter day outside. Mother hated the cold and
Leah thought that Mother tried to change the season by
staring at it with meanness. Leah fingered the ends of her
hair. She was sorry she didn't look right. After a while her
mother said, "How's school?"

Leah didn't reply. She didn't know how to make her
mother laugh. Nor did she understand how to keep Mother
interested. She knew Mother cared nothing for school. Leah
felt like a grown-up at a cocktail party. She was trying to
understand what it meant to make a conversation.

Lazar danced into the room balancing a tray on his hand.
He'd made drinks for himself and Mother and a ginger ale in
a champagne glass with a cherry for Leah.

"Ah the sleepwalker," he said. He was friendly but he did
not give Leah her usual kiss. "She'd be a good candidate for
a space voyager, don't you think? We'd send her up and she
could doze all the way to the moon."

Mother smiled at Lazar and thanked him for her drink.
Leah sipped on her ginger ale and prayed she wouldn't drop
it on Mother's quilt. Lazar plopped himself down on the bed
at Mother's feet and clapped his hands together like a master
of ceremonies.

"What shall we do today?" said Lazar. It was as if he were
in charge of keeping things going. "Shall I read to you? Shall
we tell jokes? Shall we look at dirty pictures?"

Mother laughed at Lazar to please him. Lazar was working hard. Leah was staring at Mother now, taking her in.
She loved her mother's woolly hair, her long neck, her thin
arms. She loved her mother's fingernails with the bright red
polish. Mother knew that Leah was staring at her and did
not stop Leah by returning the look. She sipped quietly on
her drink, lit a cigarette and took a slow dramatic drag.

"Let's just sit, Lazar," said Mother.

The three of them went into a kind of prayer. Lazar and
Leah always did what their mother told them because she so

rarely said anything. Leah felt that the visit was not going well. She saw her brother getting restless and angry. Her presence was interrupting his rituals with Mother. And something about Leah's being in the room was causing Mother to grow silent.

After a long while Lazar spoke again.

"Maybe I should have Elana bring us our supper."

"No, dear," said Mother. "I'm not hungry tonight."

"I'm not hungry either," said Leah. She desperately wanted to finish her ginger ale because she didn't know where to put the glass and her hand was tired of holding it.

"I thought this was going to be a sort of party," said Lazar. "I thought we were going to talk about literature and dance the samba and gossip about the neighbors. I thought we were all going to get drunk and recite quotations from our favorite heroes." Lazar was pacing. "I mean Leah can't quote much but she could give us a line or two from Bambi, or Eloise or Babar. Who will carry on here when I'm gone?" said Lazar. "I'm afraid you'll all become dull. Maybe I won't go to college at all. I'll come back and find you all watching soap operas."

Leah said nothing. She hadn't wanted to let Lazar down. She felt her mother looking at her. She lowered her head and began to blush. When Lazar spent evenings with Mother, Leah could hear their laughter coming from the room. Lazar had books of Emily Dickinson, Robert Frost and Elizabeth Barrett Browning. He selected Mother's favorite poems. Lazar knew how to make Mother the drinks she liked with the proper amount of Scotch, ice and water. Lazar went to Mother's room without being called; he was always welcome. Leah never knew what to do during the times Mother took to her bed. The approach down the hall seemed such a long way. She felt small and uncomfortable in Mother's strange chair. Mother's room was elegant and cold and full of things that a grown woman knew about. Lazar passed through it with familiarity as if he'd designed it. Lazar and

Mother looked at each other with easiness. They talked to each other with their faces. Both could raise one eyebrow, move their ears back and forth, roll their eyes and laugh without needing words to translate their thoughts. Leah had nothing to say.

"Well I've had it," said Lazar. "I consider this evening a low point in my week. I'm going to my room." He stopped at Mother's door and took an indignant pose. "I'll be back later and give you your pill," he said to Mother.

Lazar glared at Leah.

"And *you,*" he said, "can consider yourself on the outs with me for at least a week. You have no social graces whatsoever. Stick with your dolls or do whatever little girls do."

Leah and Mother were left alone in the room. Leah sank lower into the chair and twirled her champagne glass in her hands.

"Don't twirl the glass," said Mother.

Leah was silent, looking at the closets filled with clothes, the high-heeled shoes set in rows and rows on the floor. She looked at Mother's full-length dressing mirror and the door to Mother's bathroom.

"What is it, Leah?" asked Mother.

Leah heard her voice and was surprised to find herself answering.

"I want to ask you a question."

Her mother nodded and sat up straighter in the bed. Leah saw Mother's strong bare arms and the round muscles of her shoulders, the smooth skin above Mother's nightgown.

"I want to know why you're sick so much."

Mother began to cry. At first Mother's mouth made a small smile and tears came into her eyes. Then she held out her arms and Leah went and buried her head into Mother's neck. Mother's neck smelled of musty perfume and Mother started to sob. Leah kept her eyes closed but she could feel it. She could feel her mother's tears on her own face. Mother's arms were strong around Leah and Mother kissed Leah's hair and her forehead and squeezed her and rocked her until Leah began to laugh. Then Mother began to laugh too and Leah tickled Mother and punched her and squealed when Mother tickled back and punched a bit and they rolled and wrestled all over Mother's bed until Leah was screaming with delight and was sweaty from playing. Mother brushed Leah's hair out of her face with her hands and wiped her tears with the bottom of her nightgown.

"You really need a haircut," said Mother.

Then she gestured to Leah to come close and Leah lay with her head on her mother's breast and fell asleep for the night.

6

A College Tour

Mother and Lazar were off on a college tour. Lazar had just told Leah that he'd changed his mind—he did not want to go to college. He would rather have stayed in the town and learned tattooing or sold hot dogs outside a factory, but Father insisted. He said, "Blame Father if you never see me again." Father thought the trip would be good for both Lazar and Mother, who had hardly been out of town since their vacation in Florida one year before. Elana, the maid, had to pack for Mother and Lazar because they were so reluctant to go. Father told Leah he'd bought the tickets and had his secretary type out the itinerary. They were going by train because Lazar said he wanted to recreate the life-style of Leadbelly and Blind Lemon Jefferson and Mother was terrified of planes. Leah heard Mother tell Lazar that it was Father's method of killing her off. They were to be gone a month. They departed one morning while Leah was in school and left her no goodbye note. Leah and Father were alone in the big house with only Elana. Father left for work before Leah was awake and often returned when she was asleep. It was a lonely time for her. She did not have any friends as close as Lazar and she missed her mother's quiet drifting through the house. When two whole weeks passed and there had not been a letter or postcard, Leah began to have terrible fears. Often she would lie in her room in its remote corner of the house and listen to the creaks in the wall and hold her breath for strange footsteps on the stairs. During the first days she'd waited excitedly for the phone to ring,

hoping her brother and mother were calling to check in.
After a while she waited for the phone thinking it would be
the police to inform her father that Lazar and Mother were
dead. She imagined their coffins being sent home on a fat
plane with four propellers. She pictured the open coffins
sliding down the luggage racks with Lazar and Mother lying
in them, fully clothed with their mouths open, their eyes frozen in unspeakable terror. Her worst vision was of one coffin,
the two of them bloody and naked draped over each other's
starved, bony skeletons, like the photographs she'd recently
seen of concentration-camp victims in the glossy magazines
Father brought home from his office. She never knew the
cause of Lazar's and Mother's death because she didn't know
where they had gone. Lazar had tormented her before leaving saying, "You get to stay home—so *you* can endure the
loneliness." Also, Leah was twelve years old and her breasts
were starting to grow. She was afraid she was going to get
her period and she was worried that Mother and Lazar
would think she'd done something wrong while they were
away. Father didn't seem concerned. He never mentioned
Lazar or Mother when Leah saw him. He asked her about
school, complimented the clothes which Elana had laid out
for her and he seemed calm and happy. Father was a handsome man. He had dark curly hair, peppered with gray, a
finely cut mustache—he was tall and thin and walked very
straight, because posture, he told her, had a great deal to do
with the image one projected. Father's suits were always
pressed with perfect neatness, his fingernails were manicured. To Leah he had always seemed the same age—a powerful age, the age of a leader—and he never got older or
younger. Leah made sure to be dressed and washed if she
was to see him. And she was terribly worried that the new
parts of her body would be interpreted by him as sloppiness.
She wore extra sweaters while Lazar and Mother were away,
so that, if by chance, she and Father breakfasted together, he
wouldn't discover the new outline of her chest.

Mother's and Lazar's silence caused Leah to make alternative worlds in her head. She spent long hours in her room imagining herself among the peoples she'd seen in *National Geographic* magazine. She liked the black tribes the best—the ones with the tattoos lining their eyes and crawling like snakes up their cheeks. She wanted to have brass necklaces spun around her neck and wide earrings dangling down from her ears like chimes. She wanted to wrap leather around her hips and paint her chest and arms with orange and blue paint. She often lay on her bed imagining a campfire in a forest with drums playing and warm helpful women like Elana humming. Then the men of the tribe would initiate her. They'd rub her body with oil and squeeze tropical juices over her and smile down at her with their large white teeth and wide coal-lined eyes. Then they'd lift her up. She would be in the arms of seven or eight tribesmen and they'd carry her to a grass hut where her husband waited. He was a chief dressed in bells and feathers. He'd sent scouts out all around the world and had finally chosen her to be his wife. As in Cinderella, he'd chosen her from millions and millions of girls. There was one painful aspect to the marriage. He had to take a long hot poker from the little fire in his hut and brand her right above her right breast. Leah imagined the pain to be excruciating. She'd have to vomit into one of their gourds. But the kind women would hold her head and the chief would be satisfied with her bravery. Leah imagined the branding ceremony four or five times an evening. She placed it in between her versions of Mother and Lazar's funeral, her father's move to a big city and her own impoverished orphaned walks across America trying to find a home. She went into these imaginings as if they were a kind of sleep. Much of her life had been a kind of sleep and the drowsiness was taking a new form which she found enjoyable. The time passed quickly.

Finally two letters arrived. One from Mother for Father. One from Lazar to Leah. Leah was angry when she saw

Lazar's scrawled printing on the envelope which Elana had placed on her pillow. She hoped the letter had been written before Lazar's death. She was ready for her new life and felt interrupted. She closed the door to her room and put on pants and a sweater (usually she lay naked) and read. It was postmarked from Massachusetts.

Dearest Princess,

Mother and I have pulled a real coup. Of course, I must, as usual, ask for your absolute confidence in this matter and have you swear on everything we are to each other that you will not tell Father.

I told you I wouldn't write you, but I don't see how I can deny you the wonder of this experience. Mother and I have abandoned the notion of visiting colleges. We have been living a kind of honeymoon. She is like a girl again. I wear white suits and she, silk dresses. We stay in two-bedroom suites in all the most glorious hotels. We order turkey club sandwiches from room service and bottles of champagne. In Boston we dined by the seashore and watched the boats. I ate a whole lobster. In New Orleans we danced through the streets at the Mardi Gras. I was dressed as the devil in a bright red-sequined completely tight body suit and Mother was a streetwalker in a black dress, black fishnet stockings, a beauty mark painted on her cheek and a beret on her head. We stayed up all night in the bars and listened to Dixieland. In Colorado we stayed at a chalet and built a large fire with thick logs and had our meals and brandy brought to us on a sled. In Iowa we rode horses bareback and I never knew Mother could gallop, but you should see the wind when it goes through her hair and when the farm country sun gives her a deep tan. In New York City we went to galleries and listened to poets reciting on the street corners and rode through Central Park in a buggy drawn by a white horse. We've had so many invitations to move in with rich and famous artists, architects, doctors, business people, that it's a wonder we're considering returning at all. But as you know our train arrives from Albany on the twenty-fifth of February and it would be lovely if you could be at the station. College is completely out of the question. *This* has been college. Don't tell Father any of this. He thinks we are visiting campuses and meeting with guidance counselors. That's his idea of learning. But we've blown his money to bits everywhere and it is sailing all over America and has become the stars in the sky above his dreary fact-filled head. Mother said, "Why not?" She is such a pioneer. In Saks Fifth Avenue she bought herself seven new outfits and I have an umbrella with a wooden handle.

I want a hero's welcome when I return. Bring your guitar to the train station.

Love,
Lazar

Lazar was probably lying. Leah read the letter over several times. She tried to imagine Mother and Lazar in all the places he described. She tried to see the two of them eating together at restaurants, sharing a hotel suite. The images made her jealous. Elana knocked on the door at one point to get her to come to supper, but Leah remembered what Lazar had said and she became afraid. She told Elana she was sick. Elana went away. Leah kept herself clothed—she no longer wanted to be naked for herself. She felt feverish and nervous. She thought about all the rooms in the big house and where she might go to find herself an adventure. The house seemed empty in her mind's eye. She was feeling a lightness in her head as if she were disappearing. She tried to recall her tribal family but the *National Geographic* photographs were invaded by images of her mother and Lazar in elegant clothes riding through her African village in a Victorian carriage. She took out her mother's razor. She'd seen her mother once, in the bathtub with her legs spread out over the edge. Mother was shaving her legs. Leah had tried to turn her eyes away but she had obviously seen, because now her mind was filled with pictures of her mother's long legs, spread, stretching, the razor going up and down them. Leah waited in the bathroom until she heard Elana go to bed. Then she took down her pants. She held Mother's soap under the faucet and made it lather. She covered her legs with the lather. The fuzzy hair on them spread out under the white soap like little worms. She took Mother's razor and shaved off the hair as best she could. Then she shaved the fuzz under her arms and then the two or three hairs that were growing between her legs. Finally, she decided to tattoo herself so if the African chief was sending his scouts out she would be more instantly recognizable. She took the razor out of its holder and slowly carved three lines on the top of her right hand. They made a triangle. She watched the blood come up in little bubbles and it fascinated her. She went deeper with the razor until the pain brought tears to her eyes and the triangle on her hand was totally engraved. She dabbed at the wound with toilet paper until the bleeding stopped and covered her work with a Band-Aid. She vowed to come to the bathroom every day and open up the triangle to keep it bleeding. She wanted it to stay clean for the chief. She vowed to do it every day until he beckoned her. That would be the sign to stop.

Leah knew she must've been busy for a long time because she heard her father's car in the driveway. She'd never been awake when he'd come home before. She pulled up her pants, rushed from the bathroom and ran down the stairs to greet him. He had not come into the house yet. Leah was confused. She looked out one of the windows that faced the driveway and saw Father's car. There was another car parked behind it. Father was sitting in the strange car—she recognized his silhouette. He looked as if he were bending over in pain or as if he were praying—moving up and down as he did in temple when he was remembering his own father. Leah thought she ought to wake Elana or call an ambulance. Then she saw there was someone else in the car with Father. She couldn't see who. The other silhouette was bending and praying as Father was and they appeared in the front window of the car and then disappeared as if they were being swallowed by waves. Leah ran to another corner of the large living room and hid behind a chair. Her father was a mysterious, powerful man and she thought perhaps he was doing something awful. She didn't want to have to tell Lazar.

After a while she heard the other car go and Father's keys in the door. He stopped at the old mirror in the hallway and combed his hair and slicked his mustache. He was walking slowly, grabbing hold of different chairs and tables as he went as if they were bad people and he was slapping them angrily on the shoulders. He fell into the couch next to the coffee table on which Mother's letter lay. "Well if it isn't a missive," he said to the envelope. He stretched out his long legs, let out a groan and turned on a light to read. Then he saw Leah in the corner.

"Insomnia?" asked Father. "In need of a bit of divertissement?" His voice was booming as if he were entertaining her at a party.

"Come," said Father gesturing to Leah. "Let's have a little father-daughter soirée."

Leah stayed in the corner.

"Come on. Come on." Her father raised his voice. He had no patience with timidness. "Sit here by me on the couch. We're like strangers. I never see you. You stay locked in your room as if it were a convent."

Leah came out from behind the chair and sat next to her father. He smelled of after-shave lotion and there was a sweet sour odor to his breath and sweat.

"Look," Father said to Leah. He swatted the envelope with the back of his hand. "A letter from the Lady of Our House." He handed the letter to Leah. "Read it, Madam. Let's hear your diction. I want to see where the taxpayers' money is going."

Leah opened the letter from her mother. It was a short note. Leah read slowly and carefully and Father sat beside her and conducted his hands in the air as if listening to a symphony. It was hard to concentrate on the letter because Leah had never seen her Father as animated. Usually he was very stiff and proper. In this moment he reminded her of Lazar.

"Dear Husband," she read.

Father giggled. "That, my dear, c'est moi—I am your mother's husband. How do you do."

"Dear Husband," Leah repeated.

"I *heard* that," yelled Father and he slammed his fist on the table. "Don't you suppose that higher education gave me enough of the mental facilities to perceive and retain a two-word greeting?"

Leah trembled and continued.

> The college trip is going nicely. We are having some of the difficulties we anticipated in that Lazar will visit a campus one day and refuse to visit another on the next.

"The unctuous little prick," growled Father. "Go on."
Leah continued.

> His decisions seem arbitrary to me though he has his usual poetry to convince me why one day he'd rather go to a movie than have an interview.

Father groaned.

> But on the whole we are getting a good idea of what's available to him and though the travel is tiring we are also seeing some sights. We'll be home as scheduled. Please send my love to Leah.

The letter was signed with Mother's name. Father had become quiet. He seemed sleepy. He turned to Leah and looked at her as if he were seeing her for the first time. His usually clear eyes were bleary. He rubbed them and sighed.

"Not exactly the letters of Elizabeth Barrett Browning, huh?" he said.

Father suddenly became shy and rather uncomfortable. "How long have you been down here?" he asked quietly.

Leah blushed.

"Not very long," Leah answered.

Father stood up abruptly but his usually strong posture was slumped and unsteady. "Your mother and brother will be home soon and you won't be so lonely," he said.

"Yes sir," Leah whispered.

Father grabbed Leah in his arms with such force that her breath escaped in a cough. "Why do you call me *sir?*" he hissed. "I'm your father. I *love* you. I want what's best for you. I'm not *sir.*" He held her and she froze. When he felt no response he pushed her away in a disgusted shove.

"Next year when your brother's at college, maybe you'll learn I'm not such a monster."

Leah said nothing.

Father began to yell. The veins on his forehead bulged and his teeth bared.

"You learn *this,*" he said to her. "Living breathing functioning socializing hardworking human beings are *not monsters.* The good people are not only depressed bedridden dreamers. Do you understand?"

Leah nodded that she did.

Father's face looked sour and weepy.

"I think you know that," he said. "I think you'll grow to be a lovely woman."

Leah quickly folded her arms to cover her breasts under her sweater.

"Go to bed," said Father.

Leah climbed the stairs to her bedroom. She closed the door to her room, remembered her father's words and opened it again. She stripped naked and crawled into her bed as fast as she could in case he was coming to her room with more to say. Her legs burned where she shaved them and she felt prickles under her arms. The triangle under its bandage throbbed with her heartbeat. It was like the drums in the village where her chief waited for her. The quiet stinging "bam bam bam" put her to sleep.

When Lazar and Mother came home, Leah was surprised to find that they didn't look any different. They weren't tan and their clothes were wrinkled. Mother was tired and answered Father's queries in a stony, clipped voice. She walked around the house inspecting it. Father was casual but Leah felt nervous. She thought Mother might discover evidence of her rituals and tried to remember if she'd cleaned the hair off Mother's razor. Lazar was in a sullen mood. They'd found a college that would probably take him on the strength of his English compositions and Father's influence in the steel world and state government. The college was in Albany. "It's like being transferred from Siberia to Mongolia," he told Leah.

Father was elated. "It's a new beginning," he announced. A few days after Mother and Lazar returned, Leah found a fresh daisy dipped in black India ink on her pillow. The ink made a little stain on her pillowcase. The note was from Lazar. "And goodbye to you, too," it read. "From the condemned college freshman-to-be."

7

Arnold J. Saks

Lazar was in his freshman year at the State University at Albany. Lazar thought the modern campus looked like a top secret science laboratory and wondered if experiments went on late in the night. There was a maximum security prison nearby and he imagined that psychopaths were wheeled into the chemistry labs after dark and injected with serums made from rare tropical diseases. He figured no student would be subjected to electrodes and computer machines because their parents would find out. But he knew enough would volunteer. The sterile blond buildings and windowless factory-like dormitories made him suspicious. And the bubbly complacent nature of most of his fellow students he thought had to be drug-induced. They all acted and looked the same. He endured a lonely and cautious vigil living out his time, as he imagined journalists did in the prisons of Turkey and South America. He was doing this for his father. He was paying the debts of his sins to his father. Four years of neutral anesthetized life would equalize on the heavenly scale the wild first eighteen years. Father wanted Lazar to "sail smoothly" for a while. Otherwise there'd be no hope. Lazar would be cut off, cast out and not allowed to come home. Lazar lived his first week this way. Full of penitence and dreary hopes that were not his own. In the second week his roommate arrived. His roommate blasted into his life like a demon on a flaming chariot from hell. Lazar knew immediately that they'd been brothers in another life. He knew his roommate was bringing

66

him a message. Lazar was to live by improvisation. Fuck Father. His roommate had brought a key and let Lazar out of his cell.

Arnold J. Saks was a street boy from New York City. He had greasy dark curly hair, beady black eyes. He always wore sunglasses and his sideburns grew down his cheeks in straight lines. He was unshaven but wore no beard. He was lean and tall. His clothes were faded denims and black leather boots. He had a thick silver ID on his right arm and a tattoo of Buddha on his left. He drove a Harley-Davidson seven-fifty and strapped his guitar, upside down, on his back. He had strong muscles and the veins stood out on his arms like trees. He was older than Lazar by four years. He was on a writing scholarship but he didn't care. He told Lazar it was a place to sleep for a while. His voice was gravelly and tough. Lazar felt meek next to Arnold J. Saks. He watched him unpack with awe. Arnold J. Saks had candy jars full of multi-colored pills. He had a leather kit with a needle and a spoon. He had two Chinese puzzle chests full of secret drawers. In the drawers were different herbs and packets of powder.

"I have a disease," said Arnold J. Saks. "I medicate myself."

Arnold J. Saks set up a bar in their room. He brought an ice bucket, glasses and bottles of bourbon, tequila, vodka and gin. He hung up posters of Allen Ginsberg and Jack Kerouac. His books had no covers; they were grubby and ripped.

"The best part of writing," he told Lazar, "is to find all the ways you can kill yourself."

Lazar was in ecstasy. He'd dreamed of men such as Arnold J. Saks, but he never believed he would meet one. He decided not to go to classes anymore. In medieval times boys were taught by apprenticeship. Arnold J. Saks would be his mentor. Lazar sat day after day and watched his roommate. He especially loved to watch him write songs. Arnold J. Saks had an old cherrywood Gibson guitar. He'd put silver finger picks on his right hand and pluck and strum, repeat a phrase, try again. The sweetness of the man's picking filled Lazar's heart with tears. Once Arnold J. Saks was having trouble with a tune. So he put his fist through his guitar. He drank a bottle of bourbon and left on his motorcycle to go buy another. Lazar stayed behind, picked up the pieces, and glued them together into a statue.

Neither Arnold J. Saks nor Lazar liked to clean up their room. It stank of underwear, sweat and alcohol. Lazar began to get warnings under his door, typed notes from the dean's office about cutting classes and the filth of the room. But he didn't care. He was in love. "The best part of learning," he told himself, "is to see how many ways you can kill yourself."

Arnold J. Saks continued to instruct Lazar. He gave him pills to swallow and showed him what drinks set them off. Often Lazar was nauseated and dizzy but he'd read books about peyote and he knew that, after the physical agony, came the revelation. He never dared show Arnold J. Saks his weakness, and the poet was impressed and tender.

"You're a veritable geisha girl," he said to Lazar. "I asked for a single but you're far better than silence, my man. Why you're a veritable muse!"

Lazar was proud of his apprenticeship. When Arnold J. Saks drank, Lazar drank with him. When he sucked on a joint, Lazar never refused. Even when the man brought out his heroin and pulled his belt around his massive arm and stuck the needle in his vein, Lazar watched and asked if he could try too. But this request his mentor refused. "I'm your daddy, my boy," said Arnold J. Saks. "And I have to watch our budget. This shit is just too expensive." Lazar accepted some pills instead, the kind that kept him up all night and had him mouthing to himself. Arnold J. Saks looked up from his typewriter and grinned. "Keep praying for us, boy. The world needs it."

One night Arnold J. Saks brought a whore from the local

bar. He'd go there between songs and leave Lazar nodding. Lazar's whole occupation was listening and waiting for his roommate. He helped Arnold J. Saks pull the woman through the dorm window. She was petulant and rough. Her teased hair was ugly, but her breasts were enormous. "I thought you might enjoy this, my boy," said Arnold J. Saks. He had her undress for Lazar while he finished a song. Lazar found her body offensive and strange. He wanted to listen to his roommate's songs. He lay on his bed with his head to the wall and listened to Arnold J. Saks, just three feet away, moaning and slapping the whore. Lazar heard her cry and he heard them both come. He prayed Arnold J. Saks wouldn't ask him to join them. Luckily, they both fell into a drunken sleep. Lazar got off his bed and looked at their entwined naked bodies, the open guitar case. He had a diary—he wrote it all in. He felt certain his years with Arnold J. Saks would become history for future students of literature.

Father wrote Lazar an angry letter. He'd heard from the dean's office that Lazar was cutting classes. He warned Lazar that this was the chance of his life. That it was the beginning of his manhood. That every choice he made in these years would be reflected in his whole life. He told Lazar that college was the foundation for philosophy and discipline. He asked Lazar to try to use college to find a niche for himself in the world—that college was where he could begin to find it. For once Lazar agreed with his father. The drugs he was taking made him tolerant, he even felt a little pity for the man. He wrote Father a reassuring letter.

Dear Father,
    I agree with what you say about these years. Fundamentally we want the same results. I simply have chosen another path to get there. I am studying with a Master. I work eight to twelve hours a day with him. He is a Zen Buddhist, a man of the world. He instructs me in literature, music,

human relations and religion. He knows medicinal healing, geography, and travel. By giving myself to one teacher I can benefit much more than one hour a day in those stifling classrooms. I am learning about risk, about danger and the darker side of life. You may not agree with my method, but you will probably be pleased with the results. So please leave me alone. And also, please send me some money so I can pay him. He is doing all this for free as any religious man would. I should be encouraged, not scolded. This teacher knows more than the president of the whole college.

Sincerely,
Lazar

Lazar had hardly left the dormitory for a month. He was vaguely aware of other students in the building, but he was far too concerned with his learning to care about their knocks on the door or their shouts through the window. Once a guidance counselor came by to inquire about Lazar, but Arnold J. Saks told her he had the flu. "Protecting you from the demons of mediocrity," said Arnold J. Saks. They ordered Chinese food in and ordered pizza through their window. Their room was a clutter of decaying food. Once they threw a pizza up on the ceiling (Arnold J. Saks called it *art concret* and watched the tomato sauce drip down the wall tile like blood in a horror movie. When Arnold J. Saks was despondent in between songs, Lazar read him poems or chapters from the Bible. Once they stayed up all night reading *Charlotte's Web* out loud to each other. They were so stoned it seemed scary and mysterious. "A veritable psychedelic mystery koan," said Arnold J. Saks.

But Lazar's health was beginning to go. He didn't have Arnold J. Saks' "street constitution." He was thin and nervous. His face was pasty and pale. He had a drippy nose and his eyes were caked with mucus. Often he vomited from the drugs.

"Don't fail me, my boy," said Arnold J. Saks. "I have no

plans for death in my poetry. We'd better give you some
world dosage."

Arnold J. Saks took Lazar out on the motorcycle. Lazar
was inflamed with excitement. He loved putting his bony
arms around his teacher's strong back. He rejoiced in the
feeling of the wind, the feel of Arnold J. Saks' denim jacket
against his face. He hugged the leather seat of the motorcycle with his thighs and although he was terrified when Arnold J. Saks ran through traffic lights and skidded around
turns and pulled the front of the motorcycle up like a wild
stallion, Lazar loved the terror.

Lazar's mentor took him past the factories, near the ship-
yard, into the ghettoes. They rode on the bike down the railroad tracks and onto the piers that overlooked the Hudson
River. Many of the workers knew Arnold J. Saks from his
hanging out in bars and his long night walks. He also dealt
speed to truck drivers and construction workers. Lazar was
chilled, but exhilarated. In the dorm that night he wrote a
long poem. It was called "The Ballad of Arnold J. Saks." In
the poem Arnold J. Saks was a national hero, a leader and
eventually a saint. Lazar felt it was time to give his mentor
something back. He wanted to do more than type his papers,
read him poetry and listen to his songs. He worked hard on
the poem, took the right pills to stay awake. Though at times
he couldn't remember the beginning of a sentence by the
time he'd reached its end, he was convinced he'd written a
masterpiece. It was fifty pages long and it rhymed.

When Arnold J. Saks returned from his nighttime wandering, Lazar was awake and full of anticipation.

"Well, my boy's got a blush," said his mentor.

Lazar showed Arnold J. Saks the poem and Arnold J. Saks
lay on his bed slugging down bourbon and read every word.
Lazar watched his roommate reading every word. The time
passed by slowly. Lazar heard clocks tick, chimes ring, doors
creak, people come and go. No time had ever passed so
slowly.

At the end, Arnold J. Saks lay the papers on the bed and sat up straight. He looked at Lazar with his dark moody eyes and squinted at him to get him into focus. Lazar's heart was beating fast, waiting for his master's words.

"It's *good*, Lazar," said Arnold J. Saks. "My man. It's *really* good. It's a kind of bona fide naive bumbling masterpiece. That's what it is."

Arnold J. Saks was getting very excited. He put his big hands on Lazar's shoulders and stood him up. He shouted to the ceiling and out the window. "It's *good*. It's great! My little man has come of *age*."

"I'm going to put this on my album covers," screamed Arnold J. Saks. "I'm gonna make this my fucking bio. They're gonna print it in *Who's Who!*"

Arnold J. Saks began slapping Lazar on the back. Then he held him at arm's distance and stared into Lazar's tearful eyes.

"Who's your daddy? Lazar, boy. Who's been your fucking spirit daddy? Who's been your literary pope, you fucking latent genius, huh?"

Lazar smiled tearfully and said, "You."

"That's right, old boy," said Arnold J. Saks and he pulled Lazar to him and began hugging him. Lazar's mentor kissed Lazar all over his face, on his lips, on his ears. He hugged him and rocked him and laughed his gravelly laugh and kissed Lazar so many times and so passionately that Lazar got an erection.

"Whoa, boy," said Arnold J. Saks, pushing Lazar away and looking down at Lazar's swollen crotch. "Let's not get queer. There's all kinds of ways to love a man."

Arnold J. Saks looked embarrassed.

Lazar's emotions overwhelmed him. He was delighted and ashamed. His mind was speeding with his own greatness. His body was shaking from its reaction to his teacher. He ran weeping to the shower, threw the empty cartons and dirty laundry out of it and turned on the cold water and soaked himself. He stayed under the hard stream of the shower until his feet and hands went numb. When he emerged, Arnold J. Saks was gone. Lazar didn't bother to dry himself. He sat by the window waiting for his teacher to return.

After several hours passed, Lazar knew he'd done something terribly wrong. He went over the recent events moment by moment. He saw their wild pizza parties, the poetry readings. He saw the motorcycle ride and the greetings to the workers. He saw Arnold J. Saks in his bed and the naked whore-belly undressing in front of him. He saw Arnold J. Saks playing his guitar and smashing his fist through it. Then Lazar recalled his teacher reading his poem and his hugging of him and his teacher's kisses. Lazar remembered his own reaction and began to weep at his weakness and stupidity. He had done something wrong. He had abused his lessons. Lazar wept and vowed to himself that he would redeem himself in his teacher's eyes.

When Arnold J. Saks returned the next afternoon Lazar tried to appear aloof and concentrated on a manuscript.

"There's a present there for you, my man," said Lazar. "Under your pillow."

Arnold J. Saks said nothing, lifted up his pillow and took the envelope which had been placed there. He seemed reluctant, but he opened it. There was a hundred dollars inside.

"What's this for?" asked Arnold J. Saks.

"It's for heroin," said Lazar. "I want to contribute to our budget."

"No, man," said Arnold J. Saks. "You can't take the intensity. Keep your money."

Lazar's mentor handed back the envelope and Lazar was sure he was being careful and keeping at a distance. Lazar tried to reassure Arnold J. Saks that the passion of the night before would not be repeated. But his mentor was preoccupied. Lazar promised he would not abuse their relationship if things could go back to the way they had been.

"You know, Lazar boy," Arnold J. Saks said, "you ought

to start your own life. I've only got room for one of us in mine." Arnold J. Saks left Lazar alone again and appeared less frequently. Lazar considered this a Zen test. He knew his mentor was testing the strength of his loyalty.

Once when Arnold J. Saks found a fourteen-karat gold roach clip on his pillow with a one-hundred-page dedication to him, he lost his temper.

"You're like a fucking *amoeba,* Lazar boy. Get outta me. Get offa me. It's unnatural and it's embarrassing to our manly dignity."

Lazar's pursuit of Arnold J. Saks became more passionate than ever. He wrote poems every hour to his mentor and spent every cent of his allowance on an electric guitar for him. He tried to show Arnold J. Saks his dedication by doing wild dances in their room and painting maps of invented countries along the dormitory walls.

Arnold J. Saks got scared. "You ought to be cool," he said to Lazar. "You ought to run at the power your machine can take and no more."

Lazar tried to be Arnold J. Saks' jester. He wanted to bring laughter into his life. He wiggled his ears and put his glasses upside down on his nose. He painted himself in bright colors and dressed like a woman. He hid a large doll in Arnold J. Saks' bed. The more passionate Lazar's pursuit, the more Arnold J. Saks became cruel.

"You ought to be *cool,* you little queer," he said to Lazar and moved in with some other fellows on the campus.

Lazar stayed up nights waiting for Arnold J. Saks to return. He memorized thousands of ways to win his roommate's affection. But each one canceled out the other. He tried to be cold, but his coldness was shrill. He began appearing around the campus with others. He joined the school newspaper and wrote long essays on friendship which couldn't be published. He began to appear, dressed in blue denim with sunglasses, in the downtown bars where Arnold J. Saks hung out. He sat by the windows so he could be seen

pretending to compose in his notebooks. Arnold J. Saks no
longer had grief. He took no notice.

One night Arnold J. Saks returned to the dormitory room
and asked Lazar if he wanted to share a pizza. Lazar was
numb and exhausted. He knew it was goodbye. The room-
mates ordered several large pies and threw them onto the
ceiling, recreating their earlier ceremony. The cheese and
red sauce spilled down the walls making a wet layer where
the other had dried. Lazar laughed into the night and Arnold J. Saks grinned while he was packing. Lazar could not
stop laughing. He was hoping his mentor had forgiven him.

"Going to New York, old boy," said Arnold J. Saks and
then he walked into the long dormitory hall singing

> Trouble in miiind—I'm bluue.
> Buut I won't be blue always
> You know the sun's gonna shine
> on my back door some day.

Arnold J. Saks never returned. Over the weeks Lazar became certain Arnold J. Saks had stolen all Lazar's ideas, his
words, even his melodies. Lazar hadn't written them yet but
he felt his mentor had stolen the germ. He was positive that
all along *he* had been the teacher and Arnold J. Saks the student.

Lazar heard rumors that Arnold J. Saks had a gig playing
for happenings on Second Avenue in New York City. Lazar
heard he was making a band that was going to play at Folk
City and appear in Washington Square Park. Lazar wanted
to follow, but he hadn't been invited. He felt angry and re-
sentful. He felt he'd made Arnold J. Saks' career. He wrote a
letter to *The Village Voice*—

> Sirs:
> I wish to expose a certain ruthlessness in the character of
> one of your new "heroes." Perhaps you will carry him on

your shoulders to stardom and perhaps you will not.

I, however, have certain information which would clearly prove that this individual is neither poet nor visionary. He is simply a needy man. It is dangerous to give phonies access to the souls of real artists. It can corrupt our future.

Lazar decided not to include Arnold J. Saks' name. He figured *The Village Voice* would call him for specifics and he would give the information in a discreet manner. But the paper did not call and they did not print his letter.

The State University at Albany was buried in gray snow. Lazar lay in it and made angels by batting his arms up and down. He took as many drugs as Arnold J. Saks left behind. The faculty advisor for Lazar's floor wrote him a handwritten letter warning him to clean up his room instantly. The pizza stayed on the ceiling and grew blue moldy hair. Once Lazar got a postcard of the Empire State Building with a tiny gorilla smudged on its roof in ink. The postcard said, "Miami is great—especially the alligators." Lazar got some wooden planks from where they were setting up a Christmas dance in the dining room. In a whirl of carpentry he nailed himself into his room, leaving only a small crack as a peephole.

"We're going to send for your father," said the dean through the crack.

Lazar lay on his bed, his typewriter on his stomach, singing "Zombie Jamboree."

> Back to back, belly to belly
> we don't give a darn
> 'Cause we done dead already.
> Back to back, belly to belly
> At a zombie jamboree.

The next day Lazar's father arrived and the campus policeman axed down the door.

8

A Financial Crisis

The winter of Lazar's freshman year of college the atmosphere in the house began to change around Leah. Father came home from work at unexpected early hours. Sometimes he did not go at all. He and Mother stayed locked in their large bedroom. Leah could hear that they were talking on the telephone. She did not know to whom. Mother and Father took two- and three-day trips. Leah did not know to where. Once she saw a plane ticket on the kitchen table and it was to New York. Leah was surprised. She couldn't imagine Mother flying. Mother was different too. She acted involved, preoccupied. She changed outfits two and three times a day. She went out to luncheons dressed in tailored suits with silk blouses. She told Leah she was looking for a job. Leah found her in the front den typing out a resumé with two fingers. Mother was also typing long letters to someone and hiding the envelopes so Leah couldn't see to whom she was writing. When Mother wasn't in the den, Father was there. Often he was screaming on the telephone. It had to do with money. Father seemed to be losing money. Leah knew that Lazar was involved. Father and Mother no longer allowed Leah to mail letters to Lazar's college address. They told her to give the letters to them and they'd see that he received them. Leah mailed secret letters anyway. They came back with "No Forwarding Address" stamped on them. Once Leah asked Father what was the matter. He looked at her with weepy eyes and said, "It's better for you if

I don't explain. But I'll tell you something . . . I'll never sacrifice this house or your education."

Leah imagined that her family was going broke. She tried to imagine them living in one of the run-down houses in the ghetto where she'd share a room with Mother and Father. She thought of herself in rags going to school barefoot in the snow, like Tiny Tim in "A Christmas Carol," which she'd seen on television. She worried about her hair. It was growing long and blond. Mother said such hair became stringy without nutrients.

Leah secretly tried to help. She didn't understand the cause of Father's despair but she was propelled into action by bits of conversation she overheard. "You tell them I need payment *now,*" she heard him say. "I need the cash as much as any nigger in this city. I have my share of crises. I can't wait."

Leah went to an old bookstore near the community college. The bookseller was an old Jewish man. He was surprised to see a young girl applying for a job. "I deal in rare books," he said. "I don't make any money." But Leah persisted. She told Mother and Father she'd joined the bowling team and went back to the store three times a week. She sat among the piles of dusty almanacs and huge Bibles. She tried to study the yellowed pages of the books written in stuffy English with fancy lettering, hoping she could become an expert by osmosis. Finally, the old man, Mr. Fuerstein, gave in. "I'll pay you five dollars a week," he said. "To dust and watch the store when I go out." Leah was elated. She went straight to her job after school and dusted the shelves with an old rag Mr. Fuerstein found for her. He spent most of his time on the pay phone in the back of the tiny store, hidden by old magazines and sheet music, betting on horses and boxing matches. Leah climbed the wooden ladder in the crowded aisle and straightened the top rows of books. Mr. Fuerstein was pleased with her. Leah announced to Father that she didn't need her allowance anymore. He asked her why and she told him she just didn't need it. Father became suspicious, then angry, said "Nonsense," and raised Leah's allowance by a dollar. Leah put it in her top drawer with her wages and dreamed about the time she would present it all to Father just as he was about to sell the house. She wanted to include some money in a letter to Lazar, but she was not allowed to choose the envelopes her stationery went into and she didn't want Mother finding the crumpled five-dollar bills.

Mr. Fuerstein got nervous after Leah had been working for three weeks. "Do your parents know where you are?" he asked. Leah told him yes, but she couldn't meet his eyes. She was not yet good at lying.

When Leah arrived home that evening Father was waiting for her in the living room. He was pacing. Mr. Fuerstein had called him. "Why are you *working?*" demanded Father. "Whatever gave you the idea you had to take a *job?* You have your whole life before you. Why waste it *now?*" Father appeared insulted. He ordered Leah to quit the job and he gave her a ten-dollar bill. "If you want money, you come to *me,*" yelled Father. "Don't you think I can take care of you?"

Leah never went back to the bookstore. Instead she sat at Father's blond upright piano and began picking out songs with two fingers. She always wrote sad songs. She wanted to sell them like the Beatles did and make a million dollars. Father liked Leah's songs. He sat morosely on the living room couch smoking a cigar and nodding his head out of tempo with Leah's uneven two-fingered plunking. Mother never heard them. She was busy buying clothes and going to appointments. But she never seemed to find a job.

The secrecy grew in the house like the vines over a castle in a fairy tale. Leah began to decipher that the money troubles were related to Lazar. She could hear Mother and Father screaming at each other from behind their door and the chorus was always "Lazar, Lazar." As hard as she tried she couldn't make out the other words. She felt too frightened to get close to the door—it seemed as if it were a war zone. The sheer volume of the noise made her think that her parents' fighting could shatter her. Something had changed. The dark quiet of the house had exploded. It could not be restored. Lazar had spun out somewhere from the explosion and Leah didn't know in what dark part of the sky he was orbiting. She tried to find the answer to the secret. She went to go through Father's papers but the drawers to his desk were locked.

There were other strange things going on. Mother and Father were entertaining all the time. They had fancy catered cocktail parties and sit-down dinners. Rich women with dyed hair and their gray-suited husbands from the Jewish community talked about the theater, movies, and travel.

Mother said nothing but worked with the caterers to serve hors d'oeuvres and drinks. She was always getting her hair done and her long nails manicured for these parties. People complimented her. She didn't answer. Father bellowed his opinions about politics, the arts and sports. Often there were artistic-looking people at the parties. They stood around the piano and sang songs from Broadway shows. Father made Leah come down from bed, and sit at the piano, and plunk her sad songs for the guests. Her voice was wispy and nasal. She was nervous. The guests listened with phony rapture and applauded too loudly when she finished. One of Leah's songs went

> Ringo oh Ringo I love you
> Ringo oh Ringo I'll always be true.

Mother stayed in the kitchen watching the maids dry dishes while Leah sang.

After the parties Father always became angry. "I don't know how I'll pay for this," he'd say to Mother. "I don't know how I'll pay for anything." He didn't continue if Leah was in the room, but gave Mother a strange stare. Mother whistled back at him with no sound.

The parties continued and so did long dinners at expensive restaurants. It seemed to Leah that the more worried Father was about money, the more he wanted to spend it. Mother, Father and Leah ate out at least twice a week. They went to French and Italian restaurants and steak houses. Mother often left for the ladies' room in the middle of the meal. She didn't return until Father was paying the check. Father always paid in cash.

Once Leah came home early from school after an air raid drill. It was the kind where the guardians walked the students home. Usually they just had them kneel in the halls with their heads down. Leah knew Mother and Father were having a party because the caterers were setting up in the kitchen. Leah could hear Mother talking on the phone in the den. Leah knew Mother was talking to Lazar. She was crying and apologizing.

"We can't get you out of there yet, dear," Mother was saying. "The doctors don't think you're ready." Leah walked into the den and saw her mother in a long woolen housecoat and slippers. Her eyes were puffy and her mouth was slightly open as if she couldn't breathe through her nose. Mother looked up at Leah and hung the phone up in the middle of one of Lazar's sentences.

"How was school?" asked Mother.

"We had an air raid drill," said Leah. The phone rang and Mother picked it up immediately.

"Leah's here," she said. There was a pause. Lazar was talking on the other end.

"No, I haven't," said Mother. "No one has." Lazar spoke awhile more. Mother hid her eyes from Leah. Then she held out the receiver to her. "Say hello to your brother," said Mother.

Leah put the phone to her ear. "Hello, Lazar," she said.

"Hiya, sport," said Lazar. His voice sounded groggy and slow. "How's school?"

"We had an air raid drill," said Leah.

"The kind where you have to kneel in the basement?" asked her brother.

"No, we had to come home," Leah replied.

"Oh yeah," said Lazar. "That means they're preparing you for an especially fatal bomb. They figure the whole family should go together."

There was a pause. Leah knew not to ask Lazar about college. She knew he wasn't at college.

"Are you in jail?" Leah asked Lazar.

"No, sweetie," Lazar replied. "I'm in a mental hospital. Very exclusive. The niece of the Shah of Iran comes here for shock treatments."

Leah was not surprised.

"I miss you," she said.

"Don't tell Father I told you," said Lazar. "He thinks it's a very expensive scandal. I've blackened the family's good name for eternity."

"I won't," said Leah.

"Thanks for your letters," said Lazar.

"You're welcome," said Leah. There was another pause.

"Well watch out for those communists," said Lazar. "There's no doubt they're going to bomb the shit out of Father's factories any day now."

"I will," said Leah.

Leah handed the phone back to Mother and went up to her room. She started to write Lazar a letter and was going to include all the money she'd been saving, but fell asleep.

She awoke very late in the evening. The last of the catering trucks was pulling away. Leah sneaked down the stairs. Father was asleep on the couch. His tuxedo was wrinkled and he was snoring in quick crying roars. Mother was cleaning up. She put her finger to her lips and told Leah to not say anything. Mother was cleaning ashtrays that the maids had already cleaned. She'd told Leah once that they never did the job right. She made many trips from the living room to the kitchen, each time carrying only one ashtray, which she washed in the sink, dried, carried back to the living room and returned to its place. Leah followed directly behind Mother each trip and stood silently beside her at the sink. Leah counted that they did this twelve times. On the final walk to the kitchen Mother whispered to Leah, "Lazar was very happy to talk to you. But he wants me to tell you that you are not to call him or talk to him until he gives the word. He says if you do so, he will never want you in his life again." Mother paused. "He's embarrassed and needs his privacy." Leah decided to do exactly as Lazar asked. She would turn off her mind completely, not ask one more question. She hoped that her reverence and her conviction and the perfect execution of his commands would be somehow communicated to Lazar and that he would reward her by contacting her soon. She would wait as long as she had to. A year if need be. She wanted to continue to be Lazar's best student and his friend. "Tell him I agree," Leah told her mother.

Leah watched Mother take a large glass from the kitchen cabinet, fill it with ice and pour it half full of the whiskey from the Jack Daniel's bottle next to the sink. Then Mother said, "Excuse me," and opened the back door and went out into the garden. Mother was in a long satin evening gown with thin straps. She carried a little brocade bag. The garden was frosted with the afternoon's fresh snow which had hardened into a veil of ice.

9

These Two Girls

They walked through the neighborhood streets of the industrial town. The air was full of smoke. It smelled faintly of gas. They held hands because they were best friends. They were in eighth grade. Their brick and cement public junior high school had just let out. This school had no uniforms. Almost the whole population of the school were the children of factory workers. Leah thought to herself that the other children's clothes looked as if they'd been bought from Woolworth's. Mother despised such taste. The plaids on the pleated skirts looked as if they'd been stamped on, rather than woven in. But Leah and Susan dressed differently. Their fathers were Jewish and were owners of the factories. They wore navy-blue pleated skirts and round-collared white blouses with circle pins. They wore thick wool knee socks and Weejun loafers. They both had long hair. That was the amazing thing. Of course one of them—Susan—had more red in hers, and the other—Leah—was blond. Mother made her brush it a hundred times. Both had gray eyes. And that was amazing to them, too. Leah hadn't had her own friend and everything she found out about Susan delighted her. Not since Lazar had gone away had she had such an interesting love-mate.

Leah and Susan did not associate with the other children in the school. They kept entirely to themselves and had many lists of games to keep them occupied. One thing they liked to do after school was to walk to the Black Rock district—that was the place where the vocational high school

was located and there were many Polish and Italian boys to
be seen. Leah was becoming interested in boys. They were
like new animals at the zoo. She believed they were all
variations on Lazar. The walk was through the back lot of a
bowling alley. Lately the tar parking lot was cracking in
many places and steam was coming through the cracks. The
city had promised to fix it, and until then no one was supposed to be near it. But Leah at thirteen was busy imitating
Lazar. She fancied herself to be a sort of poet and loved the
cracks. She told Susan that hell and molten lava and slith-
ering dinosaurs lived beneath them. Susan loved Leah's
imaginings. It was the first time Leah had her own audience.

Beyond the parking lot were abandoned boxcars on a railroad track. With the silhouettes of the stacks from the factories and the dark smoke of the air, the boxcars looked very
empty and haunted. Leah and Susan never dared enter one
because Leah said they must be careful of drunken hoboes.
Also there were very large rusty barrels in the boxcars and
Susan was prone to clumsiness. Leah was afraid she'd fall
against the rust and have to get a tetanus shot. Leah was
protecting her friend. Also they'd have to tell their fathers
where they had been. Leah's father would be horrified. He
wanted his daughter to go to college eventually and not
hang out with the poor people in this unfortunate city.

The vocational high school was a bleak, blond-bricked
building with bars on many of its windows and large, dirty,
glass doors. Leah and Susan watched the different boys leaving at the end of the day and waited for some of their favorites.

Leah's boy was Wayne Haverson—a curly blond-haired
son of German immigrants. He had blue eyes and thick lips
and always smiled gently at her. Susan's boy was a big Italian named Mike. They greeted the girls but never asked
them out. Leah desperately wanted to be asked out. The
greetings were enough to set her into a frenzy of a conversation and giggling. She took Susan into the nearby diner and

bought her a Coke and they curled up against the sides of their booth and whispered. Leah talked most of the time and Susan listened raptly.

Sometimes when they still had extra minutes before supper Leah and Susan would walk back by way of a small lake. The lake looked like green oil and bubbled rainbow- and brown-colored bubbles. There was also a brown sort of dust over the lake and the trees leaned in and were covered with rusty damp moss.

The lake had a stale smell that made the girls a little nauseated and light-headed. The only drugs going around their junior high at this time were some pot and very expensive pills. Leah was tempted to try these drugs, but wanted to invent her own first. This lake provided Leah and Susan with a private high. Leah had read Carl Jung on fairy tales as Lazar had instructed and she told Susan she thought this was a holy swamp and that they would transform into ravens the way Hopi Indians did on peyote. Leah felt discomfort at how completely Susan took in her every word, because she knew she was not always telling the truth. She was beginning to learn to lie. But with Lazar gone she felt free to act the way she pleased and, at the same time, she was confident she was saying things Lazar would be proud of. Susan was purer and sweeter than she, Leah felt, but the two of them made a perfect couple.

Each of them had her own room and each had her own phone. As soon as they ate supper one would call the other. (They took turns from night to night.) Their fathers were pleased that the girls were sticking together, since the fathers did not like the toughness of the industrial city, but were enjoying the quantities of money they had begun to make and hoped to relocate someday. Neither Susan nor Leah had to do any homework because both were extremely bright and the school system was very undemanding.

The nights in the late spring in this industrial city (and it was spring) were heavy with humidity. The weather had changed over the years. The sun often set in a bright orange bubbling color, covering the sky with streaks of lavender. The park across from Leah's house had begun to die. It was sparsely covered by trees and scattered patches of grass. There were cracks in the earth starting up in the park too. And some of the trees were without leaves. Leah did not know the reason for this. Her mother had said it was due to the endless punishment of the winters. But it was clear that the land near where Leah lived was changing. It was drying up, losing its color. It smelled sour. A small group from the community college wrote pamphlets about the dangerous "atmosphere" of Leah's city, but she didn't read them all the way through. Father said someone always had to protest something. He said the students were probably communists.

One day Susan stepped out into her back yard to find her red Frisbee and nearly fell into a crack in the earth that was very deep. Luckily, she grabbed a branch and hung on. She told Leah afterward that she looked down into the crack and saw smoke and green bubbles. She said she saw black rock and smoldering gray water. She saw an endless black pit. Susan hung on to her branch for an hour—reciting the names of rock-and-roll singers she could remember and repeating her multiplication table. She said the odor from the pit over which she hung smelled like rotten eggs and rusty metal. It made the fillings in her cavities ache. She knew the crack in her yard had been there, but she'd forgotten about it. She couldn't be sure that her hanging there was really happening. The intense pain in her arms turned to numbness. Finally her whole body was shot through with a hot stabbing pain. She told Leah that she thought about Leah's lectures on Tibetan monks, how they sang until their throats bled and kept singing. Then she got sleepy. In her dream she was being carried through the air by a big vulture. When the vulture dropped her she realized she was letting go. At that point she woke up and held on more tightly. She could see her arms were turning blue. Finally her older brother came home from the private school and called the fire department. They lowered Susan down and she fell sound asleep in the fireman's arms. Since both of Susan's parents had been working they did not understand what happened. The crack was disturbing to them, but they wouldn't talk to Leah about it when she visited Susan after school. Susan's father built a walkway over it and told the girls to forget about it. Then Susan began to scream in the night. On overnights Leah heard her long wheezing screams. Susan stopped wanting to walk down steps or walk in the streets. The factory doctor made a house call as a favor to Susan's father. He prescribed a tranquilizer. When Susan went back to school, Leah noticed how slowly she walked in the hallways and how she always moved sideways against the walls. Her answers to teachers' questions were very slow. Kids laughed— Susan didn't notice. Leah felt very badly for Susan. And angry. She was not certain what had happened to her, but she knew that she'd changed. Leah began to think about Susan's slow, empty walk. Leah sneaked by Susan's house, which was only a block from hers, and looked at the strange Japanese-looking walkway in her back yard. Leah still went everywhere with Susan, but she felt deprived. Susan began to snap out of her fog, but was no longer the same friend. Leah felt jealous. She wasn't the only thing in Susan's life. Susan seemed to have a secret. Leah felt frustrated. The whole city was changing—becoming old and smelly and her best friend walked around with a half-smile on her face all the time. She was proud that she'd almost died and after telling Leah her story once, would not discuss it further, as if it was hers alone and not to be shared.

One night the railroad yard caught fire. Their fathers drove Leah and Susan to the site. Many other families gathered. The colors of the fire were odd and fascinating like the rainbows reflected off silver Christmas-tree bulbs. Wires cracked like Fourth of July sparklers. Little geysers of oil and fire erupted from the ground. The sight was prehistoric and terrifying. The ground got blue-black bubbles in it. Leah's father took photographs with a Polaroid. Leah was bored. She noticed that Susan was elated.

"Isn't this weird?" Susan said to Leah.

"I don't know," said Leah. "It's getting boring."

Susan said she imagined large slimy lizard-like creatures sliding out of the earth. Leah looked at her annoyed.

"You stole that from me," said Leah, and Susan smiled and made a face Leah thought looked almost religious, her eyes going to a rapturous distant place.

Leah and Susan drove away in two cars with their fathers casually, as after a picnic. Susan told Leah later that the firemen had been joined by men dressed in bright white suits with transparent masks—men who looked like astronauts. They arrived in white vans with no markings on them. As she looked out the back window of her father's car she saw the white astronauts spraying thick orange foam over everything. "It was beautiful," Susan said—and Leah didn't know why she missed it. She felt Susan was getting the edge over her in experience.

Susan and Leah were in the same homeroom. Often they passed notes up and down the aisles. There were thirty-two children in their homeroom and they were rowdy. The teacher was a lady in her sixties with glasses with wings and a phony pearl-covered string that held the glasses on her neck when they weren't on her head. Her name was Miss Dowley. The kids knew that her first name was Henrietta. "That would be typical of her," said Leah about the name Henrietta. "And I bet she never went out on one date either." Leah thought about dates. Boys and girls sitting in movies. Boys and girls sitting in cars in the bowling alley parking lot. Boys and girls dancing in bear hugs. She whispered to Susan and Susan smiled at her as if she were a little girl.

No one in this particular homeroom liked school. No one was passionate about the pumpkins and witches pasted above the blackboards on Halloween, or the white cotton snow and Santa Claus face for Christmas or the rainbows and shining suns for spring. This made Leah feel embarrassed and dumb. One day, Miss Dowley asked them to make little men out of cranberries and apples, marshmallows and toothpicks. The floor of the room became a finger painting filled with purple, red and white. Some kids went out in the hallways to smoke. Others were busy forming fraternities and sororities. Dirty notes filled with gossip flew up and down the aisles. Leah felt superior to all the activity—on this she and Susan still were alike. Once Miss Dowley got so angry she took her glasses off and slammed them on the desk. The class laughed and mumbled that the stupid bitch broke her glasses. Miss Dowley just stood there with big old cow eyes staring out in shock, thin droopy old lady lips in a snarl, veiny thin-skinned cheeks frozen like a death mask. Then Leah saw the blood coming up between her fingers and they got restless. Soon some of the blood was soaking into the composition paper. Susan said, "Miss Dowley, your hand is bleeding." Miss Dowley ran from the room making little crazy sounds and when she closed the doors behind her a roar went up. Papers went flying, kids stood on the window-sills, cigarettes were lit. Susan and Leah moved next to each other. "This must've been what it was like in Rome," said Leah, "during gladiator fights." There was a spirit in the room that was strong and even when the assistant principal came in the fury did not die down. But Leah saw that Susan was looking out the window, mouthing a little song to herself.

The next day the parents of each member of the class received form letters from the school. The letters said that each student was on probation. Susan's father and Leah's father said they knew that their daughters couldn't have been directly involved. Leah wished she had been. She was dreaming about becoming a juvenile delinquent. It seemed to her that Susan was dreaming about becoming a nun. For Leah the only exciting thing happening at the school was the big limos that drove up at recess. They were driven by high school guys employed by Mafia men around town. They offered girls free reefer and a ride around the city. They were tough and manly. Leah was drawn to them. Susan was not interested.

Slowly a change came over Leah's homeroom. Kids came to school much later. They were quieter. They still stood by the windows and stared. Miss Dowley marked each kid late but talked quietly. "What's happening?" she'd ask—but to herself. Leah saw that kids started to take naps on their desks. Really rough guys started to cry for no apparent reason. Other kids started to mumble and draw pictures, holding their pencils like babies hold spoons—with fists. Kids had colds a lot and then these big running cold sores on their lips. Leah passed a note back to Susan one day. The note said, "It's the plague." Leah felt terrible when Susan didn't write any note back. Susan was looking out the window of her classroom at the smoke towers of the factories and the layers of purple and black in the sky. She looked happy in this quiet atmosphere. She didn't look out of place. Leah was drawn to her friend's serenity, but she couldn't understand it. Leah felt restless and wanted to have experiences with boys.

Leah asked Susan to take another walk to the vocational high school. Leah was full of poetry and ideas about young rich girls having affairs with older blue-collar high school boys. Susan was quiet and seemed a bit out of breath. She had to walk slower than Leah and asked her friend to be considerate.

"What is it?" asked Leah. "Do you have the *plague* or what?" Susan replied that she was superior to the plague. She truly meant it. Leah felt Susan's strength and again some strange sort of holiness. The truth of the matter was that Susan had decided to stop eating. It was an experiment. She was telling no one. Not her father. Not Leah. It was something she'd thought of since her accident. She knew it was a way to keep her specialness.

Leah hardly noticed the change in the scenery as they went through the bowling alley parking lot. But Susan took it all in. Children were walking around near them. Not in groups, but alone. They were walking slowly. Young child-bums hung out near the railroad tracks. But there were no fires lit and no songs sung. Just children sitting. The schools no longer seemed to have regular hours. The students came and went, drifted in and out. No one greeted anyone else and there was very little laughter. The railroad yard was a burnt skeleton. Susan rejoiced in this. Leah's mind raced with fantasies of slow dances with healthy boys in green gardens with Japanese lanterns and a live orchestra.

"Whew," said Leah. "It positively *stinks* here."

Susan smiled. They saw kids rummaging through the debris. Leah couldn't imagine what these kids were looking for.

"I can't believe all these people have discovered our turf," said Leah.

"They belong here," said Susan. Susan was becoming mysterious. Leah felt inferior.

When they reached the swamp it was luminous with shiny color. The greens and browns and oranges hurt the eyes. The trees seemed to have grown rubbery-sticky material that hung off them and sucked onto the ground. The water in the swamp bubbled and smoked. The girls could hear crackling sounds beneath the surface that exploded like electricity.

"Contact with outer space," said Leah. "I'm getting incredibly high, aren't you?"

Susan was inhaling the heavy gaseous fumes. In truth, she had been here many other times without telling Leah. She felt that this new atmosphere was a food from God.

She felt it was feeding her. She didn't know for sure, but

she thought it would transform her from a regular, American girl to a creature who could communicate and mate with boys from other planets. She'd dreamed about it since her accident. It was a secret she kept from Leah.

There were big red signs up all over the swamp. The signs had white lettering which said NO TRESPASSING. Susan had seen a white-suited astronaut, like one of the ones the night of the fire, posting signs. This certified to her that there was something otherworldly about the swamp. She'd watched the man drive away in his truck with no name. Then she'd read his sign over and over again. It said the swamp was government property. Susan was thrilled.

When Susan and Leah reached the vocational high school, they leaned on its big fence and waited for the boys. Wayne and Mike finally appeared, but they did not wave at the girls. Susan noticed that Mike had a big sore on the side of his cheek. Wayne was coughing. Leah made a sound that indicated she was repulsed.

"I guess the plague hit the high school too," said Leah. Susan was quiet and dreamy. Leah went on, "Father's trying to find out if there are any shots or whatnot. The school says it's some sort of Chinese or Russian flu going on all over the country. Father says if it keeps up, he'll just have to take us out of school and go to Florida."

Susan was horrified at the idea of Leah's leaving town. She wanted her friend to see how she was going to change— how she was going to become an extraterrestrial creature. A super-being. There was almost no purpose if Leah wasn't there.

"Hey don't sulk," said Leah. "I mean it won't be for a *while,* if *ever!* The papers say this flu is passing. Getting blown out to sea or whatever." Leah was pleased to see that her friend still cared for her.

During the walk back Susan felt light-headed and Leah's talking was a pleasant drone in her ears. The ground seemed to rise up at her like the tar on a street on a hot day or the dough of baking bread. When they passed the swamp Susan thought she saw bodies hanging from trees and she imagined she saw someone floating face-downward in the green slime. She gasped, then recovered. The vision went away. Leah noticed that her friend was behaving strangely again and that she was also getting thin. This annoyed Leah and made her jealous. But above all she was finding Susan tedious. She tried to make excuses for Susan, saying to herself that she'd been through a scary experience. But Leah was growing impatient. She wanted to get on with her life. Above all she wanted to wear a black leather jacket and have a boyfriend. She wanted to show off to Susan. Leah was beginning adventures on her own. She decided to match Susan secret for secret. She was hanging out in the back of the limos that pulled up at the school during recess. She was smoking pot that the boys gave her and listening to them talk about the after-school parties their bosses gave at the Sheraton Motor Inn near the airport.

Susan was working hard at home on her regimen. She stole Ex-Lax from her father's leather shave kit and ate it like a chocolate bar. She sat on the toilet until only water ran out of her. She ran in place. She did twenty-five sit-ups every half hour. She ate dinner with her parents so they wouldn't suspect and then shoved her finger way down her throat so she would be sure to vomit. She no longer needed to sleep the whole night through. She woke up at intervals and stared out her windows to watch the different colored flames coming from the factories, the smoke against the moon. She felt a religion for the steel ladders, the cranes, the towers, the huge constructs lit at night, looking like deserted cities of a future century. She felt her blood was changing— being transfused into a new chemical mixture like the beautiful men in the white astronaut suits. Susan's father and mother were unaware of her fasting. They told Leah when she came to visit that they were very proud of their daughter.

She was precocious and cheerful. She was healthy and hadn't come down with the unattractive illness that was going through the families of so many of the workers. She was thinner, they noticed, but they attributed the ups and downs of her weight to the changes of adolescence. Leah was polite to Susan's parents, but had learned from her own family. She sensed tension beneath their cheerfulness and tried to understand the serene peacefulness of her friend's smile.

Homeroom was becoming smaller and smaller. More kids were out sick. Those who attended took to sleeping on their desks or were curled up like duffel bags in the big wooden coatroom at the back of the class. Miss Dowley brought in a cheap record player. She played scratchy thick 78s of Tubby the Tuba, Peter and the Wolf and Little Orly and his bubble gum all day long. She called it music appreciation, but she clearly was pacified by the simple music and the neutral droning voices of the narrators. Leah thought the whole thing was weird. The scene irritated her. Susan was irritating to Leah too. She sat very still and had a weird smile on her face. Like a nun or a Catholic painting in a church. Leah wanted to go to Florida but Father wasn't ready to leave his business right away. With so many of the children sick, many of the factory workers had to take off time from work. "Nothing's wrong," he said to Leah.

Susan heard a story about the fire underground. She overheard one of the white astronauts telling another one at the swamp. There was an old mine under the railroad tracks that was built over thirty years ago. That mine was smoldering. It was catching fire. And it was burning under Susan and Leah's city. It was like a kind of hell, they said to each other. It could explode and throw parts of itself up through the earth and into the homes and streets of the town. It was like living on a bomb, they said to each other, and with chemical waste all around, the city would blow up in one raging ball of fire. Smoke was pouring from the cracks in the

sidewalks. The air in the town was becoming thicker. To
Susan it was like living in prehistoric times, on the borders of
Mongolia or Tibet. If she was afraid, her fear had become
her religion.

Leah spent more time in the back of the limos. Artie, one
of the drivers, saved a special furry jump-seat for her. Leah
smoked pot and let Artie and a couple of the other guys put
their hands underneath her bra and down her underpants. A
few long hairs were beginning to show up and they joked her
about it. They had a Polaroid and said they wanted to take
some shots of her. They said they'd send the photos to New
York and maybe find Leah some modeling jobs. Leah was
grateful. She felt as if she were going deaf. Everyone in her
town seemed to be talking quietly. Everything appeared in a
blur as if seen through a flame. She herself felt like screaming, dancing to rock and roll; but everything around her, including Susan, had gone sort of retarded. That was why she
agreed to go to the Sheraton out by the airport and meet the
"clients" of Artie and the others. She knew she was going to
be a hooker. But these guys with their limos were the only
spaceships out of the city. Lazar would approve. She used to
walk down the street singing Gene Pitney's "Town Without
Pity." No it isn't very pretty what a town without pity ca-a-
an dooo-oo.

"Susan," she said one day—and she slipped her arm
around her friend's bony arm as if it were the old days—
"you've got to do me a favor." Susan seemed taken aback by
Leah's friendliness. Susan looked at Leah and thought of the
word "flesh." Her friend's breasts were showing through her
tank tops. Her belly stuck out a little over her bell bottoms
and her belly button had little folds around it. This disgusted Susan and reminded her of how indulgent and selfish
Leah had become, how "of this world." Leah felt Susan's
disgust, but pressed onward.

"Susan," said Leah, "I really need your help." Susan still
wished to impress her friend; to not lose her before she'd

completed her fast and her transformation. She knew then that Leah would love her and be in awe of her.

"What do you want?" she asked Leah in her most indifferent tone.

"I need you to cover for me," said Leah. "If Mother calls you, I need you to say I'm staying with you and that I've gone to the supermarket or whatever and then I'll give you this number where you call me so I can call her back."

Leah held out a piece of loose-leaf paper with a number on it. Susan took it from Leah and said nothing.

"And I need you to not ask me any questions," said Leah. Susan nodded and simply walked away.

Leah's first "client" was a thickset beer-drinking factory worker. She thought his name was Ron. He was a strong guy with large calloused fingers. He was wearing a white T-shirt and faded blue jeans. His belly and underpants stuck out at the belt. He sat in the motel room and he was nodding heavily. The insides of his arms were red and inflamed with needle marks. He was giving a talk to Artie.

"I'll tell ya," said Ron. "It's far-out employment and there's a whole network of it. Pays like crazy too."

Artie was quiet and gave Ron a beer. Leah sat on the other end of the motel bed watching "Concentration" on TV.

"You get in so close to those rays, man," said Ron, "you can almost feel something in you. Like the horse (he pointed to his arm), only different, you know."

Ron nodded for a while and then started up short.

"And the closer guys want to get to the stuff, the more they get paid. There's a club—you know—called the Death Kissers—they *touch* the goddam stuff." Ron snorted and drank. "The fuckers' hair'll all be out in six months. They give 'em all these suits and gloves and pills 'n' shit, but everyone knows the fuckers are gonna die. The fuckers *know themselves,* man. But they think they can lick it. Fuckin' Green Berets or whatnot!"

Ron looked over at Leah. "She's a cute one," Ron said to Artie.

"Smile at Ron," said Artie and Leah turned around from the TV and smiled at the young man who was looking at her through glazed half-open eyes. Then he dropped over into a nod. His cigarette was burning into his calloused yellow fingertips. Artie raised his eyebrows at Leah to let her know his opinion of Ron.

"He's our ticket to Florida, babe" said Artie. Leah really liked Artie.

Ron woke again. "It's no joke, though. Sometimes guys die once a week or so. It's heavy-duty material. Once this guy was up on the ceiling pipes—way the fuck up—and he was cleaning a shaft or whatever, and the guy must've slipped or something and bam he fell through the air right onto a steel gate and his head got smashed, man. Like a pumpkin, that was how his head broke."

Leah giggled through her nose.

"I mean the mess of the brains was one thing," said Ron, "but the real mind-blow was that a couple of guys—myself included—had to go and scrape his fuckin' brains off the pipes, stick 'em back in the guy's head, de-radioactivate the fucker's whole head and body and go over the creep with a Geiger counter before the body could be moved so it'd pass government inspection."

Ron laughed to himself. "What a shitload amount of overtime that was," said Ron.

"But really," said Ron to Artie, "give me your name and telephone number, fella. Because if you got two years of high school they'll take you in at these plants. And it *pays*. The contact is in Massachusetts."

Artie wrote down his name and number. Ron was very excited. He put the paper into his pocket and stuck a finger out at Artie.

"It's the work for *now*, man. It really pays. It's not bad stuff. You can lick it."

Ron looked over at Leah. "She's okay," he said to Artie. "But I'm too wrecked right now. How about next week?"

Artie said it was all right. He'd bring Leah to the same place at the same time. He told Ron he'd have to pay for the day though. Ron doled out a generous grubby fistful of cash and staggered out the motel room door. Artie held up the money to Leah like a trophy. "Miami!" he whispered to her. Then he took her on the bed and slowly and tenderly taught her how to make love in case any of the future tricks were together enough to come through. Artie was very practical about it. Leah felt as if she were learning a sport with a friend. "Now do this," he told her, "and now you do that." When she did well he applauded her. "Thatta pal," he said. Leah herself felt nothing. She passed the night in a pot-filled haze. It felt like a sleepy gym class. She only felt relief when it was not her time to move and she could rest.

The same night Susan dreamed of a new circus ride. It was an enormous conveyer belt in a factory. She was on her back riding down the metal ball bearings and chains and each bump hurt her. The conveyer belt deposited each rider into his own enormous iron waste can out of which stuck only a head. She saw Leah's head and Miss Dowley's. Then the men in the white suits came along and set each can on fire so they blazed with multicolored flames, shot through the roof like rocket ships and turned into stars. Susan's white-suited astronaut was very handsome. He had black slicked-back hair and eyes that glinted and flashed. He kissed her heavily on the lips before he torched her and embraced her garbage can as if it were her body. She felt the metal go into her back.

When Susan awoke she realized that her backbone was sore against the mattress. This made her smile. She tried to turn to one side, but her rib cage felt assaulted by the bedsprings. When she sat up it felt as if her coccyx were shooting out of her like a pole to be hammered into the earth.

Leah heard that the next morning Susan's mother had been perplexed to find that her daughter had no energy to get out of bed. (Father had sat Leah down in the den and tried to tell her the story gently. Leah heard other versions of it at school.) Susan's mother became increasingly worried when Susan would not leave even to go to the bathroom. She screamed with horror when the doctor came, pulled down the covers and revealed Susan's black-and-blue emaciated body. They rushed Susan to the hospital and began to feed her intravenously. Leah went to the hospital. She was frightened when she saw that Susan looked very much like a skeleton covered with veiny translucent skin. Susan's eyes were wide and rapturous. She told Leah to lean close to her on the bed. She whispered to Leah. "I'm involved in a secret scientific experiment," she said and laughed happily. Within a week Susan caught pneumonia and died. Leah had stopped going to the hospital and spent more time with Artie.

Leah was too caught up in her new life at first to feel much about Susan's death. The whole town reminded her of those jokes about the South where people marry their own brothers and sisters and have children who are deformed and slow. Susan had become like that too.

Leah's parents shamed her. They kept making excuses about why they weren't leaving. Business was good. The town was in the international and national papers because of the "burning city" beneath it. And it was just hard for them to leave comfort. Artie, at least, had dreams. He snapped her photo, talked about movies they were making in New York, the beaches and wealth of Miami. He was tough and protective. Leah followed him around because he wasn't sick.

Susan was buried in the wealthy Jewish section of the town cemetery. A tiny tombstone had been constructed that looked like a doll house. This had been donated by friends of the family who had not known what else to do. Her fellow students had collected coins in a milk carton that looked like a UNICEF Halloween box and laid a bronze plaque in the junior high school in her name. But many were too ill to come with their parents to her funeral. Susan's father was comforted by his business associates and workers. The crowd contained about one hundred people. There were two men taking notes. Their blazers had an insignia on them. They'd arrived in a white van with no label on its side. From Susan's grave came little towers of smoke as in a medieval fairy tale. The air was humid but there was no rain. Leah stood at the gravesite with Father because Mother found funerals too upsetting. She watched the box with Susan in it placed on its straps to be lowered in the ground. Leah hoped the burning city they'd talked about was as alive as Susan had wanted it to be. She imagined a glowing Atlantis, but she also felt angry and her anger interrupted her pleasant thoughts with images of Susan's sickly face and her wide eyes. Leah remembered that Susan's eyes had looked like the eyes of the blind people who walked on Main Street with pencils and white cans, milky and wild. She tried to shake the picture from her mind and it was followed by another—Lazar in the bed next to Susan's in the hospital. He had wires and gadgets attached to his brain and he was being zapped with electricity which made him squeal and his legs and arms were dancing around. In the background Leah heard someone singing the Kaddish, but in her mind Lazar was saying, "There's an empty bed over here next to me, sweetie, with your name on it. We're all going down like bowling pins." Leah looked up and saw Susan's coffin being lowered far into the earth. She was horror-struck by the finality of the situation. She looked past the crowd and saw Artie's limo parked at the edge of the area that had been cordoned off. Artie was waving to Leah. She smiled.

Father was looking hard at Leah. He was dressed in a black suit and he wore a hat. There were tears in his eyes. He took Leah's hand, but she pulled it away. "Why don't you cry?" he asked.

Leah was high on dope, and she and Artie, a girl named Andrea and another guy named Phil were in Artie's new

Lincoln Continental on the interstate highway heading for Florida. A cop stopped them for speeding and asked for everyone's IDs. The cop was a young Polish fellow with blond hair and a turned-up nose. Leah saw from his badge that his name was Kasakowski. He looked at Leah in the front seat. Leah knew she was dressed like a hooker and she tried to imitate the mannerisms of a real woman. Leah was afraid the cop knew her ID was phony. He took her into his squad car and told her so. He said he was going to take her into the nearest precinct and have her father come pick her up and take her home. At first Leah tried to be seductive. Then she felt belligerent and trapped. Finally she broke down and grabbed at Officer Kasakowski's shirt and begged him not to send her back home. She was stoned and her words came fast. She told him the name of her town and she said it was a death trap. She screamed about her best friend who had been eaten alive by the atmosphere. She sobbed about the earth exploding and herself getting sucked to its center. She said she didn't know if she herself didn't have cancer even now and why couldn't she have a few relatively normal years as a child.

Leah felt Officer Kasakowski look at her. He felt her forehead and told her she was feverish. He told her he believed her and said she could go. She was too depressed to even thank him. She staggered from the squad car and fell into Artie's arms. Artie slapped her awake and dropped a pill into her mouth. "You'll feel better in a while, babe," he said. "Once we hit the sun and begin some serious business."

That night, when Leah didn't show up at supper, Father became agitated. He flipped through his Rolodex on the desk in the den and began to thumb through it furiously. He called all the numbers, in alphabetical order, of every friend and member of the family, asking if they'd seen his daughter. His voice was loud and angry, then at the end of each confused conversation, he became whispery and apologetic. Father even called business associates, some who had never met his daughter. Mother stayed in her bedroom, lay on the bed and stared at the television. She called the maid and calmly told her to cancel dinner. Elana was tearful and Mother asked her to please calm down.

It was late in the night when Father finished his phone calls. Then an image came into memory of a limousine at the cemetery. He tried to force out the features of the young man behind the wheel, but the face remained in shadow. Father got into his Buick and drove on every street of the city. He speeded forward on the bigger streets, and sometimes slammed into reverse going backwards and too fast on the little side streets. He raced onto the New York State Thruway, but he didn't know where to go.

When he came home in the early hours of the morning, he phoned the State Police and the FBI. He was shouting Leah's name at the officers and spelling it out in spitting, impatient letters. The police told him it would take time and Father threatened to expose them all, though he didn't know with what.

When he got to the bedroom Mother was asleep. The television was still on. There was a lonely broadcaster at a news desk giving the weather reports and crop conditions for the farmlands outside the city. His voice droned on and on. Father got into bed. Mother's back was to him. She murmured something in her low gravelly voice. The voice was heavy with sleep and not easy to understand. "Let her go," said Mother. "Let us all go." Father began to cry noisily. Mother got up, disgusted, and went into Leah's room to go back to sleep.

10

In Florida

Leah sat at the bar at the Brown Derby restaurant. It was a dark wood bar with thick paneling and the stools were high wicker chairs covered with palm-tree-patterned upolstery. It looked like all the bars in Siesta Key. The windows looked out over the ocean. The tables had candles on them; the flames blew around in the wind. Big fans spun from the ceiling. The rooms of the restaurant were filled with families tanned from their vacations and lots of old people who'd come to the Keys to retire.

It was five P.M.—the Early Bird hour. This was when steaks and flounder specials and Surf-and-Turf Platters could be bought for half price. Most of the restaurants had the Early Bird specials to attract the retired people. The waiters and waitresses hated the policy because it meant they had to come in from their swimming and running and surfing early. And the old people were demanding and cranky. Leah liked to go to the bars at the Early Bird hour. It gave her awhile to sit by herself before the men came for their business dates. She enjoyed watching the waiters and waitresses. They were all blond, hair bleached by the sun. They were tan and muscular and many of them had Southern accents.

She was fourteen years old and had nothing but a fake ID. Artie had given her a list of the restaurants where the bartenders "owed him one." Esther was her favorite bartender. She'd come from Nebraska. Esther liked to lie in the sun and plan hurricane parties. Esther hadn't been in Florida when there'd been a bad hurricane, but she'd heard about them. They leveled the Keys, she said. Esther had parties in her condominium apartment whenever there was a storm warning. This happened a lot in August. Twenty or thirty locals would gather around the color TV and drink, eat potato chips and Cheez Doodles, and wait to see if they'd be evacuated.

Esther minded her business. She let Leah sit at the bar and served her free ginger ale spiked with a bit of Scotch. "If the boss comes we'll tell him you're my little sister," she said. Artie repaid Esther by giving her free cocaine and fixing her up with dates. Esther was on the tubby side and couldn't find a man. She told Leah she had a nine-year-old daughter she'd left with her mother in Nebraska. "I like the sun," Esther told Leah. "And it's like a small town here—you're always meeting folks you know when you go to the bars or the shopping malls."

Leah lived with Artie in a trailer camp on the beach. He'd bought the trailer with cash the day they'd come from Miami. She'd been in the hospital in Miami with bronchitis and malnutrition.

Artie paid for the whole thing, but he wanted to get her out of there before the doctors traced her name and called her parents. "There's a law against transporting you over the border," Artie told her. "And what would you do if I went to jail?"

Leah slept most days until two or three o'clock. Then she went to the public beach and lay on the sand. She needed to get a tan so she didn't look out of place. She also needed to gain weight and lighten her hair which had become mousey from the malnutrition. Artie drove his beat-up Oldsmobile to one of the shopping malls and bought her supplies. He treated her well. He brought her Baskin-Robbins ice cream, Big Macs, milkshakes. He went to Woolworth's and got her hip-hugger jeans, halter tops, and bikini bathing suits. He got her eyeliner and red lip-gloss. He helped her dress and he installed three latches on the trailer door so she'd be locked in safely when he had to go away. The only time he got mad at her was when she overslept and didn't make it to the bars on time. But even then he didn't hit her. He'd just get in his car and go off for a few days, leaving her wondering if he'd come back. He also worried abut the police a lot. He dealt great quantities of hashish and speed to the locals, the universities and the hotel businesses in Florida. As far as he was concerned he was just building up his business. He didn't want to get caught. "Just tell everybody you're my sister," he said.

Esther told Leah she was lucky. She told her Artie was a classy guy—a local celebrity. Esther was smart. She reminded Leah that she could've very well ended up in New York with one of those black men who wore fur coats and beat their women. Those women lived in stables, Esther told her, and contracted diseases which gave them sores in the worst places. "If I was gonna be a whore, honey," Esther said, "I'd sure want Artie as *my* man, I tell you." Esther and Leah hung out on the beach together from time to time. On the windy days they watched the surfers. Leah held Esther's feet while she did her sit-ups. Esther couldn't lose weight. "It's my curse," she told Leah. Esther taught Leah how to paint her toes and fingernails.

"I don't judge you for what you're doing" Esther told her. "Though you're a mite young. Money's money. You're gonna be doing it your whole life, anyway. May as well make a profit."

Leah never saw any of the money. Artie always picked her up where she was working and collected it himself. He said it was for her safety. And for respect. "I know how to keep you better than you can keep yourself," he told her. And he was right.

Leah hadn't gone to the Brown Derby for a week. She'd gone to the Trolley Car, the Magic Moment, the Summer

House and Marina Jacks. Artie liked her to move around. Otherwise, he said, people would begin to put two and two together. Also, he didn't want her to get too friendly with Esther. He told Leah it was because they'd have to move on at any moment and he didn't want her getting attached. But Leah knew it was because he was suspicious—didn't trust anyone. He was also possessive. After a night of work he'd put all kinds of questions to her about whom she'd been with and did she enjoy it. She had to reassure him that she didn't. What Artie didn't know was that Leah slept through it all. She kept her eyes open but she slept. It was something that she'd taught herself to do. She was tired. It was a month since she'd left home. Probably her parents were frantic. She'd secretly sent them a postcard from Miami saying not to worry—she was fine. That she wanted to see the ocean. Then she knew she could forget about them. And her brother. And all the darkness, the bad weather and confusion. What she needed was the sun, the blond-haired people and sleep.

Leah looked at the piece of paper Artie had given her. A man's name was written on it. Mr. Wayne DuBois. He'd be coming to the Brown Derby for supper with his business associates and he'd come to the bar and ask for a vodka sour. That's how she'd know who he was. He already had a snapshot of her. Artie had made a portfolio of Polaroids. Mr. Wayne DuBois would leave the keys to his white Honda station wagon on the bar and she was to pick them up, wait awhile and then go out to the parking lot and find license plate number X117L. She was to get in the back of this car and lie down on the back seat so no one would see her. Eventually Mr. Wayne DuBois would finish his business. He was probably into building condominiums. There were lots of men in real estate. Some of them were foreigners. Maybe Mr. Wayne DuBois was French. Leah smiled. Artie's plans were as complicated as the games she used to play with her brother when they were little. Go here. Wait five minutes. Do this. Don't look there. Go this way. Leah figured Lazar had trained her for this job.

By seven P.M. Leah was high from Esther's ginger ales. "Don't get sauced, honey," Esther said to her. "The Florida police have no mercy. Get here behind the counter and pretend you're helping me. Count olives or something."

Mr. Wayne DuBois dropped off his keys on schedule. He was a small man in his early forties with dark thinning hair, glasses and a birthmark on his cheek. He had hairy hands. Leah thought he looked like someone's uncle. She leaned over the counter top to see if he had a belly.

"Child," hissed Esther, "don't stare the poor man down. He's as nervous as a bird to begin with."

Esther stared after the man while Leah pretended not to notice. "He's no Adonis. But he won't murder you in your sleep either." Esther patted Leah on her rear and gave her a little shove. "You'd best get going," Esther said.

Leah lay in the back of the station wagon. It was a rented car, as usual. She closed her eyes and fell asleep. She dreamed of the seabirds on the public beach and how they nestled themselves into the sand. She saw a family giving them bread and how they hovered and flapped above the family's heads as they threw crumbs straight up and the birds caught the crumbs in their mouths. It was a pleasant dream and she was sorry to be awakened by the slam of the door as Mr. Wayne DuBois got in.

She felt him turn around to check if she was there, but she knew neither of them was to say anything until they reached the Bay Oaks condominium where he was subletting an apartment. She liked Bay Oaks because it had a pool, and sometimes, if it didn't go on too long, she'd go out and swim. No one was ever at the pool in the middle of the night.

When they arrived at Bay Oaks, Mr. Wayne DuBois parked the station wagon and told her she could sit up. "If we meet anyone," he said, "I'm going to say you're my wife's niece." His voice was nervous but not a bad voice. It wasn't reedy or nasal like some of them. He had no accent. Leah thought to herself how everyone was making her their little sister, niece, goddaughter or baby-sitter.

Bay Oaks was a complex of clean white stucco houses surrounded by old trees with massive, knotted trunks. Mr. Wayne DuBois' apartment was the usual one with two bedrooms, bathrooms, kitchen, dining room and a living room with a glassed-in porch. Leah went straight to the bathroom and put in the diaphragm Artie had bought for her. She took her clothes off. She knew Mr. Wayne DuBois would be naked under his covers in the master bedroom. Artie told his clients that they could have a little girl if they wanted, but there was to be no funny business. No games. No beating. No sob stories. This made the clients respect Artie and Artie told Leah that it would keep her from getting cynical. Artie was going to be a millionaire—of that Leah was sure.

Mr. Wayne DuBois made love to Leah very gently. He kissed her sweetly and touched her softly and tried not to lie too heavily on her. They were all like that. Artie said she didn't have to move or respond—she was not to fake an orgasm. That wasn't the point with the men wanting a child, he told her. And the less she did, the better it was for what they wanted. Artie was right. Leah went into her wide-eyed sleep and when she awoke Mr. Wayne DuBois looked happy and tearful. "What a little doll you are," he said.

Leah wanted to go and swim, but it seemed this man wanted to stare at her. He was propped up on his elbow, stroking her hair, tears streaming down his cheeks. Leah wished they wouldn't cry, but they usually did. She curled up on her side and pretended to take a nap. After it was over, she was never tired. This was when the time went slowly. She had to be patient.

Finally she heard Artie's knock on the door. Leah was relieved. She jumped out of the bed and ran to the bathroom. She put on her clothes. Artie picked her up personally and this was the way he protected her. She heard the soft talking and then Artie's voice next to the door. "Let's go, babe."

It was only three A.M. Leah hoped Artie would take her dancing at the Flamingo or for an ice cream at Dairy Queen but he looked preoccupied. His thin dark profile was completely pulled away from her. He wasn't drilling her with his usual questions or complimenting her on a job well done. He didn't start up the car.

"Artie? Did I do something wrong?" asked Leah.

"Your mom's here, you little brat," Artie snapped. He started biting at his thumbnail. "She came to the trailer this afternoon. I don't know how the fuck she tracked us down."

"I didn't tell her," said Leah.

Artie said nothing but looked at Leah with his suspicious eyes. "She's a pretty kicky lady though," said Artie. "And a real con-artist. She came on to me like Humphrey Bogart or something. Said she wouldn't call the police if I brought you to her. She stood at the door of the trailer holding a cigarette with this sorta half-smile on her face. She talked real low and calm as if she was gonna draw a gun outta her holster. She wasn't all weepy and screeching like mothers get."

"She's pretty sexy," said Artie. He was chewing more nervously at his nails and taking long puffs off a joint. "Pretty dangerous too."

"I won't go with her, Artie," said Leah. "Don't think I told her because I didn't. And don't think I'm going back with her, because I'm not."

"Well whatever," said Artie. He was angry and removed. "She could get the police. It would fuck all my plans."

"I won't let her do anything to you," said Leah.

"I'll be far away before we find that out," said Artie.

"I make you over two thousand dollars a week" said Leah. "And I never ask for any percentage. I know who you sell your drugs to. And I'd know how to find you."

Artie turned to Leah. His eyes flashed with anger. Then he grinned at her. He looked admiring.

"Blackmail?" he said. "What a little brat you are. You've got your mother's style." He started up the car. "We're meeting her at The Pirate." The Pirate was a bar on Turtle Bay which stayed open all night. It was a little hut that jutted out on stilts over the water. It was often empty except for a few locals. The Pirate was where Artie often made his deals.

Leah was silent during the whole drive. Her mind was racing with conversations and questions. Each one shouted the other one down. She didn't know what was going to happen. Artie sped up to The Pirate and slammed on the brakes. He was angry and agitated. Leah recognized the mood.

"I'll wait out here," he said.

"I'm warning you, Artie," said Leah. "If you leave me here, *I'll* get the police and I'll testify against you. I'll show them proof." She didn't know if he believed her.

"I'll wait. I'll wait," he said. But he did not look at her.

Leah walked into the entrance to The Pirate. It was designed as a kind of plank. The bar was empty for a few of the local alcoholics sitting quietly at the bar. They were in the sleepy phases of their drunkenness. Leah could see Mother at one of the tables. Mother was looking out at the water. She'd bleached her hair blond. She was wearing a white cotton dress which made her look young. Her arms were bare. There was a drink on the table and a cigarette in Mother's hand.

Leah walked into the bar.

"Hey, Leah," said Joey. He was the owner and a sweet drunk. Joey motioned his eyes and moved his eyebrows up and down indicating the stranger sitting at the table. Mother did not turn around.

Leah sat down at Mother's table across from her. Mother still hadn't moved. Leah looked out at the water to try to see

what Mother was watching. Mother turned and looked at
Leah and Leah could see she was drunk. Her eyes were a little yellow and her focus was unsteady.

"You're thin," said Mother. "You were sick."

"Yes," said Leah.

"Are you better now?" asked Mother.

"I'm better," said Leah.

They were silent for a moment. Mother's eyes took on a
slightly mocking tone.

"I met Artie," she said.

"Yes, I know."

"He's nice," said Mother. She crossed her long legs and let
out a dramatic groan.

"So you wanted to *see* the *sea*," said Mother. "Have you
seen it?"

"No," said Leah. "Not enough."

Mother leaned forward on the table. She put her hands
out toward Leah, but Leah didn't take them. Mother left her
hands there.

"Lazar's still sick. He's still in the hospital."

Leah cringed. She thought immediately it was because of
her. "I know," she said haughtily. But she felt she knew
nothing.

"He's a sensitive boy," said Mother. "But he'll be all
right."

"Did he ask for me?" asked Leah.

"No," said Mother. "We're sour little tops right now. All
spinning our different circles. He's asked for nobody."

Leah said nothing. Mother turned back toward the window. The light was beginning to come up.

"What was it you wanted to get from this climate?" she
asked Leah. "What did you want to see? The gulls? The
waves? The dolphins?"

"All of it," said Leah.

"I saw a blue heron once," said Mother. "It was all alone
on a huge private bay. Very late one night. It swam beauti-

fully. It had a neck longer than a swan. It swam right up close to me. The heron wouldn't let me touch it, though. It glided away before I could give it the little crackers I found in my purse."

"I think you told me that once," said Leah.

"I probably did," said Mother. "I don't have more than two or three stories."

Joey came over and brought Leah a daiquiri. Mother raised her eyebrows.

"Do you like sex?" She smiled.

Leah dropped her eyes to her drink. She could feel her mother's mocking eyes. "Not really," she said.

"I didn't think so," said Mother. "Why don't you come home?"

"Why should I?" asked Leah.

"A good question," said Mother. "And for that matter why should I? Has Artie got any friends?"

Leah glared up at her mother. She felt ashamed for her.

"I'm sorry." Mother laughed. "That was just a joke. Your father is a fine man."

"Are you going to call the police on Artie?" asked Leah.

"Whatever *for?*" answered Mother. This was the tone which terrified Leah. It was challenging and derisive and it implied that Mother might know everything.

"I don't know," said Leah. "State borders or whatever."

"No no," said Mother. She took a sip from her drink, lit a cigarette and yawned. "I don't like jails. I don't like institutions. I don't like hospitals. . . ." Her voice trailed off and she looked down at her hands. The fingernails were painted white to match her dress. They set off a dark tan, which Leah noticed for the first time. Leah wondered where Mother got the tan.

"Do I seem to be getting older?" asked Mother.

"No," said Leah. "As a matter of fact when I first saw you I thought you looked younger."

"Good," said Mother and there were tears in her eyes.

"With all my children running off, I thought I'd gained some gray." She quickly wiped the tears from her eyes, took a compact from her purse and fixed her face. Then Mother sat very straight in her chair. She became businesslike.

"We have to do something, you know," said Mother. "I have to answer to the powers that be. Can I enroll you in a school down here to legitimize this situation somehow?"

"Don't you want me to come home?" asked Leah.

Mother turned toward the water again. She took a long time answering.

"Not if you don't want to," she said lightly.

Leah got up from the table and began talking very fast.

"It'll be all right, Mother. I'll take care of it. Tell Father I've enrolled in marine biology school or something. I'll finish high school in a while. I'll come back after I've had a bit more fun. I'll write him that in a letter myself."

Mother turned and looked at Leah. Her eyes were cold and punishing.

"Whatever you say, dear," she replied.

Leah left Mother sitting at the table. Mother was ordering another drink. Leah walked toward the door of The Pirate. She stopped to steady herself. She needed sleep. She prayed that Artie hadn't taken off. She was sorry she'd blackmailed him. She wanted to tell him that it had turned out as she promised. That nothing at all was going to be done. She had absolutely no idea what she was going to do if he wasn't waiting there.

When she got outside she saw that Artie's car was gone. Leah told herself not to shout for him. Mother would hear. She walked up and down the narrow street several times to see if he'd parked elsewhere. She knew he hadn't. She went back toward The Pirate and saw Mother still sitting at her table. The smoke from Mother's cigarette made a cloud around her face. Leah couldn't see Mother's expression. Leah sneaked around the side of The Pirate past the big garbage bin and into the swampy land at the edge of the pier.

She told herself she wanted to see a pelican but she didn't
know when they slept or when they started flying. She
waited until she heard a car drive up—she presumed it was
Mother's taxi, but on a hope she looked around to see if it
might be Artie. Leah saw Mother get into the taxi. She
waited a long time until she knew it had driven far away.
Then Leah hitched a ride off the Key and onto the main-
land. She didn't bother to stop at the trailer to get her
things. She went to the all-night runaway center which she'd
always known was there and had some tired blond-mus-
tached college student place a call to Father. The college
student had spectacles like an old grandmother. She told
him she didn't want to talk to Father. She wanted money
wired to her for a bus ticket home. She told the college student to tell Father that she wanted to stop in New York first
to see her brother. She waited to see if the college student
would tell her she was outrageous but he was very matter-of-
fact about it. He began dialing the area code, and Leah got
up and told the college student she'd be back later. She
didn't want to hear Father's voice at the other end of the
phone.

Leah found a motel that looked deserted. It was one-story
dirty white stucco and had a cheap neon sign. She went
straight to the little pool in the back and lay down on a
lounge chair. It was still so early that the pool was deserted.
She fell sound asleep. The next moment she was being
shaken heavily by a burly state trooper. A man was standing
next to him who must've owned the motel. "Drugs," she
heard the state trooper say. He picked her up and Leah
smiled. It felt good to be carried. She slept again in the back
of the squad car, and for the whole time she was in the tiny
jail. The jail looked more like a dormitory, so she felt safe.
She could sleep soundly because she knew she had no purse
on her and no ID and therefore the police wouldn't call Father.

The college student with the spectacles came to get her.

He had her ticket and some money. He advised Leah that she should take a shower, wash her hair and drink some coffee. While she was doing that he went out and got her some fresh blue jeans and a top. The clothes fit well, but Leah didn't feel like thanking him. She dressed herself in front of him as slowly as possible so he could see everything, but he didn't seem interested. He drove her to the bus, told her she'd get on another one in Miami and asked her if there was anything she wanted to talk about. She shrugged at him and said nothing. Leah thought she might exchange her ticket and take herself to the drag races at Daytona, but she saw that the college student was waiting until she got on the bus. For some reason she felt grateful and let him see a smile before she boarded the Greyhound to Miami.

11

The Land of a Thousand Dances

Leah got off the Greyhound Miami–New York express at the Port Authority. The trip had been long and the air on the bus was too cold from the air conditioning. She had a sore throat. She was fourteen years old. She was tired from sitting up for hours, but was trying to push past her weariness. Florida was over. It had been a bad time, but now the experience melted into images of dreary highways, anonymous Hot Shoppes and the Christian talking of gabby old ladies. The two-level condominiums and trailer camps were over. She'd tell Lazar that she'd slept on the beach, got sand in her hair and been kicked off by the police. She'd tell him she went to the Daytona Races, Fantasy Land, and a Cowboy and Indian Amusement Park. Leah wanted to see Lazar. He'd been a poet or something in college. She didn't know for sure but she thought he'd gone mad and been in a hospital. But Leah had a sense that her brother was something special. She wouldn't tell him the truth about her bad year and her attempt at independence. She'd be whatever he wanted her to be. That was how she'd gotten by. She was the People's Choice, full of disguises and identities. She knew that she had a core of love for Lazar in her heart and perhaps, if she felt that, she'd laugh again or draw a picture or sing a song.

Lazar stood behind the glass and watched the buses unload. He was terrified. He'd been in the hospital and didn't want it to show. He wanted Leah to worship him. He wondered if insanity had an attractive look. He watched two el-

derly ladies get off in peach-colored coats with knitted hand-
bags. They looked like twins. He saw some soldiers in their
uniforms. He half hoped Leah had missed her bus. Then he
saw the creature staring at him through the glass. She was a
fragile, strange child-woman. She was tan, but sickly under
her tan. She had enormous gray eyes and golden hair down
her back that was dry as straw and hung straight and lifeless.
She was rail-thin. She wore a bright turquoise tube around
her top—her nipples showed through it—and hip-hugger
sailor jeans. Her platform sandals made her look tall but she
balanced on them precariously. She was pointing to herself
and saying, "It's me," but Lazar couldn't believe this was his
little sister. His heart broke and he was angry. What had she
done to herself? She had circles the color of mud under her
eyes and her lips were dry, cracked, and peeled like his.
Lazar had dressed for the occasion. This was a responsibility
that his father had said he'd better not blow. He wore a
three-piece matching blue-and-white seersucker suit and a
wide tie. He'd combed his curly hair and parted it on the
side. He'd bought new tortoiseshell-rimmed glasses that
would make him look like a business school student. His father had told him that Leah was coming to visit from Florida. Lazar didn't know why. This creature was still standing
at the glass, sullen now, one hand on her hip, mouthing
something about say hello, why don't you? Lazar stepped
through the glass doors and gingerly put his arms around the
bony girl whom he still could not recognize and she fell into
him and wept on his neck. She was making loud sounds as
she cried and Lazar was in a panic. "Why is she crying?" he
asked himself. "What did I do?" He found himself worrying
about the police, thinking that the police would blame him,
pick him up, call the hospital, call his father. More shame.
More disgrace. More failure. Then the words left his
thoughts and he found he was crying too and their two faces
were soaking wet and their bodies were shaking on the bus
platform.

"Well, not since World War II has there been such a scene," said Lazar. "What war did you come back from?"

And Leah snorted a little laugh and wiped her nose on her arm. "You look rich," she said.

He picked up her beach bag which seemed to be her only luggage and crooked his arm in a chivalrous fashion. This was familiar. She stuck her arm through his and they walked silently through the crowded noisy terminal into the sticky August air.

"I've never been to New York," said Leah. Then she added quickly, "I mean I've never been much anywhere." Lazar hailed a Checker cab. His father had wired him one hundred dollars. Enough money for a hotel, taxicab fares and the theater. Leah acted impressed.

"It's from my royalties," said Lazar. "This weekend you can have anything your heart desires."

Leah pulled her knees up to her chest and stared at the tall thin buildings and masses of cars and heads of people.

"I want a ukelele," she said. Lazar began to relax. Leah still had some molecules of a child in her and this he could take care of. Their weekend had been scrupulously planned. He had the key to an outpatient's apartment which he would say was his own (he'd spent days putting certain of his personal objects in the apartment and scribbling his name on the door). He had the name of a friend of the family's at the Dakota apartments on Central Park where he could deposit his sister if he needed to return to the hospital. He wanted Leah to think he was fully recovered, that his experience had made him darker and more romantic. As if he were a Vietnam veteran or a prisoner of war. He had no intention of her ever knowing that he was still shaky and wasn't leaving the hospital for quite a while. He was no one else's hero. And she certainly had become no one else's princess.

Lazar told the taxicab driver to go to Forty-second Street at Times Square. Leah was overwhelmed by the arcades and lines of stores filled with records, radios, guitars, clocks, stuffed dolls, postcards. She saw in a tub a windup whale that spouted water out its top. There was an enormous billboard advertising Marlboro cigarettes and the cowboy in the picture exhaled real smoke. Music blared from every record shop. Different songs with different beats came together on the street in a pounding symphony. The intensity frightened her a little. The volume and suddenness of sound and the closeness of voices quickened the pace of her heart and she felt sweaty. Lazar was smiling happily. They went into a store with a high ceiling and above the glass cases filled with key chains and paperweights were strung rows and rows of ukeleles. Leah picked out one that was outrageously over-priced—forty-two dollars. Lazar had the taxi running and its fare was getting up to five dollars. He didn't know how the hundred dollars would hold out, but he paid for the uke-lele casually.

They got back in the taxi and went uptown to the East Eighties, where the apartment was located. Leah was tired and her nose began to run. She was afraid she couldn't be right for her brother. She tried to listen intently as he talked about his writing, his rehearsals with his theater group, and his plans to go to Paris and write a novel. She hoped he didn't notice that she couldn't understand him. Their past with its fairy tales, rules and games had taught her never to question him. Her recent past made her ashamed and lonely and she didn't want to make a new enemy. The present, full of color and noise, was challenging her. It made choruses in her consciousness which rushed over her like waves and she felt nauseated and drugged.

Lazar kept up his nervous conversation until they reached the apartment. He saw his little sister with her runny nose holding the ukelele to her stomach and wasn't sure he could fill up her time for a full twenty-four hours. He decided, just as the taxicab pulled up to the address, to take Leah down to the Village. "We have a couple hours before the theater," said Lazar, "and the Village is magic to the young at heart."

The Checker reached Washington Square and the meter
read fifteen dollars. Lazar didn't dare any mathematics and
tipped the driver five dollars. Washington Square Park was
full of activity in the August night and Lazar wanted his sister to think he was a vital part of its life.

"This is where a poet comes," said Lazar, "to meet his love
and find his inspiration." The park was like a slow-motion
movie. Hippies were everywhere, dressed in leather, feathers,
tie-dyes. People blew bubbles, had the fire hydrants open
full blast and were dancing naked. People were painted, tat-
tooed. They played zithers, banjoes, guitars and recorders.
There was a man juggling, riding a unicycle. There were artists selling woodcrafts and paintings on black velvet can-
vases. A girl with flowers in her hair was doing a nodding
dance with a young black man in tights. Lazar was looking
everywhere for someone to say "Hello, hello." He wished for
Leah that this were his world. He was afraid someone from
the hospital would see him and ask him where he got that
suit. He made his answer out loud—"None of your business,
my man."

"What?" asked Leah.

Lazar told her he was making a song.

Leah saw a fat man in fringed leather pants with a dirty
beard and dirty chest. He was leaned against a tree sticking a
needle up his arm. She winced. But the scene excited her.
She liked the conga drummers and the black men playing
the trumpets. Everyone seemed to be dancing together to an
invisible music. The air was sweet from marijuana. She herself wanted to dance, as she had so many times in this bad
year. She began to move a little. Her brother joined her.
They danced on the stone wall around the fountain. They
got soaking wet. They smiled at each other for the first time.
They made a hora, a mambo and a waltz.

"Shall it be theater and a Chinese meal?" Leah shouted.

He knew he had only forty-three dollars left. He told Leah
that she should learn the subways since they were the hell of

New York. She agreed as she was agreeing to everything and Lazar felt that everything was going fine—just fine.

Lazar had made reservations to see *The Boyfriend*. The theater was air-conditioned and freezing cold. He gave Leah an exercise—to count all the ladies with diamonds and blue hair—and he slipped into the men's room to take a pill. When he returned to their front-row seats he found Leah dozing, curled up, her head on her knees. He didn't wake her until the overture began. They sat quietly during the show, neither watching. Leah was feeling very ill, her chest was sore and her ears clogged. Lazar's pills always made him go into a kind of deafness where the active world retreated into darker colors and slower sounds. The usher came and checked their tickets suspiciously. Lazar put his arm around his sister. He was feeling proud. They did not leave their seats during intermission and they did not talk. It was only close to the finale that Lazar began to sing along with the show. He sang to Leah,

> I could be happy with you
> If you could be happy with me
> I'd be contented to live anywhere
> What would I care
> As long as you were there
> Skies may not always be blue
> But one thing's as clear as can be
> I know that I could be happy with you, my darling
> If you could be happy with me.

When Leah and Lazar left the theater, Lazar discovered that some crumpled dollars had fallen from his jacket pocket. He didn't want to admit this to his sister or return to the interior of the theater. He felt the ushers would disapprove. He tried to keep calm and count the remaining money in his pocket with his fingers. Lazar had just enough taxi fare to get to the apartment. He was scared of the place.

He didn't want to sleep in a new bed. He was afraid Leah would know it was not his. He remembered they hadn't eaten and tried to think of schemes to get them food. Leah wanted to lie down. She didn't want to admit fatigue to her brother, and so she was relieved when he suggested they go "home" without eating.

"Fasting clears the brain," said Lazar. "The longer we go without eating, the more we'll taste everything else."

Leah listened as she had always listened to him. The cab ride to the apartment was excruciating for her. She couldn't stay awake. Lazar kept singing. She wished he'd shut up. Those where the words in her head. Shut up. The apartment was a single-room studio at the ground level. Since it was shared by the outpatient with many youths who lived in the hospital and went to the apartment for evenings and weekends, the place was a patchwork of messiness. There was a couch that folded out into a double bed, two dressers filled with clothes of all sizes, paintings of different tastes, cups from different mothers' table settings, peacock feathers, hippie beads, crucifixes, beer cans, whiskey bottles, ashtrays piled with butts. There were college books, *Playboy* magazines, old newspapers. A portrait of the Kennedys was on one wall and Lazar made sure his drawings were Scotchtaped nearby. Leah looked at the dishes and cups and spoons caked with spaghetti sauce and knives covered with pound cake crumbs. She saw a brown bug with a shiny back crawling over the pile.

"What's that?" she asked Lazar.

"Your first cockroach," answered her brother. "Remember always you saw it with me. Kafka—'Metamorphosis.' "

"Who is Donald White?" asked Leah. She was leafing through the mail that did not have Lazar's name on the envelopes on the desk which was not Lazar's.

"Busy busy busy," said Lazar. He picked Leah up and put her on the bed. He fell down on top of her and tickled her. She didn't laugh.

"My male lover," said Lazar. "Did you know I have a male lover? I have a male lover and a female lover and sometimes I have them both at the same time. And sometimes I won't have either of them at all."

Leah thought her brother had a strange smell. (She wondered how she smelled to him.) His face floated above her as if she were seeing a jellyfish from underwater. She wanted to tell him to get off her. But she didn't want him to think she didn't love him. She had loved him in the theater when he sang to her; she had loved him in Washington Square Park and when he'd bought her the ukelele.

Lazar's seersucker suit was covered with grass stains and soaked through with sweat. It was wrinkled with thousands of tiny dirty lines. The material was thin and he could feel his sister's hipbones under him. He was very excited by the fantasy of having two lovers; he felt free of his parents, free of the hospital, free even of God. He began moving up and down on his sister, lost in his dreams, in a panic of freedom. Leah's mind drifted downward as if under a thick sea. Her helplessness became a dark fog of silence as it had so many times in this bad year. Lazar's breathing hardly came through. She put herself on what Artie had called "automatic pilot." This was just like Florida. She didn't want to make much out of it. In Florida she'd learned to orchestrate sounds as well as physical sensations to distract herself and in this city it was easy. She could concentrate on a siren she was hearing in the street. Sirens were different now. They didn't wail so long and high. They had two notes now that went back and forth, back and forth, as if someone were playing the beginning of "Für Elise" and couldn't get further. Soon it was over. Lazar hung over her. His head felt like the muzzle of a tired horse. Leah wanted to pat it.

Lazar sprang up. His pants were stained. His face was beet red and he was sweating. "It wasn't exactly incest," he said. "Not quite incest, because we had our clothes on. I'm not sure how the Jewish God would categorize it. But I know it's not incest. So there'll be no frying in hell. Jews don't have hell anyway, do they? I mean we could research other faiths and see if we're in trouble. But I'd identify it just as play, wouldn't you? Weren't we just playing?" Leah said nothing.

Lazar was looking once again at the teenage girl on this foreign bed. Her hair was spread around her like a wild crown. Her irritated skin was rubbed pink. Her skinny legs in their sailor jeans were slightly apart and lying dead. Her eyes looked sleepy or cold and the circles under them had become purple-brown. Her nose was running and she made short heavy coughs from her chest. He didn't know her.

Lazar began searching frantically around the apartment. He was tossing papers in the air and pulling clothes out of drawers. "Where's your goddamn ukelele?" he said. "Where's the ukelele?"

Leah sat up and shrugged. She didn't want to ruin everything. "It's okay, Lazar," she said.

Lazar stopped dead in the center of the room and hit both his legs with his fists. "We left it in the cab," he said. "We left it in the goddamn cab. I'll have to get you another one."

He told her to stay in the apartment, not to answer the phone and that he would be right back. She had already fallen asleep into the dreamless sleep children have when the day is simply over and they have no choice. Lazar slammed the door several times to make sure it was securely locked, but Leah did not awaken. When Lazar got outside he realized that he did not have enough money to take a cab back to Times Square to find a ukelele. He further realized that he didn't have the forty-two dollars that the ukelele cost. The night was already becoming early morning and no pawnshops would be open. He walked around his neighborhood, passed the hospital and decided not to go in. He was afraid he'd fall asleep there. He thought perhaps Leah might like an egg roll when she awoke and so went to the Chinese restaurant where his doctor often took him for lunch. The restaurant was closed, but the bar was still open and Suzy, the owner, was serving drinks to a few lonely-looking men. Lazar liked Suzy's hair; she looked like an Oriental airline stewardess with her tight flip, heavy makeup and cocktail-waitress shiny dress. Suzy recognized Lazar. He asked her if she had any cold egg rolls in the back. "My little sister is here visiting me," said Lazar, "and I want to give her an exotic surprise. I could only think of you and your egg rolls." Suzy found two egg rolls and put them in a clean wax bag. She told Lazar it was all right—it was for free. He insisted on paying.

On the way back to the apartment Lazar became cold with fear. He thought he'd left the front door of the apartment open. He worried that someone had gotten in and was doing harm to Leah. A burly Hell's Angel. He tried to walk fast—he was tortured. He saw the Hell's Angel with a knife. He saw Hell's Angels hurling heavy objects around the room, looting, tying Leah up, shooting her in the head. He remembered his father's words, "Don't blow it," and was breathless and weeping when he put the key into the door. Leah was asleep as he'd left her, her mouth a little open, her hands folded, fingers crisscrossed on her stomach. "Here's the church here's the steeple, open the door and see all the people." Lazar placed the egg rolls on a table, pulled up a chair and sat over them, watching them, guarding them, waiting for his sister to wake so he could serve her a breakfast such as she'd never had in her life.

12

Lazar in Paradise

Lazar was released from the hospital on an outpatient
basis. It was an expensive New York hospital specializing in
alcoholics, with a children's wing. Lazar especially liked the
middle-aged women psychiatrists who came and went
dressed as if they were on their way to luncheons at the Russian Tea Room. He felt the hospital had a classy atmosphere
and he had enjoyed his own room for four years which he
called a "suite." He was not ashamed of his time there. He
thought it gave him "poet status." Until he'd begun what he
called his "clinical retreat" he had not been given the proper
machinery to live his life. Now he felt confident. He was
going to Paris for a year. He was going to study mime at the
Sorbonne, and French, and write poetry sitting by the river
Seine. He'd read all about the artists who did that, and he
was to be one of them. He knew he'd earned his medals.

His doctors were strongly against it. He was on complicated medication, they said, and it had to be monitored.
They thought he should keep talking to their staff about his
nightmares and fears. For once Father agreed with Lazar.
Father said that too much money had already been spent on
needless obsessions and despair and to get on with life. Father had even bought Lazar his ticket to Paris. Lazar said he
would enroll in the Sorbonne on his own, once he'd learned
enough French.

Mother came to New York to help Lazar pack. He was not
ashamed of this need. He told himself that no great poet was
ever immortalized for folding things. Mother told Lazar

she'd been to Paris once and bought a painting on the river-bank. Lazar couldn't remember the trip. He wanted her to go with him now. She wanted to go too, she said, but Father had insisted that it was time Lazar was on his own. Lazar and Mother went to the Russian Tea Room for a farewell lunch. He wanted to see if any of his wealthy psychiatrists were there. He wanted to have them see him out on the town. He was disappointed not to find them there nor have anyone famous recognize him, but he enjoyed the lunch with Mother and ate his first "civilian lunch" with ceremony. They didn't talk much because Lazar had long ago made a list of forbidden topics which the family was to avoid if they were to spend time with him. Mother was gay and flirta-tious. Lazar drank no wine because of his medicine. He re-membered to take his pills. They got along fine.

After lunch Mother and Lazar went to Bloomingdale's to buy Lazar a briefcase. He wanted a shiny leather briefcase with a buckle to take on the airplane. He thought it would impress the stewardesses. Mother bought a pocketbook and then the two of them took a taxi back to the hospital. There, Lazar picked up his suitcase (he kept his other things stored in boxes) and he said goodbye to the other patients. He knew he had made friends in his four years at the hospital, but he felt beyond them now. He didn't want to hurt them with his health. His suitcase was packed with clothes and books and new notebooks and pens for his writing. His most precious good luck charm, he knew, was a Dictaphone recording from his little sister Leah. She'd taken up the guitar and had transcribed one of his favorite songs for him as a going-away present. The song was "Stranger in Paradise" from the mu-sical *Kismet*. Leah knew Lazar's taste because, over the years, he'd sent her extensive reading and listening lists. He thought his heart would break with pride when he heard her nasal wavering little soprano scratching on the flimsy blue record. "Take my haand, I'm a stranger in paradise . . . If I look starry-eyyyed, there's no danger in paradise." Lazar admired the odd orchestration of Leah's folk guitar and thought it was a proper avant-garde send-off.

Lazar left the hospital with Mother and she put him in a cab toward Kennedy airport. Lazar was writing his biography in his head. "He was released from the sanitarium and caught the next plane to Paris." He thought his taxi driver was a fine subject for a short story (he was a slumped cranky Jewish old man) and Lazar jotted down notes in a tiny notebook he had in his suit pocket. Lazar babbled animatedly all the way on the Long Island Expressway about his studies in Paris, world diplomacy, the role of the artist in international politics and the superiority of Frenchwomen. He gave the driver a twenty-dollar tip (Mother had given him an envelope stuffed with cash) and told him to take the day off.

Lazar felt efficient and in control. He went to the men's room and took his medicine. He checked his baggage, found his gate number, and was the first to board the plane. He learned the name of every stewardess and where she'd come from, jotted them down in his notebook, and got as many phone numbers as they would give.

When the plane took off Lazar felt a rush of excitement. He began to sing the song his sister had recorded for him at the top of his lungs. He sang until one of the stewardesses, a cute one from Minnesota named Cindy, hushed him. He was so thrilled on the plane ride he could not nap, listen to music or watch the movie. He looked out his window at the clouds and watched for angels. Then he remembered to take his medication. This time he decided to indulge himself with a little white wine. The shape of the Mateus bottle was romantic and French to him. He paid the dollar fifty and tipped Cindy ten. She winked at him and Lazar closed his eyes and daydreamed about walking with Cindy along the Seine and how he would buy her a painting. When the night came and the stars surrounded the airplane Lazar felt like the pilot. His spirit was guiding their course. Cindy came by and told him to sleep. She gave him a red, white and blue blanket and a square pillow. But Lazar knew he was filled with Paris and poetry and poets didn't need to sleep.

Lazar swallowed his morning medication with orange juice. He hadn't seen the sunrise, it was too cloudy. The pilot announced that it was drizzling in Paris and the landing was a bit rocky. Lazar didn't care. He was full of courage. For four years he'd been in treatment rooms, group therapy circles, strapped to machines, confined to beds. Now he was in Europe. He was free. He unstrapped his seat belt and prepared to disembark. He was a little shaky from fatigue.

It was only when he reached the bottom of the stairs and stood on the runway near the gate to Orly airport that Lazar realized he wasn't home. He hadn't thought Paris was quite so far away and he didn't know where to go to claim his baggage. He'd forgotten to say goodbye to the stewardesses, and became distressed when he realized they'd be flying away. Also, everyone around him was *truly* talking in a foreign language. They talked in it all the time. He hadn't quite expected this. Lazar thought French was something people slipped into to give themselves literary style. He felt the language go up around him like a wall. Father had sent him a French-English dictionary, but Lazar didn't dare touch it. He was waiting for the Customer Service people and the baggage men to use their English again. Also he had really expected to see some familiar faces. He looked through the crowds for an old high schoolteacher, or a friend of the family, his sister Leah, or Mother. He told himself to stop this— that he was a "poet abroad," but fear invaded him. He told himself that if he could just lie down, gather his thoughts and get some sleep he would work this turn of events out. He decided not to bother to pick up his baggage. He didn't think he had the strength to endure the crowds. The envelope Mother gave him was thick with money and she'd even included several hundred French francs. She'd said he'd have to learn how to change money at the banks but the francs would keep him until he was ready.

Lazar got into a taxi and gave the driver an address Mother had written down. It was a small residential hotel on the rue Muftard. They'd wired ahead for the reservations. Lazar pronounced the words as carefully as he could but the taxi driver didn't understand. Lazar tried again. The taxi driver clucked loudly, shot his hand back, grabbing the paper from Lazar, and read it out loud. The driver tried to correct Lazar's pronunciation but Lazar didn't respond. The driver took off speedily in his strange little car and began speaking in French to Lazar. The taxi driver was waving his hands around being friendly and jovial. It reminded Lazar of when he'd been sick and couldn't understand the English people were throwing at him. This time he reminded himself that he was not supposed to understand. This gave him a short interval of comfort until he remembered that all his medication was packed in his suitcase. Bottles and bottles for the year ahead. Lazar had no way of telling the driver to turn around and he felt embarrassed. He was sure if he could get to his hotel and lie down his problems would disappear.

Lazar looked out the window at the sights of Paris. He saw picture-postcard buildings and painter's skies. He became peaceful. He thought if he could close himself inside one of those oversized artistic photograph books he'd be all right. He posed himself against the churches. He sat himself in the cafés. He rode a bicycle on the windy streets. He sat himself on a bench near the river and put his head in a wide-brimmed cap. He leaned against the Eiffel Tower. He smiled and held up the vegetables in the open air market. He walked hand in hand with a French girl on a cobblestone street. The girl wore a beret, a striped sweat shirt and tight black pants. He smiled with his arms around a group of scruffy poets his age in a parlor with French antique furniture and long glass doors with blowing drapes. He sat with Arabs and West Indian musicians on the street corners of Pigalle and played a pipe. His photograph book was filled by the time the taxi pulled up at the hotel and Lazar felt he'd done Paris. He wanted to turn around and go back to the airport. It seemed absurd to him. Traveling took much less time than people indicated. He didn't know what they spent their weeks and months doing.

His hotel was located on a square. There were cafés all around and little side streets for exploring. Lazar decided that, if he took one street a day, he could fill up a week. This plan encouraged him. He gave the taxi driver a five-hundred-franc note and didn't ask for the change. Father had said that the dictionary had a guide in the back of it explaining the ratio of the dollar to the franc. The dictionary was in his suitcase. Lazar decided to sense it by color.

The residential hotel had no name. Lazar was relieved to see that numbers read the same way as in America. He could recognize Twenty-two and he was sure that was the number Mother had given him. The building was a squat, square little house with dark windows and a dark hallway. Everything seemed in miniature to Lazar, even the landlord—a man who looked like a farmer, and his plump rosy-cheeked wife. They greeted him heartily in French, asked for his passport and made him fill out a white card. The card was in French, but Lazar knew how to put down his name, his country and his date of birth. He hoped the country-looking couple wouldn't notice if he put the facts in the wrong place. He felt as if he were entering a doll house. He was worried he would shrink in size. In the dark drafty hotel office he saw an old black phone. He stared at the phone to give him strength. Then he began to worry if telephone lines lay under the ocean. He imagined sharks eating at the wires and sunken ships cutting them in two. He didn't know the area code for his country. He didn't know how to say the numbers of his parents' telephone number in French. He wanted to go to his room. He gestured to his hosts that he was very tired. The woman led him to his room.

Lazar's room was on the top floor of the building. He and the country woman climbed ten flights of numerous steps.

The stairway was dark and the lights went off automatically. The woman could turn them back on by pushing a switch at the top of each flight but the lights went off again by the time they reached the next flight.

Lazar thought about the illuminated ceilings at the hospital with their antiseptic neon lights. He could always count on seeing where he was going. The notion that he might miss the hospital shamed him. He tried to demonstrate to his hostess that he had great energy and enthusiasm by dancing up the stairs. She laughed happily and this made him think she was stupid.

His room had low ceilings and two windows that overlooked the square. There was a door that led out to a small terrace. There was a big old closet with a large mirror on it. The double bed looked bumpy and had a crude metal headboard. There was a sink with a yellow cake of soap in a cracked dish. The woman opened up the closet-cabinet and showed Lazar piles of sheets and towels. She mimed all of this because she'd figured out he spoke no French and was trying to be helpful. Lazar felt her helpfulness was condescending. He wanted to tell her that he had been brilliant and articulate in his other life. He wanted to stagger her with who was going to be living in her hotel. He also wanted to ask her if she was going to make his bed or if he was supposed to. He wanted to know who would do his laundry. And he didn't know where to go to buy a toothbrush.

The woman motioned to him to come down the hall. There were two narrow doors made out of thin wood. The green paint was peeling off both of them. Behind the first door was a shower. The woman showed Lazar the light for the shower. It also went on and off at its own unpredictable intervals. The second door had something more mysterious about it. Lazar realized with horror that this was the bathroom. It stank. There was no toilet, just a tiled floor with a hole in it. The woman showed him the chain and handle which flushed this contraption. There didn't seem to be a light for the room. Lazar couldn't think of himself squatting in the dark. In his hospital suite he'd had his own bathroom. He warned himself not to self-indulge. He reminded himself that all great artists survived under immense physical discomfort.

The woman left him and Lazar made his way back to his room. The light had gone out on the floor and he couldn't remember where the switch was. He was grateful for the sunlight streaming through his open windows. The room was chilly and damp. He went out on his little terrace and looked down on the square. The Sorbonne was supposedly nearby. College students parked their motorbikes and bicycles in front of the cafés. He wanted to go join the young people at the outdoor tables. He had one notebook left—his others had been in his suitcase. He thought he would spend the day sitting outside and writing poetry. Then he would repair the mess he'd made by shopping for clothes, food and toilet articles. Then he would find out where the American hospital was, take the one bottle of pills he had and get it refilled. His confidence was returning. If he took his time and thought things out he could make it. He might even walk over to the Sorbonne and find an English professor. Lazar was grateful to the hospital. The doctors had given him the resources to get through the dark moments. They described it as bobbing up again after going under a wave. "Human beings can float," Lazar said to himself. The hospital had given him more energy than he had had in his earlier life.

He sang "Take my haand, I'm a stranger in paradise" as he bounded down the ten flights of stairs. He didn't care if the lights went on or off. He knew he could see in the dark if he had to. He stopped singing, however, before he reached the office of the man and woman. He was starting a new life. He didn't want them to have a hint of his eccentricity. He bowed politely to them as he went out the door. He heard them laughing and talking French as he left. He didn't know what they thought of him. He reminded himself that they

were stupid farm people. He pictured them eating intestines
and pork brains.

Lazar chose a café filled with students. None of them
looked up at him when he arrived at the railing in front of
the tables. He took a long time deciding which table to
choose because no table was empty and he'd have to share.
He chose a dirty young man with greasy curly hair, glasses
on his nose, a rumpled suit and dirty fingernails. The man
was reading a book in French. Lazar gestured to the man,
asking if he minded if Lazar sat down. The man shrugged,
but Lazar sensed the man didn't like him. Lazar imagined
the man was a scholar who was sick of young Americans
abusing the magic of France. Lazar wanted to assume the
man would understand Paris in a classical discreet fashion.
Lazar found that he was humming to himself nervously and
the man turned away with a disgusted sigh.

The waitress was busy and harassed. He thought she
might be like Cindy, the airline stewardess, and take some
time with him, explain the menu to him. But the girl, no
older than himself, was shouting at the other waitresses and
scolding the customers. The students in the café were talking
and laughing. They didn't seem to notice. Lazar tried to
seem casual. He recognized Onion Soup on the menu and
pointed to it. The waitress asked him something in rapid
French. He stared at her. She stamped her foot, spoke angrily to herself and he heard the word "American" in her
ranting. Lazar reminded himself that the pudgy little waitress could know nothing about him and probably had an in-
trinsically cranky nature. He took out his notebook and
began to write. His thoughts were disjointed and he knew
what he was writing made no sense. He hoped there were no
bilingual students sitting nearby who could peer over his
shoulder. He shut his notebook and put it back in his pocket.
He knew it was time for a pill but he didn't want anyone to
see him taking it. He'd been good about his medicine and
figured this dosage could wait. All he'd need, he thought,

was for the French police to ride up on their little motor scooters and question him about drug abuse. He wouldn't be able to explain, he'd have to get someone to translate for him and then all the students would know he'd been in a hospital. Now he was not proud. Now he wanted to be one of them, their arms full of books, their faces intense, their conversations loud and full of laughter.

The soup arrived and was covered with thick cheese. The waitress asked Lazar in mocking English if he wanted some wine. He nodded his head yes. He didn't dare oppose her. Lazar put his spoon into the soup and brought a large chunk of bread and cheese to his mouth. The cheese stuck to the bowl, making a web along his chin. He decided not to eat it because he would look too self-conscious. He pressed down on the bread in the bowl to get the broth and the onions underneath. The waitress brought the wine in a half-gallon pitcher. When Lazar went to pay he knocked it off the table. He knew it was going to happen as he handed the waitress the money, but he couldn't stop his elbow from hitting the glass. The pitcher fell to the floor with a smash. The wine splattered in a wet explosion and hit the ankles of several of the students at other tables. They made tsk-tsk noises at him, wiped their ankles, and lifted their feet up. The waitress shouted to the others and there was a great commotion. Soon they were all scolding him. He got down on his hands and knees and tried to help them pick up the glass. They shoved him away. The man who had been reading got up from the table, waved his hand in the air, said something in a low angry voice and stormed off. Lazar took his envelope out of his pocket. He picked out all the remaining French notes he had and left them on the table. He walked in the opposite direction of his hotel. He didn't want the students to know where he lived.

He walked until dark so no one would see him return. The square was still buzzing with students. He took a long route around so he didn't have to pass the café. He walked quietly

into his hotel. He passed the little office and stared at the
phone. There was no sense calling home. He realized he was
supposed to be well. He climbed the ten flights to his new
room. The lights went off and on as he ascended the stairs.
He stopped at the bathroom, opened the door, held his nose
and relieved himself. This made him feel proud. He walked
into his tiny room and looked at the bed. The fat country
woman had left a peppermint on his pillow. He popped it
into his mouth; it felt fresh and sweet. He opened the door to
his terrace and stepped outside. In the darkness the square
was even more alive. Loud rock-and-roll songs blared from
the open cafés. He recognized American tunes, but the words
were in French. The square of cafés looked like an arena.
Colorful students filled the seats on all three sides. Lazar felt
he was in the center on his balcony. But his long travels had
made him weary. He knew he needed energy if he wanted to
be in this arena. He took out his pill bottle and swallowed his
medication. He waited a proper time until the recognizable
wave of relief came over him. And then he jumped toward
the painted Paris sky.

13

A Hero's Homecoming

Because of sadness, Leah played more music. Father bought her a fancy Martin D-28 folk guitar—the kind she'd seen Peter and Paul, of Peter, Paul and Mary, strum on television. The guitar was too advanced for her and she had painful blisters on the tips of her left hand. It wasn't that the action of picking and strumming and fingering chords relieved her—it took up time. It put noise where there was silence. Once again Lazar's spirit had entered the house and stopped all conversation and day-to-day activity. Mother and Father had gone to meet the plane from Paris and hadn't returned for ages. They said there'd been an accident—that maybe Lazar would die. Leah imagined Lazar in a body bag, the way they were sending home the soldiers from Vietnam. Only Lazar's head stuck out and the rest of him was crumbling bones. She saw the bag covered with an American flag. Mother and Father, dressed in Marine Corps uniforms, were playing a trumpet and a snare drum. She got these ideas from hearing bits of conversations from behind her parents' door. She heard the word "crushed." She heard the word "critical." She heard the news coming over their TV as well and the chanting of war protesters and the announcements of the dead and missing. She herself was not allowed a TV because she was confined to the house for running away to Florida, and Father didn't want her getting cheap ideas from the late-night programs. But he'd bought her the guitar and she began composing a ballad for Lazar. She had a boyfriend, Kari Narti, a football player from high

138

school who played a little piano. They put together an act.
They rehearsed in the living room with Father sitting in the
den, listening, making sure Leah didn't leave the house. Kari
was a gentle boy and did whatever Leah said. He kissed her
when she told him to and stayed businesslike when Leah
wanted to get serious. He allowed her to pick their repertoire
because she had mysterious secrets and the beginnings of a
good body. They learned "The Times They Are a-Changin,"
"Sounds of Silence," "It's Crying Time Again," "Nobody
Knows You When You're Down and Out," and they also
learned "Blue Moon," "My Funny Valentine," "San Francisco Bay Blues," and "Just a Closer Walk with Thee." They
couldn't do any rock because Leah didn't have the voice for
it. She could only sing soprano. This didn't go with the
image she wanted, but she had no choice. So she secretly
worked on her strange ballad and slipped the chords to Kari
when Father went outside to take a walk or could be heard
talking on the telephone.

Mother and Father were away most of the time when
Lazar was in the hospital. They only returned for occasional
visits. Father made a special point of coming home for
Leah's first "professional gig." She and Kari had been hired
to play at a friend of the family's bar mitzvah dinner. Kari
wasn't Jewish, but Leah said that this was the sort of people
they'd be playing for the rest of their lives in show business.
Kari kept his thigh next to Leah's the whole ride out and she
let him. The dinner took place in a series of tents and in between the orchestral dance music and the buffet supper Leah
and Kari were to do four numbers.

Everyone was dressed in tuxedos and long dresses. The
tables were round and set elaborately with Hallmark crepe-
paper clown centerpieces. The bar mitzvah boy and his
friends had their own tent with amusement-park games and
a professional magician. But Leah was too old for that. She
didn't even visit it. She went straight to the adult tent and
set her guitar beside the stool and the scratchy P.A. system

microphone they'd set up for toasting the parents of the bar mitzvah boy. Kari looked unsettled at the grand piano. Father was dressed in a powder-blue tuxedo at a front table (Mother had declined), and he waited anxiously for Leah to begin. He had deep circles under his eyes and kept yawning. The M.C. for the evening—the local rabbi—announced them, mispronouncing Kari's name. There was scattered applause, and although the talking continued, Leah could feel the attention focused on her. For reasons she didn't understand, the eyes of the adults made her angry. She mumbled through a folk version of "Moon River" and got polite, indulgent applause. This made her feel angrier. Father was sitting forward in his seat looking proud and giving her a thumbs-up signal. Leah turned to Kari and told him she wanted to skip the next two numbers in the set and get to her ballad. She could feel that the attention of the party wouldn't last. The waiters, dressed as clowns, were passing around scoops of chopped liver with little flags and flowers sticking out of the balls. This made Leah think of Lazar. Kari whispered to Leah that she was crazy for wanting to do her song, but he was stoned on pot and couldn't argue for long. The people at the party continued to chatter and seemed to have forgotten Leah. She tapped the microphone and announced, "I'm going to sing an original song for you." Father looked pleased. The other people at the party went "sh, sh," and got relatively quiet. "It's called 'A Hero's Homecoming,'" said Leah. She put down her guitar and Kari began to play one chord over and over on the piano like a dirge. Father leaned forward. He looked concerned. Leah said, "This song is from the point of view of a critically injured hero." Leah began to sing. The song was all on one note. The people at the party began to get quieter.

> Gets up, Stands up
> Looks out the window
> Bars on the window

Not any bars. Hospital bars.
I must sit up.
All those molecules.
Hard at work.
Twenty billion molecules getting up, sitting up.
How shall I live?
Socks on the floor
Shirt beneath the pillow.
Shoes on the bed.
Pants still on.
How shall I dress?
Lean over get the socks
Fall on my head
Not any head
My head
Full of scars
Maps for the molecules.
How shall I live?
See the sunlight through the bars.
Hear the talking on the street.
Not many voices.
My voices.
Their voices.
Should I cry help?
Ticking ticking, time ticking
Body can't move.
Not much getting done.
Life somewhere
Life out there.
Easy come—Easy go.
How shall I live?
Try again.
Just sit up.
Just open eyes.
Or should I say eye?
Or should I say none?

Am I blind
Am I dumb
Am I moving?
Will anyone help me?
Are the legs gone?
Not much getting done.
Twenty million molecules
Waiting for command.
Sleep Sleep. Never mind.
Sleep Sleep. Hushabye.
Fuck this anyway.
The joke of jokes
Bars on the windows.
Should I cry help?
Never cry help.
Fuck you.
How shall I live?

Leah thought to herself that the song wasn't very good.

She looked at Kari and he shrugged. Leah felt furious and told Kari not to speak to her again. He was stoned and he obeyed.

The guests at the bar mitzvah party had begun talking nervously during her song. Some drunken ones laughed when they thought parts of the song were supposed to be funny. Others had stopped listening altogether. When Leah was done, there was a small bit of clapping followed by a generous ovation when they realized she was done for the evening. One theatrically oriented middle-aged man—an uncle of the bar mitzvah boy—remarked to Leah that the song didn't rhyme. Leah told him it wasn't meant to. Father said nothing—he looked tired. Kari was giggling and eating a roast beef sandwich. Leah began to feel very foolish. She was sullen and silent when Father drove her home. She held the twenty dollars cash in her hands, having given the other twenty to Kari who stayed on at the party to watch the magician.

"Maybe you ought to get out more," Father said to Leah as he drove.

"Maybe it's time to join a Sunday School youth group or something." Leah didn't answer him. She was looking out the car window for young men in uniform who would understand her.

14

Grieving

Leah decided to take Father's advice. She began to look for places to go to. There was a poor black section in the industrial city behind the Sears Roebuck store back four or five blocks. The liquor stores were all there and the cheap clothing stores. The houses were wooden and they all had porches. In the summer the families sat out on the porches fanning themselves, rocking, listening to the radio. Leah had visited this section when she was little with Elana, her black maid. Elana had retired awhile ago. Now Leah wanted to go back there alone. It was the churches. They seemed mysterious and full of energy she knew nothing about. She'd seen it on Sunday television. She wanted to see it live.

In the industrial city the races and religions were divided into blocks of neighborhoods. She went to a synagogue that had a dome on top of it and stained glass windows full of biblical scenes. Since her father was rich and now owned many of the factories, her family belonged to a "mink coat" temple. They only went on the High Holidays. Leah loved it when the organ blared the Kol Nidre and the tenor sang his long and trembling notes. She always waited to see who would stand up for the Kaddish prayer. She was fascinated by the people who stood up and she wondered what grief would feel like. They bent their heads and chanted and bobbed back and forth a bit; their weeping came through in the repeated drumming chant. She'd almost got to stand up because of Lazar. Lazar had almost died but suddenly pulled through. Leah only knew this because there'd been no funeral for him. Other than that, he might as well have died. Father said nothing. Mother had definitely gone into a state of grief. She wore her veil and black clothes as an attitude. Her mother walked around slowly. Her mother stared out the front window at the park across the street. Her mother left dinners early and went into ladies' rooms frequently. Leah's friend Susan had died, but Leah hadn't thought about her for a long while. Leah seemed to be on the outside of passion; she never could break into the screaming dark center of it. She was not allowed to talk to Lazar, not allowed to talk about him, she couldn't find out what happened. She never went to see Susan's parents; they thought she was a loose girl with a careless heart, full of bad values.

Leah looked in the Yellow Pages for Baptist churches. She wanted to go to one with a big choir. She found only two listed and picked the one with the worst address in the town. The atmosphere at home was taut with discipline and her crimes were implied everywhere. Her parents required her to tell them everywhere she was going. She had no friends, so she had few excuses. She told them she was going to try out Sunday School for a while. They were tired of not believing so they let her go. She took a bus to the Sears Roebuck stop and walked twenty blocks toward the church. On the streets the black women were dressed in cotton skirts with matching jackets, and white linen blouses. Their hats were cardboard with linen covering them. They wore corsages and big fake pearl jewelry. It was spring but it was never warm in the industrial town. The men wore dark suit jackets and patent leather shoes. The cold protected them from the soot. Leah felt her whiteness. She was embarrassed walking in this private section on a church Sunday, but she'd come with respect and hoped it would show. She dressed well in a flowered cotton skirt and matching blouse, had her long hair pinned back in barrettes. The people stared at her, but smiled. She found the church an old brick building, scrubbed clean and standing bare in a yard where no grass was growing and the trash had to be cleared every day. She took a seat in a back pew and was not asked to leave.

Drums played with the organ. Leah couldn't take her eyes off the drummer. He was her age—fifteen or sixteen. He had only a snare drum and a bass drum and a high hat, but he hit each beat as if he were saying "yes."

The preacher sang like James Brown. The audience responded like a perfect backup group. The deacons spun in the aisles and ladies were fainting. Voices called out like trumpets and although Leah had no interest in Jesus, she was envious of so much love in one room. When the choir began—and there were about fifty members in bright blue robes with white collars—the room filled with a moaning chord. She felt it in herself and she saw it rise in the rest of the congregation.

Sitting next to Leah was a timid, frail old lady whose hat had a pink net hanging from it. She smiled and Leah nodded proudly to her. The congregation, choir and preacher were involved in a wild question-and-answer sermon. The responses were so rhythmic and so natural that they seemed memorized. Leah wished she knew the words. The old lady next to her was not shouting but had her eyes closed and was nodding as if her shouts were internalized and had become warm flows of sound within her.

Then the choir began a hymn that was clearly for the dead. It was about a ship that sailed out on a sea and carried new visitors every day. It was about the width of the ocean and the depth of it. The choir swayed back and forth. A young female soloist cried above them and the choir began clapping their hands above their heads. Leah could see the oars and the captain, she could hear the wind and she heard them singing about the huge crowded boat as it broke through the clouds and sailed up toward God. The drummer was dressed very properly and sat still, but he was looking at Leah. This broke her mood and made her uncomfortable. He seemed to be frowning in her direction.

The preacher asked for new converts to come forward to the platform. He wanted to put his palms on their heads and bless them. Leah wanted to go forward, not because she wanted to switch religions, but to give respect and get closer to the podium. The drummer's stare was holding her back; the choir was throbbing with a new gospel tune whose rhythm was almost irresistible. The old lady next to Leah smiled at her again and nodded in the direction of the preachers. About twenty people had come forward and the congregation was standing, sitting, clapping and dancing. Leah eased her way through the crowded aisles, trying to appear like a spectator. The music was moving her, though she felt awkward and cautious. When she reached the line of people waiting at the podium she felt a strong familiar hand on her shoulder. She was frightened and froze with shame. Elana glared at her and slapped her full in the face. In the passionate chaos, few people noticed, but those who did minded their business. Leah caught a glimpse of the young drummer and he was smiling bitterly, looking down, playing what he was supposed to play. Elana, who was completely gray now and whose eyes were small and clouded behind thick glasses, said not a word to Leah, but held on to her shoulder firmly so she could not move forward. Leah turned around and head bowed, walked out of the church.

She was blushing and felt her whole head heat up. She rushed to the Main Avenue bus and took it to the synagogue. She walked into the brick one-story Sunday School and slipped into a seat in the high school seminar. There, one of the members of the board was finishing up a talk about the differences between Reform and Conservative Judaism. He was a dentist and a senior member of the temple who got to carry the Torah out of its ark. Soon class was dismissed and, as Leah expected, her father was waiting in his Buick convertible, fingers drumming impatiently on the steering wheel. He motioned to her, as if he didn't know that she had seen him, that he'd come to surprise her by giving her a ride home. Father talked to Leah about his days as a bar mitz-vah, but Leah was hearing James Brown in her head and she was pounding her thighs with her palms, keeping time with a congregation of mourners. She was imagining herself giving a sermon. When they reached home Leah leaped out of the car, slapped the sidewalk with her hand and then held it skyward and leaning nearly half over in a back bend she yelled, *"Praise* the Lord!"

"Stop acting like Lazar," snapped Father.

Leah diddily-bopped into the house. She felt as if her body were moving in a million different directions. She was proud, but unhappy.

15

Home Movies Without Sound

Leah went up into the family attic. It was a crowded space, stuffed with cardboard boxes. The roof slanted sharply; she had to duck her head to walk. There was a tiny window that led out to the roof. It was winter, but she opened it. The cold air cleared away some of the feeling of mildew. Leah was looking for an adventure. She knew her parents' love letters from World War II were stored in a box, but she'd read them already. She knew old books with fancy rhyming poetry were piled in other boxes but the poetry was corny. She knew there were brownish photographs of family on both her parents' sides, but she was so young that her history meant little to her. It was her sixteenth birthday and she was hoping to find a mystical secret hidden. A special light. An arrowhead. A map to an ancient country. She hadn't had any contact with Lazar since he'd gone to Paris and been shipped back and the magic was fading. Later in the evening she was to have a ritual Sweet Sixteen. But the porky long debutante-type gowns and the half-cocktail–half rock-and-roll orchestra did not thrill her. She searched around the boxes looking for traces of Lazar but his papers had been secretly stored—she was not to see them.

Leah rummaged around, flipping up the tops of the boxes and shoving her hands through old sweaters, tablecloths, shoes and documents. Birth certificates, marriage license, diplomas, letters from names she didn't recognize. It seemed her family saved everything, but used nothing. Finally, she discovered a couple of cartons that had little yellow Kodak

149

boxes swimming in them and loose reels of film. Her father had always taken movies of the family. He labeled them elaborately as if he were Shakespeare. She couldn't stand the titles. They seemed so haughty. There was one movie, she remembered, of her father playing the recorder. She guessed her mother had been holding the camera. The title wasn't "Father playing the recorder." He'd labeled it, "A Man in Search of Music." This disgusted her. But she decided she'd give herself a movie show. She debated at first because she was trying to hear if the telephone downstairs was going to ring. She kept thinking Lazar might call for her birthday. After all, it had been a sort of annual ritual. She thought the sound of the projector might drown the phone—that she'd miss the call. "Can't wait around all day," she said to herself. And anyway, Lazar hadn't called in months. Why would he start now?

She threaded up the projector and was already tired. Life was getting dull. She'd had some pretty strange times for a girl her age but now they were in the past and she couldn't seem to get going. Every time she tried to create a little poetry for herself it backfired.

The projector was looped carelessly, black streamers of film hanging down, capable of going anywhere. She knew she was making a mess. It hardly mattered. Her mother hadn't been up to the attic in years. The projector whirred with a horrible grating sound. The light on it smelled like burned hair. The picture on the slanted wall was blurred and running at a jagged weird speed.

THE PRINCESS IS GIVEN THE PROPER
SALUTATIONS ON HER FIFTH YEAR

Little girls bobbing around in petticoats. Umbrellas of petticoats and little underpants parade by the screen. Lazar is wearing a party hat and blowing on a kazoo. He is leading the march. He's a little Nazi. His glasses and stiff walk make him look strict. The little girls seem to be having a good

time. They wave at the camera as they go by. Leah's mother
and father are smiling and waving at a long white table.
There's a cake on it. Leah leans over the cake and blows at
the candle. Lazar is counting the candles she missed. He ap-
plauds her vigorously anyway. The film runs out.

Leah didn't bother to stuff that one in its box. She let the
spotted black film pile on the floor. She grabbed another
yellow box.

THE LEOPARD MAMBOS WITH THE BOXER

Mother and Father are dancing. The projector makes the
dance seem all out of time. Mother is wearing a leopard-pat-
terned pajama suit. Father is dressed in red satin boxer
shorts. They are bobbing up and down like people who have
taken dance lessons and are proud of the steps they memorized. Father goes to take Mother into a dip and drops her
flat. He laughs. She doesn't, but she looks at the camera and
poses a smile. Her lipstick is bright red. So are her fingernails. She waves to the camera to get off her. The camera
moves to Father, who is coaxing her to get up. The film runs
out.

Leah didn't bother rewinding. She enjoyed the mound of
film on the floor. She liked the thought of her parents dancing together and was moved in particular by her mother's
long-waisted body and the natural way she swayed her hips.
Her father moved his head up and down like a turtle.
"Style," she whispered at them and imagined herself as a
woman dancing for a camera late at night in a living room.

THE FATHER AND SON AS LAUREL AND HARDY

Lazar and Father are sitting on a couch. Lazar's glasses
are slipping on his nose. Father hams up a face and pushes
the glasses back on Lazar's nose. Lazar makes his glasses slip
again and Father pushes them. They slip again, Father
pushes them. Lazar hops a foot sideways on the couch. Father moves next to him. Lazar hops again and Father ad-
vances. Lazar is squashed against the arm of the couch and

Father is squeezing him there making faces. The film breaks here.

"Ha ha," said Leah. "You two are a scream." She doesn't know why but that clip makes her angry. And her moodiness gets into her hands, which can't fix the broken film or unstick it from the spokes of the projector. "At war with the material world," as Lazar said. Once he had found her waist deep in cutouts, paste, Scotch tape and toys in the family room. Her mother had left her there to clean up the mess. She was helpless to do it. "At war with the material world," Lazar had said to her and tried to help. They'd crumbled the bigger pieces into crumbs of paste and paper. They'd laughed until they had to grab their stomachs. Mother had sent them both to their rooms and summoned the maid.

PRODIGAL CREATIONS

This is a film shot and designed by Lazar. She could tell by the way it went in and out of focus. It is an art show of cutouts and paintings with captions. The first, a painting, is called *Heart's Blood* and shows a dagger and a beast. The second shows a cake with smoke coming out of it and is called *The Devil's Surprise.* The movie pans along here and sees nothing and finally gets into focus on an India ink drawing of some dots, called *Snow Is the Indifference of God.* The last piece of cardboard has the word FINALLY printed on it and the camera finds Leah pudgy and smiling shyly at age three posing by her brother's sign. The film runs out.

Leah rewound this film. Partially to test her luck with the projector and also because she liked this one the best so far. She paused awhile to hear if the phone would ring. After some silence she reached into the carton for another yellow box.

MARTHA GRAHAM'S COMPETITION

Leah is four. She is wearing a derby that falls over her eyes and she has a fat cigar in her mouth with the plastic still on it. Her party dress is short and her underpants show. She is doing a fast dance, half soft shoe–half ballet. She's going at it in a seductive way. The camera stays steady on her. This is her father's camera work. The film runs out.

"What a princess," Leah said to herself. This was a dancing, drawing, acting, playing family. She imagined film clips of her life when they honored her for whatever she'd done when she turned eighty-three. She thought this one should definitely be included. She rewound it and put it carefully back in its box. She was proud and taking bows. "Oh, Lazar Lazar," she sang. She much preferred to spend her birthday in a derby with a cigar than in a stuffy long dress dancing the jerk with her vocational school boyfriend. She was getting tired of her afternoon at the movies. It wasn't getting her anywhere. She rummaged around for a Lazar film for the last one. She found one labeled with his handwriting.

LAZAR CINE PHOTOG PRESENTS THESE TWO GIRLS
By J. Lazar Esq.

This movie is outside the house. Lazar's grubby hand can be seen on the camera. The small two-story house is in a smoky background. Leah is out on the sidewalk, posing, not knowing what to do for the camera. She is nine or ten. Lazar's other hand snaps at her, makes a motion and the film jumps up and down. Leah begins to dance, not like her four-year-old dance, but slower and shyer, a kind of swaying. Her mother appears on the porch and is watching Lazar film Leah. The camera takes in Mother. Mother immediately begins to dance behind Leah in exactly the same way; imitating Leah precisely and with love and a little bit of mocking. The camera enjoys this double image. Leah has no idea her mother is there. She is serious and intent upon pleasing her brother. Her smile is like a little girl model. All frozen and overly cute. Mother is not smiling; she is dancing. Leah is working hard for Lazar. Lazar is picking up on Mother. There are some titles at the end. They say, "And so they danced on and on . . ." The film runs out.

Leah left everything. She left the last film on the projector and the carton and mounds of celluloid in the middle of the floor. She wasn't one for saving things. She'd had enough history. It was late afternoon when Leah descended from the attic. She was tired and wanted no part of the rented country club, the little hot dogs, meatballs, the wide cake or the thin wrapped packages of pantyhose she'd receive. The telephone hadn't rung and there was no wild telegram waiting for her.

Her mother was sitting on Leah's bed when she got to her room. She'd laid out clean underwear, stockings, the long white dress with the pastel flowers.

Her mother was wearing a bathrobe. She didn't ask Leah what she'd been doing or why her hands and face looked as if they were smeared with newsprint. Her mother was always completely clean. She took Leah to the bathroom and began scrubbing her as she had done when Leah was a baby.

"This is a special night," said Leah's mother.

They went back to the bedroom. Leah's mother helped her into her teenage girdle and zipped up the back of the dress. She insisted on combing her daughter's long hair and it pulled and hurt. Leah whined and made angry faces. Her mother was peaceful and patient. When they were done, Leah's mother took her daughter in front of the mirror and gave her a full view. They swayed back and forth as if dancing.

"You look beautiful," said her mother. But Leah was only looking at the tall thin woman behind her who seemed to be dancing.

"You won't hear from Lazar," said her mother. "So don't waste your life waiting."

Her mother hugged Leah from behind and wished her a happy birthday. They looked as though they were dancing a private bear-hug slow dance in a small room late at night.

16

Lazar Buys Leah the State of Vermont

Leah traveled to Bennington College at the age of seventeen. She had little hope of getting in. Her high school records were incomplete. Her grades were uneven. Her schooling had been more like a correspondence course between herself and Lazar. He'd told her what to read, what to listen to. When he'd become injured, she no longer made an effort. Father quoted Winston Churchill and Henry Wadsworth Longfellow. Mother played *Lost in the Stars* by Kurt Weill on the record player and watched TV game shows on television. Leah's learning was made up of these sounds and images, with her own travels in Florida and her walks through her haunted hometown added in. Also, she was still playing the guitar. She had an idea that if she could make a folk group like Peter, Paul and Mary, she'd be able to tour to New York and be reunited with her brother. What she wanted most was to be near him, and not to disappoint him. But she so rarely heard from Lazar that she was often unclear about what he would want her to do.

She'd been very uncooperative about college. Father wanted her to go to summer school and night school, bring up her grades and "take a shot" at one of the Seven Sisters colleges. Mostly Leah sat around with Kari Narti and wrote songs. When she'd sent some of her songs to Lazar he'd written her back and said her tunes were lovely but that her lyrics were "choking to death" on their own images. "One more adjective," he wrote, "and your little song will expire from obesity. One more internal rhyme and the song will commit suicide." Leah wanted to go to New York and audition for a coffeehouse circuit. Father told her to "cease from Lazarisms." Kari was going off to college to study to be a doctor. Leah had no wish to write her name over and over again on different colored forms and compose essays on why she was particularly choosing a school she knew nothing about.

She went for the interview at Bennington because she wanted to see mountains. She went by herself. She rode on a Greyhound bus for eight hours. The Bennington campus was made up of white New England houses and imitation barns and big mansions. Leah liked the enormous range of mountains and open fields. She knew she could get lost in them. Mother and Father had been watching her every move for over two years. She wasn't to be ill, to get sad, or exhibit any signs of anger or restlessness. She'd made an unspoken pact to cooperate. But now she wanted to get lost. She imagined herself lying naked in these Bennington mountains. She wanted to walk far back into the woods, disappear for days. She needed to retreat.

The admissions office was in a red building called the Barn. Leah found her way to the appointed room with ease. She felt no nervousness. She was afraid perhaps that they'd ask her why she wanted to go to their college and she couldn't think of a coherent answer. There was nothing specific she wanted to study. There was no one she wanted to be. "I want to camp out on your acres of land," she said to herself, and heard her father warning her against "Lazarisms."

The admissions office was a white room with a large iron fireplace. A white rug lay on the old oak floor. There was a round desk at one end and a couch at the other. The admissions director sat on the couch with two golden retrievers at her feet. The woman smiled at Leah and told her to come in.

She said her name was JoAnna. She wore faded Levi's and a
T-shirt—something Leah had not seen a grown woman wear
since Florida. JoAnna was in her late forties. Her hair was
brown and cut short like a boy's. She was a skinny woman
and muscular. Her hands looked calloused and her fingernails were cut short and were unpolished. Her face was
strong. She had wide round eyes, a button Wasp nose and
large mouth. She wore no makeup. From the instant Leah
entered the office she felt JoAnna was evaluating her. But
not unkindly.

JoAnna told Leah to take a chair near the couch which
was directly facing her. Leah cringed at the close contact.
She was tired of being scrutinized. The golden retrievers
sniffed at Leah for a few moments and went back to their
mistress.

"You must do this all day," Leah said to the dogs.

JoAnna said nothing, smiled pleasantly and began looking
through a file she had on her lap. When she read she put on
the thick glasses which hung around her neck with a piece of
string.

"There won't be much in there that will make you want
me," said Leah, indicating the file.

JoAnna looked up at Leah and stared hard at her.

"And what will make me want you?" she asked.

Leah liked this woman. She was scruffy and tough. Her
office was messy, but full of light.

"Maybe my life," said Leah.

JoAnna closed the file and got up to close the door. She
leaned out and told her secretary to hold her calls. She sat
back down and asked Leah to tell her whatever she thought
would be helpful.

Leah wasn't used to someone with such flexible rules. It
freed her mind. She figured that maybe she could make a
good exchange. It was a real con, she thought. All the years
of secrets could maybe buy her a year in the country. There
was no reason to hold onto them anymore. Leah began to

tell the story of her life. She exaggerated every point, but kept the fundamentals true. She described her mother as a poet and national athlete. She talked about her father and said he was a drunken business magnate with ties to the Mafia. She said she'd run away from home in protest of his murder of several innocent workers. Leah sketched out her hometown for JoAnna and told her how one had to make rituals and exercises to deal with its evil and unhealthy forces. She described watching her best friend starve to death under mysterious and unexplained circumstances. She told JoAnna about her own strong relationship with the black people in her town, her political organizing, her field study of their music and poverty. Then Leah went on to describe her year as a prostitute, her connection with the hard drug trade. Leah made up a dramatic scene in which she had to escape under cover from her pimp and had to be under police guard for two years to make sure he wouldn't kill her.

JoAnna was listening raptly. She stared at Leah the whole time and encouraged her with nods and shocked sighs. Leah was delighted at her own spill of words. She began to describe her brother and found herself clutching. It was as if she were Taking His Name in Vain. But Leah pushed through. She wanted to buy herself into the mountains; she wanted to talk her way into a scholarship—a Ph.D. She talked about Lazar's games. She told JoAnna about his letters to her and his lessons. She told JoAnna that Lazar and her mother had slept together. And that Lazar had been the inspiration for many rock-and-roll stars and poets. She described to JoAnna the time she went to visit him in New York and he'd taken her to the theater, showed her Greenwich Village and had taught her about sex. It was only when she began to talk about his hospitalization and what happened to him in Paris that Leah began to wind down. She couldn't complete the story. She skipped over the end and lamely began to describe her music and guitar playing. She felt ashamed of herself and she stopped in the middle of a sentence.

"What happened?" asked JoAnna kindly. "Why did you stop?"

Leah looked away from the woman, whose eyes were still penetrating and whose face had not changed expression

"This is a low-level con game," said Leah.

"I don't think so," said JoAnna. "If even one quarter of what you've told me is true, it's a wonder you're walking around."

Leah looked up at the woman. She couldn't help herself. She felt a wide grin spread over her face.

"You have a good smile," said JoAnna. "It changes your whole looks. You light up."

The admissions director changed positions and leaned back casually on the couch. She seemed to be calculating.

"Tell me something," she said. "If you like to live life so dangerously, how come you want to come to a little sequestered girls' school in Vermont? That doesn't seem your style at all."

Leah shrugged. She felt bereft and disappointed. She thought she'd blown her chance.

"I think I know why," said JoAnna. She gestured with her hands as if her thoughts were adding up correctly. "I think you're tired. I think you want a vacation. You want to lie around in the mountain air, read books, think about yourself, go to boring Williams mixers and be told irrelevant facts by outdated old professors. You want to be a regular girl."

Leah laughed in spite of her embarrassment.

"I won't tell anyone," said JoAnna. The admissions director got up from the couch and went to her desk. She opened up Leah's file, took a piece of paper from a drawer, and slipped the paper into the file.

"I'm going to take you," said JoAnna. "Power has its advantages and I've decided to admit you. Don't bother to graduate from high school. You probably don't go there enough to make the formality worthwhile. Start this spring. We'll say you're a genius."

"Lazar's the genius," Leah found herself saying. "I got by today on Lazarisms."

"Well, whatever you did," said JoAnna, "you did it well. Just do me a favor and try to stay here for a couple of years. We have a work program which will give you the time when you need to go destroy your sanity. But we lose so much potential alumnae money on dropouts."

"Thank you," said Leah.

"Thank *you,*" said JoAnna. "My dear, you've got *something.* God knows what it is . . ." Her voice trailed off and she began looking through some papers. Leah interpreted this as a dismissal.

The compliments shot through Leah like a drug. She ran out of the Barn and into the wide open space of what they called the Commons lawn. She lay down on the grass and closed her eyes. She felt the cool Vermont air on her face. "I'm going to study *drums,*" she said to herself and pounded the ground on each side of her with palms. "Or maybe Celtic literature," she thought. She got up and went on the first of many long walks toward the mountains.

17

A Country Education

This was her second Greyhound bus trip. And it was her longest. She thought of Simon and Garfunkel's song, "They've all come to look for America." She was heading south to a little town called Stephenson, West Virginia. It was a mining town. She had volunteered, as many people her age were doing, to do work with the poor. She had romantic visions of the Appalachian life. Blue-green mountains, grannies with soft quilts, toothless fellows brewing whiskey in stills that looked like Walt Disney machines. She imagined rocking chairs and banjo music, epic ballads, herbal cures, Anglo white-witch magic and wisdom. Where she had gotten these notions she didn't know. But Bennington College offered a work-study program. It allowed Leah to leave the campus and get credit for working in the field. So four months into her first year she went up to a recruiting radical, got the name of a family, an organization that had an opening, and off she went. She made sure to bring her guitar because she thought the mountains were full of banjo players and jug bands.

Leah had another reason for going which was, for her, not so poetic. She'd been living with an older guy—a Drama Fellow on the campus. His name was Sam. They both wanted to be writers and musicians and actors and teachers. She was exhausted from their race. When she went to sit at her typewriter he got up and went to sit at his. When Sam pulled out his guitar, she felt she had to drop whatever she was doing and play with him so he wouldn't get more advanced than she. When he took a long walk, she went out and hung around the dorm, and waited until he returned so it wouldn't seem that he was healthy and she was a recluse. When he made a friend, he did not include her. Therefore she sought out people just so she could be seen as popular. On the surface she and Sam were very friendly. They made love a great deal, even when Leah didn't want to. Underneath, Leah knew she didn't like Sam very much. He was as demanding as Lazar, but not as gentle or brilliant. But Leah felt she had to keep pace with him. He'd been a drill sergeant in the army before coming to school, something she could never to claim to have been. She'd begun to feel exhausted and dizzy. She thought she was either pregnant or insane. Either would've put her on an equal footing in the competition. When Sam announced to Leah that he was leaving her and going to study mime at the Sorbonne, she was shattered. He'd beaten her. He'd won. She saw the West Virginia outing as a way of catching up with him though she knew she wouldn't see him again or have any occasion to tell him. Her traveling and her illness seemed in vain. But she put Sam out of her mind, and tried to focus on the Bennington work-study philosophy and her own will to win someday the Nobel Peace Prize. She was ashamed of herself, but couldn't control it. She wrote Sam a long letter about mountain poverty and then realized she didn't have his address. She whited out Sam's name on her typewriter and decided to send the letter to Lazar. She never got around to mailing it. She packed a duffel bag and put everything all out of her mind, deciding that she deserved to be noticed, and that God would get her out of her messy, sleepy state of mind.

The first surprise was her fear. In the dark bus, on the cold night in mid-January, the bus swerved out of Ohio and took the curves on the snowy mountain highway with an arrogance that seemed to her careless and cruel. She cringed on every swerve, making her jaw tight and sore. The second

shock was the pit of loneliness in her stomach. As they
stopped for their half-hour rest stop at a Hot Shoppe, she sat
alone drinking coffee under the yellow neon light and felt
cold and disoriented.

The bus arrived in Beckley, West Virginia, the closest city
to Stephenson. She was depending on her foster family to
pick her up. If they didn't come she could turn around, she
knew, but they were there, looking polite and nervous and
what a sight she must have been—her thick hair pulled back
in a dirty ponytail, her face wrung out from two days on a
bus, her small girl's body covered over by the bulky army fatigue jacket, baggy blue jeans and combat boots scuffed
black and fat at the toes.

Her foster father was named Hershall Stilltson and her
foster mother, Ruth. He was a railroad worker with a blond-
gray crew cut and bright blue eyes (one of them glass). His
face was muscular and square. He was a short powerful-
looking man in his early forties. His wife was round and dark
and made Leah think of bread. She was shy and looked
away. Both of them were flecked with snow, red-faced, and
they stood like immigrants as if it had been they who had
just arrived and not she.

"This is a small hole of a place, a lousy place, and you'll
hate it," said Hershall. And his wife giggled and clucked at
him. He insisted on carrying Leah's duffel bag—a fact which
embarrassed her and amused her. "Ladies are ladies here,"
he said. "College-bred or not."

She sat between them in their Chevrolet pickup truck and
was horrified as the truck skidded up sideways, climbing the
steep mountain road. "Miles and miles to go," said Hershall.
"You'd better have nerves of steel. I thought we'd just go as
fast as hell, fall off a cliff up yonder and get there faster, but
Ruth made me put my chains on the tires."

Leah tried desperately to not show her fear. Hershall was
telling her about the newest strikes, the black lung cam-
paign, the problem with the slag heaps, the indifference of

the government, and he had a terrifying habit of turning full
to Leah while he talked, not looking through the windshield
for moments at a time. He seemed relieved to have someone
to talk to. He seemed also to be testing her. They were driving along the edge of a mountain—the valley looked like a
deep pit lit by fires and scattered light bulbs. Leah couldn't
make out the shapes of the houses nor could she see the
mines. The blackness of the night was unfamiliar to her. The
heavy snow was the only variation in color in a seamless sky
and ground. They could've been driving in a cave.

After a time which seemed longer than the bus ride—because each second was wired, because her fear was being
checked by the two strangers on each side of her, and because she suddenly dreaded where she was going and didn't
know when she would be coming back—Leah felt the truck
stop.

"This is as far as any road will take us," said Hershall.
"Now we'll have to walk."

Hershall jumped from his seat and went to retrieve the
duffel bag. Ruth ducked out into the storm, her head covered by a kerchief. Leah felt her way out of the cab of the
truck into a darkness that smelled of smoke and unfamiliar
fires. Her head went light and she fainted dead into a dirty
snowbank.

She awoke to the scraping sound of the mines outside the
small bedroom she was sleeping in. She was enveloped by a
feeling of gray, as if heavy smoke surrounded her. She was in
a large bed, a very hard bed. She could feel the springs.
There were quilts piled on top of her. Her body was sweating
but her face was ice cold. She was alone in the bed but she
vaguely remembered bodies had been on both sides of her
during the night. Flannel nightgowns and the smell of little
girls. She could hear talking from the next room. She saw
some blond heads sneak looks at her through the open door,
but she pretended to be asleep. She looked out the window

and was shocked at what she saw. There were no trees on the mountains, they were stripped raw. And there were other mountains, black sticky ones made of coal waste; they smoked and looked like wet charcoal. The mine seemed to envelop the town, like the walls of a prison—gray steel for trees. The daylight was just coming and the miners still had the lights on on their hard hats. She saw men coming and going who looked as if they were in blackface. Tracks squealed, machines were grinding, the noise was overpowering and relentless. Yet she felt an eerie stillness in the valley. Her first impression was totally opposite of what she had expected. She tried to find a way to describe what she was feeling—to equate the present with some idea of experience from her past. She couldn't do it. It was not even like a dream.

"You sure slept." Ruth was at the door. Her face was expressionless. Leah remembered she'd fainted, and felt embarrassed. "Shouldn't have traveled so long without eating," said Ruth. "Hershall laughed all the way here carrying you."

Ruth had made breakfast for her. There were biscuits and a brown gravy. The bacon was as thick as a slice of beef. Milk was set on the card table in the kitchen. She met her new family one by one. There were twelve children; they all had blond hair. They laughed when they introduced themselves. They were spotlessly clean, though their clothes didn't fit—it was clear the same outfits went up and down the family as if there were a conveyor belt that went round and round with shirts, blouses, sweaters and pants and each child had his or her pick as they outgrew the outfit they'd worn before.

It was clear that Ruth kept a clean home, but nonetheless there was a film of dust over everything: it bled into the walls, it covered the chairs, it made the children's hands gray, it changed the quality of the light in the room. Ruth saw what Leah was looking at. "Nothing to do about it," she said. "A baby's born with dust on his face, an old man dies with it in his lungs."

Leah tried to eat the heavy breakfast, but the weight of the food was unfamiliar to her, the biscuits were painful, the gravy lumpy. She left most of it on her plate. The children gathered around her like a small blond village and this made it more difficult for her to eat. "Eats like a bird," said one of the teenage girls. Another girl was fascinated with Leah's hair and was touching the length of it, patting it against her own face. The boys kept more distance; they stooped at the opposite end of the table, elbows on the table, faces propped up on their fists, and stared.

"Go 'way," shouted Ruth to her children. "She ain't no museum."

There was one child who showed no interest in her. He was about thirteen or fourteen and hummed as he walked around the kitchen. He was the ugliest of the children. He had popping eyes and yellow sticky buckteeth. His nose was fat and pug and smeared with mud. His corduroy pants were too small and the tops of them had to stay unbuttoned. His belly showed and the rim of his underpants. His boots were half untied and his fat hands were black with dirt. He drooled and told himself everything he was doing as he was doing it. "That's Ian," said one of the girls. She spoke with exaggerated gentleness as a young girl talks when she is playing mother. "Ian's going to feed the hogs. Aren't you, Ian?"

Ian turned toward Leah and spoke very excitedly at her. Leah couldn't understand him. But she smiled and nodded as if she did. He seemed to be instructing her in the ways of feeding hogs or telling her about his day at school or a television show he'd seen two weeks ago—she couldn't fathom it. No one at the table helped Leah in her discomfort. The little boys smiled meanly at each other; the girls watched Leah to see what she would do. "Well, Ian," said Leah,

"let's go meet your hogs. Maybe you can teach me how to
feed them." Ian shrugged and looked at her as if she were
crazy. On the way to the hogpen Leah stopped off at the outhouse and closed the plywood door behind her. As she sat on
the stinking wooden hole, she could hear gales of laughter
coming from the kitchen. She saw that an old *Good Housekeep-
ing* magazine was to be her toilet paper. When she emerged
from the outhouse Ian was standing, waiting for her with
two enormous pails of slop on each arm. He handed her
one—it was heavy and unwieldy. The pinkish-brown oat-
meal-looking stuff spilled over the sides. He laughed. It was
the strangest laughter she'd heard. All their laughter was
strange, and again she couldn't put it anywhere. Not her
past nor her present. The Twilight Zone, she thought to herself. She stared at the hogs and Ian as if she were at the zoo.

Hershall worked on the railroad. He left way before dawn
and often returned late at night. He was always covered with
soot and so tired he could barely talk. Ruth bathed him in a
tin tub that was set behind the coal-burning stove in the living room. Once Hershall had asked Leah to stoke the coals
in the stove and she'd gone to open the grate with her hand
and her hand had stuck to the grate from the heat. She remembered a time in her hometown when some children had
bought creamsticks that were too cold. The same thing had
happened to their tongues. She didn't cry out when her hand
was singed. Hershall laughed. Ruth put some Crisco on it.
The burn was small but it stayed for two months.

Hershall, on a day off, was full of mischief. He taunted
Leah into watching wrestling matches with the family on
their black-and-white TV. "We'll get lots of politics done
today," he'd say. He offered Leah chewing tobacco. She
tried to take it like a sport, but she gagged and her cheek
swelled up like a chipmunk. He tickled her with hard relentless jabs. He wanted her to stay up all night and listen to
philosophical talks which were at the same time brilliant

and made no sense. "You people in the cities," Hershall would say, "think you're better off than us poor hillbillies. But when the starvation and drought comes, you won't know hell about growing crops or finding food. I'll have to come up there in my old truck and pull you out of the rubble. Your friends will all be wandering around like stray dogs, pickin' at the garbage and howlin' at the moon, but you won't have to worry because Ol' Hershall will come and rescue you." And again there was laughter. Always this odd good-natured laughter as if someone had told a joke in a foreign language that everyone understood but her.

Leah had long ago disassociated herself from any political organization. She learned from Hershall that the best work was done by renegades. He had a real scorn for the Northern liberals who came to his town to tell him how to live. When the Vista volunteers came by (there were three in her area), she sat around slow and empty-eyed and watched Hershall give them a hard time. Ethan, a Jew from Brandeis, was Hershall's least favorite. He came in his clean, pressed army fatigues and horn-rimmed glasses and read to the family from a loose-leaf notebook. He told them about food stamps, their right to health insurance; he encouraged them to boycott the company general store, he talked to them about black lung disease. Hershall's daddy had died of the disease and he had no patience for Ethan's preaching. He always took out his glass eye, rolled it between his thumb and forefinger like a worry bead. The blue eye stared all around the room and made Ethan cringe. He'd glare at Leah as if she were a traitor. She found herself laughing in that odd and familiar way. "You're not one of them," Hershall said to her. "You're as dumb and lazy as one of us." And it was true, something possessed Leah and slowed her down.

Leah tried to keep her obligations in her own way. She started a dance class in Hershall's living room with the local girls. During the first session a bunch of mothers came with switches and beat their daughters home. They screamed at her that she was doing the work of the devil. Ruth was laughing in the kitchen. "Pay them no mind," she said. "Tomorrow they'll be asking you for food stamps."

Leah also tried some marriage counseling with Ruth's cousin and her husband. Her name was Mary and she beat the children so badly they came black and blue to stay at Ruth's. "The woman's got a good mind," Hershall said about Mary, "but a temper as bad as any man's." When Leah tried to talk to her, Mary sat sweetly at her kitchen table staring out at the smoking mountain. She picked her nose with a bobby pin and agreed with everything Leah said. "You're very smart for a girl your age," said Mary. "But this is a shit hole and won't ever be anything other. I'd like to go to Beckley to the five-and-dime and buy myself some nice cotton and a Simplicity pattern for a pretty dress. Why don't we do that on Saturday?" She'd dig deep into her nose with the bobby pin. "Ain't this the shit hole of the world?" she asked. Mary's husband left her and went to North Carolina to join a country and western band. Mary locked herself up in her little house and made cuts up and down her arm with a kitchen knife. Hershall had to kick in the door and take her to Ruth to get bandaged up. Leah heard Mary screaming in the bedroom. When Leah stood in the door the bandaged and deranged woman looked up at her and smiled politely. "We'll be going to Beckley for our shopping date, won't we?" said Mary.

Leah was drawn to the edge of the mountain. Tired and aching she often climbed up the steep sides to the highway and walked the miles in between little mining towns. Wherever she looked she saw wrecks of cars lying like dead metal dinosaurs in the valley. "Nothing to do but drive fast," Ruth had said. "I dread it when Ian gets his hands on a wheel." There were always deaths, squeals of brakes in the night, games of chicken, cars flying off the sides of mountains like enormous mechanical birds. Leah's blond-haired family was always talking about who "got it" and who "made it."

"The thing is," Hershall said in one of their late-night talks, "the thing is that nobody cares about this or that. But get you around a curve going ninety miles an hour and pass you a big fat truck and squeeze you between the truck and the car comin' the other way and that gives you something to talk about." Hershall would stare at the stove as if there were an open fire he could see. "That's what we're up against here. Nobody cares about anything. All day in the night. The mines are like night. All night in the cold. Everybody dying young. Nobody going anywhere but maybe to get killed in Vietnam. And the spirit goes dusty."

Ruth always sat next to him sleepy and silent. She smiled sadly. She nodded as if he were singing a song.

One night Leah awoke out of a dream. She often had nightmares about Stephenson—about being caught in the mines, dark shafts of dirt with holes of light miles above and no ladders. Sometimes her dreams centered around the blond children—their look-alike selves, the strange games they played that had no rules or end. And always their laughter was in the dreams. Dry, quiet, resigned laughter. Empty and old. She'd wake and decide to go back to college. But as the morning cleared a kind of inertia set in and the desperation of the night faded like a song whose tune was less and less resonant.

After one dream Leah couldn't stay in bed. She'd gotten used to sleeping with the six blond sisters in the bed. They were like sextuplets, all blondes in flannel nightgowns fitting against each other like spoons. Leah liked the smell of their baby sweat and the rhythm of their breathing as if they were a silent rowing team. They were used to sleeping through all kinds of noise, so Leah could come and go as she needed to.

Leah was drawn to the living room where she knew the coals would still be going in the stove. She was surprised to find Ruth sitting on the old couch. Ruth had a shawl wrapped around her and was neither looking at the fire nor concentrating on anything specific. Leah had come to recognize and learn Ruth's talent for silence. "Sit you down," said Ruth. "There was a train wreck and Hershall will be gone most of the night fixin' the track."

Leah knew that Ruth never went to sleep unless Hershall was home. It was religious. She never spoke about worry and she never showed any signs of distress, but Leah could feel from Ruth's body that simply being awake was a way of keeping Hershall safe. Sitting in his chair by his stove was a way of guarding him while he wasn't there. Often when he returned she fixed him a hot tub, fed him chicken and hot milk, folded up his filthy clothes and tucked him under their thick quilts. The waiting ritual was one Leah was used to. For the two months she'd been in Stephenson she'd learned to keep silence and not jeopardize Hershall's safety with any abrupt movements or loud sounds.

This night Ruth talked. "You look good," she said to Leah. "Country isn't killing you, at any rate."

Leah smiled and nodded. She lit a cigarette off the stove as she'd learned to do, and settled back looking nowhere.

"Might I ask you a personal question?" asked Ruth.

Leah said she didn't mind.

Ruth leaned away, the opposite of what you'd expect from someone about to be intimate. "Are you taking the proper care of yourself for one in your condition? And might I do something to help you better through this time?"

A cold shock ran through Leah.

"Have you told your mama?" asked Ruth.

Leah didn't answer for a while. "Does Hershall know?" Leah asked.

"No," Ruth laughed. "Only women can tell such things. But Sissy knows." Sissy was the eldest girl. "She could tell straight off."

"But it doesn't show or anything, does it?" asked Leah. It had been such a long time since she'd thought about it—or the boy at college. She had so completely denied it that the realization was making her shiver and her teeth were chattering. Ruth went and got her a shawl.

"No it ain't the belly" said Ruth. "It's the walk, the spirit, all such things. Sissy, Mary and I, we wonder how such a skinny young thing all in army clothes keeps herself goin' all day—coffee, cigarettes, running with Hershall, climbing mountains, up all night scribbling in them notebooks—all with a baby inside."

"It's because I don't want it," said Leah. "I don't want it at all."

Ruth could not hear this, nor would she acknowledge it.

"I really don't want it," Leah repeated. "I'm going to have to leave soon and go north and get it taken care of."

Ruth looked straight at Leah. Her dark eyes were tired but very direct. "Then you'd best not come back here afterward," she said.

They heard Hershall's truck drive up and that was the signal for the conversation to be ended. Leah got up slowly; she felt dull and tired. She went to hand the shawl back to Ruth.

"Keep it for nights like these," said Ruth. She paused. "Be kinder to yourself," said Ruth. "Treat your body with politeness. Love thyself a bit."

Leah scheduled her departure for one week later. Ruth said not a word, but acted more coldly toward her.

"We'd best do something political before you leave," said Hershall. "Or everyone'll think you came down here for a vacation." The call for a strike in the area was strong. The Black Lung issues were becoming well known in North Carolina and Kentucky. Leah had helped paint posters for meetings and mimeographed fact sheets, but had long ago withdrawn from any real, active involvement. However, she could feel a new tone of excitement in the town and Hershall was often going to meetings near the border of Kentucky.

There had been some incidents involving people Hershall

and Ruth knew. Mary had led a march of women who locked their arms in protest style and stood like a human chain while an enormous Mack truck full of coal waste tried to get past them on the muddy treacherous path. "You'd best pave the road with our blood first," said Mary, "rather than ruin our roads any more with your poisonous filth." The truck driver, who worked for the bosses, turned around, but the incident made the papers and infuriated the coal company. They liked to keep a Christian image. They didn't like to see the picture of one of their employees trying to run down a group of women and children with his huge truck.

Ethan was recalled and transferred to a Chicago ghetto by Vista. The local police had been instructed by the company owners to get him out. So they arrested him for selling drugs to high school students. The company paid the kids to set Ethan up. That's what the rumor was. The company owners tried the same with Leah. One day when she was doing songs at the grammar school, the deputy interrupted her class and took her down to the station. He accused her of trying to teach sex education and of giving the little kids pot after school. The sheriff was fat and red-faced and smiled triumphantly as he drove Leah through the town. He drove slowly so as many people as possible could see. He told Leah she was too pretty to be a communist and implied that if she'd sleep with him he'd let her off. She was about to go into the sleepy submission that had served her well in the past, when she saw Hershall waiting at the station. News spread fast in the mountains. Hershall looked brave and ferocious. He was wearing brass knuckles, his glass eye made him look wild, and he threatened the deputy, saying, "You want to lie, you'll pay for it in the old style. Ain't no businessman gonna buy you a new face."

Hershall's old-time sense of honor made him a respected figure in the town and his fearlessness made this particular deputy go soft like a piece of dough. Leah was let go and no mention was made of the charges again. "You're a regular cowboy," Leah said to Hershall and he laughed. But he stayed angry and was very disturbed by the changes in his mountain town.

Brother was set against brother as the politics in Stephenson became more passionate. Those who wanted to work in the mines were beaten by those who wanted to strike. Those who walked the picket lines were threatened and used as targets for the fast-running cars of teenage boys paid off by the company owners. The usual passive quality of the hills became the opposite—there were eyes hidden everywhere; people walked with their bodies stiff and suspicious; the party telephone line was tapped. "Life's getting a little bit fun," said Hershall. He spent his days off traveling to other towns, smoking cigarettes and listening quietly to the ideas of the workers in the area.

Leah was sorry she was leaving. But the alternative was not acceptable to her. She imagined giving birth to a child in the hard flat land in Ruth and Hershall's house with Mary and Ian and all the blond-haired children standing over her. She thought of her child growing up in the smoke and the dirt, talking with a slow Southern accent. She thought about leaving the child with Ruth so it could grow up and have no idea it had a Northern-type hippie girl as its mother. But then she thought about visiting it and bringing it a stuffed bear and hearing it laugh at her with the eerie innocent demonic laugh she came to know as the music of this town. "I can't change my mind," she once said to Ruth. They were unpacking the week's groceries bought from the company store.

Ruth said nothing to her and did not look up. The rules of the mountains were absolute, the souls of the people were as strong as tablets.

Hershall, Ruth and Leah drove to the last public meeting Leah was to attend before she left for New York. The date was close to her eighteenth birthday. It was late at night and the roads were dark and icy. The meeting was a secret one in

which the men were planning a big county-wide strike
against the mines. The women were to figure out how to get
publicity. Hershall's truck was weaving up the mountain
and he was teasing Leah, going on in a voice that had become the chorus of a song to her. "You leave here and go to
your tall buildings and Automats and restaurants. But when
the starvation comes, I'll have to come in this here truck and
rescue you. Because you won't be able to plant corn on your
windowsill or raise a hog in your living room. Then they
won't feel so sorry for all of us poor hillbillies down here.
They'll wish like hell they had the friends you have. We'll
read about the cities crumbling down like a baby's game of
blocks and then me and Ruth will get in our old truck, find
us a map and come get you."

Ruth said nothing. Leah was playing a harmonica she'd
got from Mary's ex-husband. She was playing "Satisfied
Mind." Hershall was singing

> How many times
> Have you heard someone say
> If I had his money
> I'd be a rich man today.
> How little they know
> That it's so hard to find
> One rich man in a hundred
> With a satisfied mind.

Somewhere along the second verse, they heard a sound
that went pop. To Leah it was like a champagne bottle
opening—she didn't know what it was to them. She felt the
truck gasp and Hershall said "Gunshot" and the truck began
to skid violently on the icy mountan road. "Tire's shot," said
Hershall and he was guiding the truck in and out of skids,
trying to avoid the sharp edge of the mountain and the drop
underneath. More pops started going off. Ruth was very still
and slid down in her seat. She grabbed Leah's arm and

forced her down too. "Scare tactics," said Hershall. "If they'd been a-meanin' to hit us, we'd be dead long since." The truck lurched again as another tire got hit. It skidded violently in a circle and Hershall managed to stop it so it was just hanging over the edge of the mountain. The valley was lit up like an industrial Christmas tree—the fire from the mines was bright orange and yellow; the embers on the slag heaps burned endlessly and looked like bright red mountains. Leah thought about her first terrors when she'd arrived in Stephenson and couldn't imagine where they'd come from. She didn't feel afraid now. The truck hung over the deep circle of black like a basset hound asleep with its head in a water dish. The truck creaked a lullaby back and forth, rocking perilously. She and Hershall and Ruth leaped out. The gunshots had stopped and it was quiet except for the machine sounds from the mines. Hershall was holding Ruth's hand. "Well you almost got yourself countrified to bits," said Hershall.

"I know you arranged it," said Leah. "This was your special-made farewell party to me." And she heard herself laugh. The sound was eerie and empty, full of demons and idiots.

18

A Small Exchange

Leah thought the clinic looked like an airport. There were colored numbers lighting up one wall. Her mind was telling her jokes—"Pick a number like in a bakery," she said to herself. She was stoned on pot. Probably not the right thing to do before anesthesia. A furry-headed classmate, a music guy, had driven her to New York and given her a few joints as a send-off. "My lady friend went through it," he told her. "She went to dance class the next day."

Leah looked at the Swedish waiting-room chairs. They were designed in cheerful family reds and blues and yellows. They were divided into sections as on a wide-bodied 747. She looked at all the crying girls and the young men with handkerchiefs. There were older ladies, too, walking to and fro with urine samples in bottles covered with aluminum foil. "Passover," Leah said to herself (her mind would not stop its comic routine); each aunt with her little dish.

Leah's number lit up. She remembered her mother's fear when a flight was announced. Today there would be no flying. It was a walk through a line of offices. "Stop in here. Stamp this paper. Get this label. Get your white gown. Get classified. Fill in a form." Leah had begun to do some draft counseling and she and other students taught young men how to fake through their physicals. She knew this was an induction. She knew there was no way of getting out of it. She was alone. It was her choice. She'd decided not to tell anyone important. The boyfriend was history and the family had been through enough.

She lay down on the assigned white bed. Two Hispanic nurses came in; they looked like twins. They looked at her age on the chart and clucked their twin tongues. One of them said to her, "Look at jor feet! How do feet get so dirty? Wash those feet." Leah wanted to answer that she was presently a hippie, but didn't want her strange humor to alienate the Christianity of the nurses and perhaps influence the outcome of her ordeal.

A social worker came in. She was middle-aged, had dyed blond hair and blue Villager clothes. She was harassed and businesslike. Her warmth was rehearsed. "How are you?" she asked. Leah nodded in what she hoped was a mature and circumspect manner and the social worker went into her description of the events which would soon follow. Leah couldn't help thinking of stewardesses; their emergency lectures before takeoff.

"You will feel several pinches," said the social worker. "Each one will be a little more painful than the one before, though none very severe in intensity. If the pain is too much we can administer a general anesthetic, but that is costlier and there is a small element of risk." Leah remembered signing some form about the general anesthetic. She also thought about people who took their dogs to veterinarians and signed similar forms. No one is to blame if the patient dies from sleeping. Leah laughed at this and the social worker got angry. "This isn't exactly a game," she said to Leah.

The doctor looked like a clown in a blue bag. He was Arabic. Leah was in a machine shop. She was the car. He was the mechanic. She could hear a machine going clack clack behind him. That was some sort of vacuum cleaner. A new method. She was lucky. But she was frozen rigid. "Relax," shouted one of the Hispanic nurses. Leah couldn't. They attached a needle to her arm. Something was dripping from a bottle into it. Now it was dripping into her. "Knees up," she heard the nurse say. She got dreamy.

Pay phones appeared to her. She had spent so many hours on the pay phone, dimes piled up like poker chips. She remembered the graffiti on one of the phones at Bennington: "Something is better than nothing—call Steve 877-9236." She called friends who knew the name of the clinic, the political friends, feminists, the ones who knew where it would be safe. More dimes. How to get the money. It had to be cash. She'd thought about selling her guitar—that would come to $175 exactly—but decided against it. "That would be two deaths," she said to herself. The stereo was an easier loss. She was writing so much music, she hardly listened to anyone else's.

She went to a pawnshop on the New York State border. It wasn't enough. Only seventy-five dollars. So she dealt some drugs. A couple of ounces at a Dartmouth rock concert. A gram of hash during Vermont Peak Week. Finally she reached her goal. She remembered the bright red thermometer for the United Fund drive back home. The red mercury had gone over the top. "You're getting tough, Leah," she told herself. "What a fund-raiser," and only got a little scared in her dormitory cell at night. Meanwhile, she'd made no effort to deal with the possibility of having a child. "It would be too sad," Leah told herself. "It would be born with a frown. This isn't the time. It isn't the world." Leah was eighteen. Mother had been nineteen when she'd had Lazar. Leah thought Mother had been too young. Lazar had a way about him as if he'd been thrown like a basketball into the world. No one had caught him. In trying to save him, Leah kept making Lazar younger in her mind so she could have an instant replay of all his events. It didn't work. She was wedded to the time Lazar was born, his age and who he was. The only reason to keep the child was a wish to have Lazar all over again and make him whole and happy. Leah had learned a few things, and that wish was not going to come true.

Leah was feeling pain even with the drugs. It was sharp,

gripping and pulled down on her. The glare of the doctor's lamp blinded her like a blazing sun. She was wild with anger. Pictures came to her mind of the ladies who'd been wheeled back afterward. Leah saw the sleeping ladies while she waited her turn. They were always holding on to their sheets, as if they were the manes of horses. As if they'd come back from riding horses bareback. As if the horses had reared. They were so afraid they still couldn't let go.

After a while Leah heard the start of wheels. It was her own bed. Like the slow ascent on a roller coaster. The Hispanic nurses were pushing her up. White corridors passed by. Masked faces. Leah felt relieved and stoned. She fell asleep. When she awoke she was in a room of women. She felt alone and flat. She thought immediately of Lazar.

"Now I've matched him," she told herself. "Injury for injury. Pain for pain." She didn't know why she was thinking so much about her brother, hoping to relieve him of his time in hospitals with a little stint of her own.

"That's not rational," she told herself. But she prayed for him anyway and hoped she'd made some cosmic exchange.

Later, there was a room with magazines. A bunch of tired ladies were sitting around. Leah felt as though she'd got up too soon. She was dizzy. She felt lost without the close white walls. The blond-haired social worker passed some butter cookies around. She also passed birth control devices to each of the ladies. She wanted to recommend them so there wouldn't have to be another visit. The steam from the coffee machine filled the dull room. Leah thought this was an odd cocktail party. She sat drumming on the arms of her chair. She sucked on a butter cookie and stared at the loops, diaphragms, condoms and pills. She laughed. The social worker glared at her. Leah wanted to be proper and tried to cry. But she was still stoned. In her mind she was imagining a bouquet of roses from a lover who had not yet arrived in her life.

19

Treestumps and Isolde

They were going to meet at the Chelsea Hotel. As Lazar
had written, The time has come, the walrus said. Leah was
to choose the place since it was to be Her Revelation. Leah
chose the Chelsea Hotel because she'd heard there were
paintings and sculptures in the lobby, that Leonard Cohen
sometimes rode up and down in the elevator and the man
who wrote Tubby the Tuba lived on the top floor in a self-
made jungle with alligators.

Leah was exactly on time. She was nervous. She hadn't
seen her brother since his mysterious accident. Over the last
couple of months telegrams had arrived for her at Bennington. She was surprised he even knew where she was. The telegrams were written in Lazar style, but unsigned. One had
said simply, POOR BOBBY KENNEDY. Another, THE SEARCH
PARTY HAS BEEN SUCCESSFUL—THEY SPOTTED ME LAST
NIGHT—UNDER A ROCK—THEY SENT DOWN A STRAW AND I
BREATHED. Another, ARE YOU STILL A VIRGIN? Once there
was even a late night phone call from a young man who said
he was a drill sergeant from Vietnam. But the voice was un-
mistakably Lazar's. Leah couldn't get the young man to say
he was her brother. He talked about the jungle and mines.
He said he was lucky and he was still able to function as a
man. He said the drugs in Vietman had been evil, making
the rock music sound like gunfire and the gunfire like music.
He said he'd killed an innocent family. He asked her if she
would go out with such a man. She had spoken tenderly and
cautiously to the young sergeant hoping to make a bridge to

the future. Yes, she could go out with such a man. Yes, she would even marry him if the reasons for his violence were explained to her. The drill sergeant said that he had never intended marriage to enter the conversation and he hung up. Leah thought she'd failed. She cried that whole night because she hadn't been able to get him to say his name. Then finally a last telegram came. It said, "THE TIME HAS COME THE WALRUS SAID TO TALK OF MANY THINGS—COME UNAC-COMPANIED EITHER BY ORCHESTRA FRIENDS OR FAMILY. PICK THE PLACE—IT WILL BE YOUR REVELATION."

Other communications must have been going on at the same time. Her father had bought her a ticket. The week-end had been decided. Her parents said next to nothing to her about her upcoming trip. Her father told her "she'd do fine."

She walked into the lobby of the Chelsea Hotel and saw young people dressed in black turtlenecks, blue jeans. They were hanging around the lobby smoking. Old gypsy-looking ladies with scarves on their heads were seated in the plush chairs looking mystical. Paintings covered the walls. Other young people carried instruments to and fro. They wore bright-colored sunglasses—they were both seedy and vi-brant. Leah wished she was one of them, that she'd come for another reason. She knew this was her nervousness. About her brother's condition or his mood she knew nothing. He had been severely injured. The details of his injuries had been kept from her. It seemed to be too difficult for her par-ents to describe. They were vague, they moved their hands, they sighed.

She checked in at the desk and got her room key. The man at the desk looked at her name and said, "The gentleman is waiting for you at the bar." He pointed to the glass door to her right. She could see a dark room, lit low with candles in glasses, and dark brown wooden booths. Now she rehearsed. She stayed at the check-in desk and went over her list. She'd made a list of safe things to talk about. Ella Fitzgerald—scat singing. Beginning college. Haiku. The songs of whales. The war (no not the war—she remembered the telephone call and struck it from her list). She knew instinctively not to bring up her hard times or his. Their years of games and rules had taught her that he took the lead in all serious matters. She looked at herself in the glass doors. She'd made sure to dress very sexy; she remembered he liked that. She wore a tight leather vest buttoned up with nothing underneath. She wore tight denim hip-huggers and clogs that made her walk like a dancer. She pushed her way into the bar and saw his wheelchair pushed up against one of the tiny cocktail tables as if he were supporting a tray. He did not see her. It gave her time. The first thing she noticed was that his curly hair had all been shaved off into a crew cut that was so tight he looked bald. A poem came into her head from one of her English classes.

> There's little Tom Dance who cried when his head
> That curled like a lamb's back was shaved, so I said
> Hush Tom, never mind it, for if your head's bare
> You know that the soot cannot spoil your white hair.

She mentally told the poem to shut up and moved toward the table. She saw two fat steely-looking legs lying dead from his thighs and she knew her first facts. He was wearing black-rimmed sunglasses and was staring down into the candle on the table. She saw there was a scar across the whole top of his head—a red crown. It looked as if his head had cracked. She felt a chill of fear. And then relief. And then joy.

"Kiss me, sweetie," he said quietly. His voice was an older version of himself. His presence was stern and demanding. He would not look up. He circled the rim of the candle-glass with one hand; the other arm seemed to be covered up by a black silk sling. She leaned over him awkwardly and kissed his dry cracked lips. She was counting scars. Like cobwebs they made lace all around his mouth, his chin, his cheeks. He noticed her clothing immediately.

"Vixen," he said.

She couldn't stop herself. "Where'd you all go?" she asked.

He snorted and said nothing. His smile revealed brown blood on his teeth. Bad gums. A closer look. She saw the sling had no whole arm in it. The voices in her wouldn't stop—"three limbs gone. The score three to one. Lazar Lazar Lazar." She took his hand. Burn scars. He was barely there. It was as if he'd been slammed together by a wild sculptor throwing clay.

"Do you find me ugly?" he asked.

"No, Lazar. It's just that I missed you so much; it's overwhelming."

"It's very important," said her brother, "that you feel comfortable with me."

"I do," whispered Leah.

"You must be able to look at me."

Leah looked at Lazar. He was forcing himself to sit very straight. His lips were tightly pursed and his eyes behind the dark glasses were defiant. Leah began to sweat. She dared not make him angry. She didn't want to be a coward. She did not, once again, want to fail him.

Lazar looked at his sister. She seemed more awkward than the last time he'd seen her. If she knew everything about him, it didn't show. He didn't think it was possible. Her eyes were innocent and curious. He tried to lean across the table and he whispered to her that he loved her more than God. As he did so his heavy artificial legs smashed into the table and upset a water glass. Leah knew not to flinch. She knew not to cry out. She faked a laugh. She kissed him.

They ordered lunch and Leah began to learn a new sense of time. She had to carefully cut Lazar's steak. If a piece was too large he had to gnaw at it with his teeth, pull with his fork and yank it to its right size. When he went to light a cigarette he'd hold the whole pack of matches in his hand and bend one down striking it against the bottom. Once a whole pack flamed up in his hand. It didn't faze him. That was the reason for all the burns. They didn't talk much because eating was so time-consuming and full of so many maneuvers.

After lunch he insisted that he wanted to walk with her to her room. He asked the bartender if he could leave his wheelchair in the bar. He had a large knapsack on his back which he said was filled with vital transportation. She didn't understand. When he stood up it was as if he were balancing himself on stilts. He moved slowly, tipping back and forth like a man on a perilous ladder in a silent movie. People stared. The walking was taking forever. Leah became embarrassed, then enraged, then ashamed of her anger. By the time they reached the hotel elevator Leah was exhausted. She wished she could leave her brother downstairs, go upstairs and think about him. The time dragged on. The movement was slow. Every arduous step stretched the muscles in her own brain. He creaked. He was a tin man. It was unbearable.

In her room, she felt relief. They'd reached their destination. The room had a sunny window and a nice wood floor. "Why don't you relax on the bed?" Leah said to him. She rushed into the bathroom to gather her thoughts. It was strange. Her thoughts were making sounds like crying. They didn't have words. She was sitting on the toilet imagining his days, his nightmares, as if his whole life had been opened up to her with this gory portrait. Outside the bathroom door she heard wheels whizzing. She came out and was amazed.

Lazar had undressed to a pair of white boxer shorts. His two artificial legs were standing in a corner like stern African statues. He was propelling himself on the wood floor by means of a wide skateboard with red Kryptonic wheels. He was singing and tottering around his turns.

Leah saw everything now. Brutal scars on his back. His

Elizabeth Swados

pink stumps. She had never seen so much. Not even in the *Life* magazine photos of war victims, famine in Africa, or the Holocaust pictures of Auschwitz. It was a kind of pornography to her. Her terror became fascination—she couldn't stop staring. Lazar was doing a kind of dance for her. "I'm showing you," it said. The mutilation of Lazar's body told her the whole story of his violence. She didn't know if he'd been crushed under an elevator, thrown out of an airplane or pushed through a window. But she saw his falling, she saw his landing on a hard ungiving floor, she saw the glass going into him. She saw him crushed and then put together piece by piece. She thought of a poisonous rotting tree in which the limbs get covered with fungus, rot and fall off.

Lazar still had his sunglasses on. He was doing curves on the floor and shoving himself along with one hand. He was testing her. He wanted her to see. Leah showed her brother that she was not afraid to look. And her horror faded from her consciousness into her dreams. She felt high.

"You're incredibly brave," said Leah.

"I am redefining beauty," said Lazar. But he was helpless to join Leah as she sat on the bed. And he could not put himself into a chair, but rather knocked it down to him. And he sat there in the middle of the floor, the afternoon sunlight spotlighting him, and he could not move and she could not move him. He was a strange octopus. His temper became dark. His mood had fallen.

Leah called the manager, who brought up two security guards and they lifted Lazar onto his legs. He greeted them in a dignified manner, instructed them as if he were an aristocrat and they were servants. He insisted upon tipping them. Leah stood around tense and felt odd as if she were having a rare piece of furniture moved around her room.

"Thank you, my good sirs," Lazar said when the men left. Then he turned to Leah and, his face drenched in sweat, he said, "I will leave on my own. You will not even open this door for me."

Leah didn't protest. She felt angry again and helpless. Lazar teetered toward the door and opened it. He paused.

"This is the beginning and the end of a long relationship," he said.

Leah had no reply.

20
Kari Narti

The Hot Springs in Saratoga Springs, New York, was a basement coffeehouse. Lots of folksingers came to do sets here because the location wasn't far from Stockbridge, Woodstock or New York City. Also the Bear Mountain Farm was nearby and that's where they made dulcimers and had three-day festivals—they said sometimes Pete Seeger would come by.

Leah had her old Martin D-28 wide-body steel-stringed guitar. She hauled it into the other seat of her white MGB—the case looked like a coffin—and set out from Bennington for the Hot Springs. It was the summer of her freshman year and, after all she'd been through, she felt too worldly to be a music counselor at a summer camp. She definitely wanted to audition. She wanted to forget about Lazar, politics, and heavy sex. She wanted to be a star. She could pick well enough and she'd written songs that her classmates at college liked. Kari—now her boyfriend—made a caravan with her. He went to Dartmouth and drove a BMW 650. He played the recorder and fluent piano. He was going to hit one of the resort hotels for a cocktail lounge job. He and Leah had decided to spend their summer this way.

As Leah drove along the New York State Thruway, she saw caravans of army trucks filled with guys. This thrilled her. She felt beautiful in her open convertible. Her hair was a flag. She gave them the peace sign. Sometimes a truck would slow down and the guys would mouth kisses at her.

188

Leah'd lift up her T-shirt and show them the peace sign Kari
had drawn on her stomach.

Kari carried a big fake book. It was illegal and had piano
scores and lyrics of tunes by Gershwin, Arlen, Hammerstein,
Hart. He'd brought along "much grass," as he said. Otherwise it would be hard not to play modal music, Incredible
String Band style. The caravans did not bother him. He was
exempt from the army. He'd fallen off a set of rings in the
gym on acid, got a concussion and landed in a mental hospital. He'd known Leah since high school, and she'd come to
rescue him. This was her wildness. For a while they'd made a
band playing standards, folk and rock and roll, but her soprano couldn't fool anyone. And his touch was soul-fired,
but light. In fact he was a great pianist—jazz—but there was
time for that. However, not much time for Leah. She was
light and moving. They'd made love in a sleeping bag in
Vermont by a river near the Putney School. Leah's songs
were so sad. She laughed and counted the stars through the
night as if she'd never known a happy moment.

The town of Saratoga was dreary. The streets were narrow
and steep. Leah drove up and down looking for the café. Her
car needed a muffler. The interior was a mess filled with
cardboard boxes of clothes and papers. Finally she saw the
Hot Springs sign. It was a basement next to a drugstore. She
made a U-turn and Kari followed her. They sat in a shopping center parking lot for an hour. Leah was scared. She
asked Kari please not to touch her. She couldn't eat a
McDonald's either. Finally, she asked him to wait in the
parking lot for her while she went to audition. The town was
muggy and the tar in the parking lot gave off black light.
Kari lit a joint to ease Leah's snub of him. However long
she'd be gone, he'd wait. He pulled out his fake book and
began to study "There's a Small Hotel." He was looking
around to make sure the summer cops weren't prowling
somewhere.

Inside, the Hot Springs was a familiar, dark coffeehouse. The posters were impressive. The bulletin board was full of announcements of festivals all over the country for the summer. No one was there when Leah arrived. She put down the clumsy guitar case and it made a loud wooden sound. She sat at a tiny wooden table that had a round candle on it. She took out a pack of Marlboros filled with butts and pulled out a longish butt and lit it. After a while the owner showed up. She called herself Athena. She was an enormous Middle-Eastern–looking woman who, from the neck down, was nothing but a huge tent dress, Mama Cass style. Her hair was frizzy, black and wavy. Her eyes were large and brown but not warm. She seemed harassed, like the mother of many children.

"Hi," said Athena. Her voice was very low and husky. "You drove from college."

"Yes," said Leah.

"Are you tired? Do you want something to eat or drink?"

Leah said no she didn't, and Athena seemed saddened by this response.

"Well then get to it," she said. Her tiredness put Leah off.

Leah climbed up on the tiny triangular stage and pulled her guitar out. She put her thumbpick on her thumb and began droning the low strings in her usual style with the upper strings turned Indian or dulcimer-style. She began to sing her song and Athena called from the back.

"You want the mike?"

Leah was terrified.

"Try the mike," shouted Athena. "Just sing and play. I've turned it on. You don't have to do anything."

Leah went through her set of songs. The amplification made her feel as if someone else were singing. It put her into a counterpoint state of mind where she could think simultaneously while singing. This was disconcerting—childhood memories came to her. She wondered how fat Athena was under her dress. She thought about Kari waiting in the parking lot.

Finally the set was over and Athena approached her on the triangle. Athena came up very close to her and Leah could see the beads of sweat on Athena's dark woman's mustache. Athena's eyes were very intense. She was intimate with no explanation.

"How odd," said Athena. And that was all she said. Athena kept looking at Leah as if there were something perched on one of her shoulders that she couldn't remember the name for. Then abruptly she began to clean up the table tops of the coffee house and talk to Leah as if she'd just walked in the door.

"You can open for Arnold J. Saks starting tonight," said Athena. "I'll pay you if we make a profit—which we won't."

"I don't need the money," said Leah.

"I didn't think you did," said Athena. "You want some Sangria or anything?"

"No," said Leah. "You want some help cleaning up?"

Athena gave Leah a broom and Leah was obviously inadequate at getting the ashes and napkins and crumbs off the floor. But she felt the need to ingratiate herself to this lady who seemed strangely wired, who came in and out of focus like radio stations when someone is switching the dial. She knew Kari was waiting and Kari wasn't well, but she was drawn to complete this situation which in name should have been exhilarating, but in actuality was lonely. She kept sweeping, leaving lines of ashes everywhere until Athena left the room for her office saying, "The first set goes on between nine and ten," and never looked back.

Kari was sitting on the asphalt leaned up against a tree near his trusty Peregrin. (Peregrin was "pilgrim" in Latin and he had named his motorcycle fondly for all the journeys they had taken together.) He was trying to study the fake book but he hadn't told Leah about his eyesight, which, since he'd fallen off the rings at Dartmouth, had taken to doing weird tricks. Whenever he'd have a seizure he was reminded of Fritz the Cat—his pitch-black eyes and the way, like peas, they could go in any direction they wanted. So Kari had taken some of his money he'd earned teaching recorder at the Putney School and had bought a little Panasonic tape recorder with earphones. Then he'd gone for a trip to some resorts in the Poconos, the Catskills and the Berkshires, had sat at many a bar drinking many Heinekens, and had taped the styles of twenty or thirty cocktail pianists. He figured he could copy them by ear if his eyes gave out. Driving Peregrin was another story, but he and Leah had reached Saratoga without catastrophe and if they could settle in one place long enough he'd go to an eye doctor.

The main problem, of course, was whether Leah could get the singing gig. Kari didn't care much what he did. A hallucination-free day or a day of clear vision was enough for him. He loved the green of the country. He loved Peregrin. He loved reading Chaucer. And he loved making love to Leah—his wild-child—full of her wails and ideas in the daytime and so blond and childish at night. The weed he was smoking made him feel very fatherly. And yet it was she who'd driven up in her blaring Que Fortuna de Los Angeles (her car) and taken him back to college from the hospital in their hometown. He wasn't sure he wanted to leave. He had a scheme for Bach and a synthesizer and Steve Reich–type harmonies that he needed time to compute. But she'd said, "Come along, chum, too many geniuses are rotting away because the sixties is a decade from another cosmos." And that night they'd pulled into a Holiday Inn—her treat—and she wanted him so badly sexually and he was so scared from the blackness of the concussion and she was so grateful and responsive to his fear. He wasn't sure what had gone on with her over the years. She was eighteen now and full of secrets. But she had cheese and Triscuits and cold canned ravioli and she sang at the top of her lungs to the radio. And she'd

always put her hand down his pants while driving with the
other. And there was always a Marlboro in her mouth.

She dared to drive anywhere with him when they picked
up Peregrin from Dartmouth and she told him she didn't
mind if he went slow, that—as with their sex—they both
needed to be scared for a while. She'd become so complex.
All he remembered of her was this girl waiting for him after
football practice so they could get together and be a band.
She wanted to be Ian and Sylvia she said, or Richard and
Mimi Farina or, as the year went on, Ike and Tina Turner.
He didn't even know how she'd heard about his accident or
his freak-out. She was just there.

For a moment while he was waiting for Leah, Kari looked
at the black asphalt and the black all of a sudden became a
vertical wall. He couldn't find the edges of the wall either
and he couldn't see the sun straight up in the sky. Acid flash,
he told himself and pictured demonic multicolored sperm-
like bugs being time-capsule–released through his blood-
stream for the rest of his life. Yet when the moment passed
the shopping plaza definitely had a milky edge to it. Like a
town in very hot weather. A dizzy day. This more than anything made him want to sleep awhile and wake up in a white
bed. But then Leah came along sounding like a vacuum
cleaner on top of a sanitation truck and he had to laugh at
Que Fortuna de Los Angeles and admire the car's noble attitude in the midst of its mistress's abuse.

"Yes, love," said Leah, "I'm employed."

Kari smiled happily and jumped up rabbit-like and angu-
lar. But Leah moved her head when he went to kiss her.
Then she gave his thin neck a hug and whispered, "Let's go
to a motel and get a phone book and start lookin' for resorts."

So they drove down the wide lanes of Saratoga—fast food
joints all the way—and Kari played the road games he knew
Leah loved: circling around her on the bike, riding close to
her side, her rear, bumping her front and doing a few wheel-

ies. He wasn't sure in all of this, but he felt obligated to celebrate a holiday that was entirely Leah's festival.

They checked into a cheap motel. The bed was damp and
the bedspread was mustard-colored. The second they got in
the door and before their duffel bags were unloaded, Leah
pulled out the Yellow Pages and was circling the names of
resorts and cocktail lounges with a black felt-tip pen. Kari
pulled out an alto recorder from his knapsack and began
playing a Pachelbel melody on it. Leah looked up at him,
cigarette dangling from her mouth and said,

"Such a rare, gentle soul!"

He knew she meant him, but the notes of the melody were
little portholes of vision for him and he was concentrating.

Leah got on the phone and began to seek appointments
for Kari. She looked like a caricature of an agent. She
seemed nervous. Finally she flung down the phone and Kari
flinched, not knowing if the news was good or bad.

"Listen to this, pal," said Leah. "There's a super-huge res-
ident hotel with sulphur baths and they need a pianist for
their cocktail hour and dinner set. The thing is, you see, that
everybody's about two hundred and fifty years old so nobody's gonna stay that late. Their other guy left for a cruise
to Bermuda or somewhere so you can audition right now.
The lady's name is Mrs. Collingwood and she sounds half se-
nile and deaf, so just look cute and you're halfway there."

Leah's enthusiasm had an edge which made Kari afraid.
But she undressed him so gently and bathed him, cooing as if
he were a baby. And they splashed in the rectangular tub
and then she dried him and held him.

Leah took out a sports jacket that she said had belonged to
her brother, Lazar, which was too short in the sleeves, but fit
otherwise. Then she clipped a blue satin bow tie onto his
Brooks Brothers shirt.

"If you wear your blue jeans with that you'll look colle-
giate, but respectful," she said. "I'll wait in the lobby and
wear white gloves."

Of course she didn't own white gloves. She was dressing these days like the most outrageous flower child, with long skirts, capes and scarves all around her braided, beaded hair. But for the occasion she brought out a simple A-line cotton flowered skirt, Capezio shoes, a round-collared short-sleeved shirt and a barrette to hold back her mane of hair. Kari preferred this clean-cut look but would never dare say it.

Kari imagined them married and when he put her on the back of Peregrin, for the first time in a long while he felt the peace he'd felt in high school. A simple date. A mad, simple date that could end in a family and grandchildren! He drove into a McDonald's parking lot and did a slalom course through the garbage cans.

The residential hotel was dreary and cavernous. It looked like the inside of an old ocean liner. White linen tablecloths covered thick wooden legs. The guests walked with canes and tripods and walkers and it made Kari feel as if he were in robot land. Leah sent him into the wide dining room full of windows and he felt as if he were a paper sailboat she'd set afloat. His vision was making the room appear convex and Mrs. Collingwood came to him through a zoom lens. This was fine for her, he supposed, because she had so many layers to her glasses that her eyes seemed to be waving from another ship off to Europe. Her voice crackled like the games kids played when they gargle Coke.

"You're the pianist."

Kari said yes he was.

"Well I don't suppose you'll try too much modern on our guests. You know, they come here for peace."

Kari said he needed peace himself.

"Do you know the songs that would please an older generation?" asked Mrs. Collingwood.

Kari said yes he did and slid down onto the blond piano bench of the blond baby grand piano and did what he knew to be a charmingly obnoxious arpeggio. (Leah had advised him that cocktail music was made up of fifty percent arpeg-

gios and thirty percent modulations into different keys.)
Kari kept very serious while doing this although inside he
was giggling hysterically and hearing Dylan Thomas recite
"Do Not Go Gentle into That Good Night." Kari did a rendition of "Bewitched, Bothered and Bewildered" where he
changed keys three times and put an arpeggio at the end of
every line.

Mrs. Collingwood was thrilled, and it was only then that
Kari noticed she had a curve in her spine which made her
stare straight down to the floor when she walked.

She informed him what he would be paid, which he didn't
hear and didn't care about, and Mrs. Collingwood told him
he would have a room on the top floor. Kari asked what
about his wife and Mrs. Collingwood said fine and when
Kari introduced Leah to Mrs. Collingwood he was shocked
to see how quickly Leah became his perfect Seven Sisters
Wasp wife.

When they left the hotel Leah grabbed him by his crotch
and said it was a thrill to know him. Kari was exhilarated
and utterly confused. He had a headache and a pain in his
eyes and was relieved when Leah said she'd rather stay in the
motel the first night and move into the Old Age Home the
next day.

"Well fine," Kari said, "well fine," and quoted something
in Dutch from his ancestors that he couldn't remember the
meaning of. Then they flew back to this motel and made
love for a while and Kari kept his new seersucker jacket and
bow tie on so he wouldn't be late for his first cocktail gig.
When he took off again Leah stayed at the motel to cut a
square out of the cover of the telephone book and write on its
white side the order of her songs in the set. Then she tried
hard to stay awake because she didn't want to sleep, she
didn't want to take speed, but the emergency of the events
was losing its kicks for her. So she got into Que Fortuna de
Los Angeles and drove in the dark toward some country-
looking land, got out of the car and stared at the stars. The

mosquitoes were biting and making big half-dollars all up
and down her legs, but she didn't want to be early. Athena
was too scary.

Kari kept thinking he was on a cruise ship. He'd taken a
couple to Europe with his parents when he was a prep school
boy and they'd felt like this. Old people in pastels prome-
naded to their tables. They all smiled, though he knew not
why they smiled. They looked bent and twisted; they came
in wheelchairs and with blue knotted hands. But they smiled
at him in that particular way very old people smile and you
know they've told themselves a dirty little joke. Of course the
middle-aged sons and daughters came along for supper and
they were rather fat and dour. Kari preferred the grandpar-
ents and the greasy and overdressed grandchildren for whom
he threw in some unrecognizable Beatles tunes. Mrs. Collingwood kept applauding at him from her round table in
the corner and sending him little A-Okay signs. And he
drifted through such tunes as "Moonlight in Vermont," "All
the Things You Are," "More," "Tenderly," and even made
up a song of his own composed of one measure each from
Twenty Selected Cocktail Tunes and he called it "Dits, Lits
and Shuffle Toes" and vowed to tell Leah about it. He already had a souvenir for her, which was his name tag. It had
Saratoga Silver Spa printed on it and his name, Kari Narti,
typed in italics and underneath his name was written "Orchestra." It was pleasing to be an orchestra. He began to
hear accompanying string parts and tuba solos in his head
but was beginning to sound too much like a combination of
Charles Ives and Thelonious Monk and Mrs. Collingwood
was looking concerned through her wrist corsage.

To apologize, Kari launched into a totally respectful rendition of "Just in Time," and to his delight some takers got
up and began to weave their way around the brown-and-
mustard checkered dance floor. Kari's favorite couple was a
three-year-old-boy and probably his great-grandmother.

The little boy seemed only able to step sideways and the grandmother marched up and down as if she were lifting her legs in and out of a bathtub. Her legs were very skinny and had blue veins all over them. Neither she nor the little boy seemed to mind. In fact they seemed hopelessly in love, a fact for which Kari was very grateful. He was getting tired and he was only one hour through his four-hour commitment.

Arnold J. Saks was in the back room when Leah got to the Hot Springs. He was hunched over a book with his head leaning up against the mirror and a cigarette dangling from his mouth. His guitar was leaning against him.

Leah introduced herself as his opening act and he stared at her very intensely and then just as had happened with Athena, seemed to lose interest in his own intensity. "Where'd he go?" she thought to herself as he got up without a word and disappeared into another room.

Shortly thereafter Athena appeared, acting distracted. "You need anything?" asked Athena.

Leah said she'd be fine. Leah asked Athena if she'd listen to her act.

"Never on the first night," Athena replied. "I can't stand the nervousness." Athena was combing out her long hair, talking through the mirror. Then she came eyeball to eyeball with Leah again and said, "I will listen tomorrow night and we'll decide."

We'll decide *what?* thought Leah, but she didn't say it aloud. She knew she was hired for a month and anyway Athena's statement had a far more mystical ring to it. Athena was still staring at her so Leah nodded.

"There's a bunch of us going to have a barbecue along the beach after the second set," Athena said. "You'll come."

Leah didn't answer. Theoretically, this was supposed to thrill her. But she was getting afraid, the way you do in dreams where you're in a foreign country and no one speaks English. Then a fellow with a long scraggly beard and a ponytail down to his waist came in the room with a big-bodied guitar.

"Let's jam," he said and Athena left without saying good-bye.

This fellow never said his name. He smiled at Leah and pulled out multicolored finger picks and put them on all his fingers. Then he lay his guitar on his lap and began strumming it like a dulcimer. Then he was picking. He talked simultaneously as if demonstrating. He was playing a kind of honky-tonk but it was not logical, the chords didn't go anywhere or resolve.

"I made this technique myself," the fellow said. "It's the way I deal with being left-handed."

Leah tried to sing along and felt like an ass. Arnold J. Saks came and stood in the doorway and she stopped abruptly.

"Go on! Go on!" said the fellow and he was nodding his head and hearing a tune that Leah obviously couldn't hear.

"Don't she sing great?" said the fellow to Arnold J. Saks. But Arnold J. Saks just stood there with his eyes crinkled, looking as if he were trying to remember someone's address or telephone number.

Athena's son came by. He was sullen and about fifteen years old and told Leah that she'd be going on in fifteen minutes. Leah knew he was Athena's son because he had exactly her face. He was dressed in a white linen shirt and long brown pants, white socks and black tie shoes. His hair was cut short and his hands were greasy.

"Athena says to wait until she announces you," he mumbled and disappeared.

The amazing fact was that the café was filling up. It was really getting jammed with people and Leah began to get very scared.

Eventually she heard Athena's husky voice. Athena was saying, "Tonight we have my dear old pal, Arnold J. Saks!" and the audience went wild. Athena went on. "His opening act is a young woman who I think has great promise. She's still in college, but she writes good songs and I hope you'll welcome her . . ."

Then Athena left the stage. She hadn't said Leah's name. But Leah walked out on the little triangle and sat down on the stool anyway and began her set. She didn't bother to introduce herself either. All the time voices in her head were pointing out who wasn't listening to her. Also, since Leah was a soprano singer, everyone in the back of the café talking full volume was clearly audible. "Never mind," she told herself and decided to sing for Arnold J. Saks, although she couldn't see him. The applause in between each song was solid and mechanical. Less as each song went along. She wanted to hurry up and finish. Her tunes were modal and melancholy and her lyrics were full of unspecific longing and psychedelic nature symbols. She knew as she went along that there wasn't enough variety in her writing. She vowed that night to write a country and western tune and a honky-tonk, John Sebastian style. At long last she left the triangle and the applause didn't go on at all. There was no conclusion to the experience. Arnold J. Saks was in the back room getting ready to go on. The ponytailed fellow was strapping him into his guitar like a bull about to be sprung out.

"You have a nice clear little soprano," Arnold J. Saks said to Leah, and then he burst into the little coffeehouse to the screaming audience.

Leah wanted to call Lazar in New York and tell him she'd just done her first professional job. She seemed to remember that Arnold J. Saks had known Lazar in college, but she wasn't sure. But she didn't want to risk crashing if he wasn't there. She didn't go out to listen to the first set. She stayed in the back and listened with her eyes closed. She noticed that Saks had a fine hard edge and an unsentimental quality to his work. It wasn't just songs, it was intelligent. He also balanced his rowdy up-tempo cakewalk tunes with low gritty blues. He used silences, he made guitar solos. Leah made use of this in her brain. She loved the man's gravelly voice and his scat-singing. She lit a Marlboro cigarette and didn't know where to put the match. So she placed it in her pocket, sat back in the chair and felt her first minute or two of relative peace.

The fight against acid flash, the doctors had told Kari, was like a good swim in completely calm waters. If you splashed around and got your eyes all full of it, you could convince yourself you were shipwrecked and about to go under. But if you just stopped long enough, you would realize that the water was as calm as a lake and perfectly acceptable to a swimmer with years of experience.

"Okay," Kari said to himself, "Lake Ontario, Lake Ontario," and he was reminding himself of this most extraordinary blue-green fishing lake while staring down at the chicken dinner served to him by a faceless waitress during the half-hour break before his final set. The room had become faceless. It wasn't blank. It was more as if all the kinds of folks had just recovered from some sort of plastic surgery which had put all the features of the face in gross proportion. There was a waitress with very tiny eyes, huge nose and a mouth like an incision across her chin. One old lady's glasses seemed to have a prism of doors moving infinitesimally backwards like in a Herman Hesse story. That was not all. The chicken was moving back and forth and in and out of those little bracelets of glass when you tilted it one way and got the Empire State Building and then tilted it back and got New York written on it. Kari was almost certain this was an acid flash and yet everything sounded absolutely crystal clear. There was no symphony of voices. There was no bass drum where his heart would be. There were no garden smells and the tablecloth felt like linen, the chair wood, his own sweat was clearly that, sweat. He tasted it, salt. The trouble was when he looked at his watch to check the time for his set, he couldn't see it. Not only could he not see the numbers, but he couldn't see the round shape on his wrist. He recited the names of many of his favorite lakes and felt his way back to the piano. He played very conservatively for the first hour and kept his eyes closed most of the time. He saw no startling pictures before him and felt relieved. He looked down at the keys every now and then and they were indistinct and color- less. He could no longer see Mrs. Collingwood across the room. Perhaps she'd gone to bed.

It was at the very end of his evening, when perhaps most of the guests had gone to their sleep, that the mustard ship's room began to get very dark, as if a tropical storm were about to descend. He asked one of the waiters if they'd dimmed the lights. When the waiter replied no, he felt frus- trated and mad. He played one Scott Joplin and a bit of Art Tatum because the doctors had said that pent-up feelings could cause psychotic reactions. But when the room began to really fade into night and there were no stars where the cheap chandelier had hung, Kari knew in his gut what a small voice had been singing all along—something in his eyes was going. He remembered many times falling asleep with contact lenses on; he remembered falling hard on his head off those rings.

Kari finished his evening with a calypso tune called "Yel- low Bird" and felt his way out of the spa. The bright lights on the Saratoga strip gave him direction enough to find the parking lot where Peregrin was parked.

"I'm gonna walk you home tonight, girl," he said. And he began the three- or four-mile hike along the wide roadway by clucking his tongue and pulling at Peregrin's handlebars as if they were reins.

"I'm gonna git you home and cook us some franks and beans," said Kari.

And he sang some old cowboy tunes and pushed Peregrin along the gravel. He yodeled like his dad had taught him when they'd been skiing in Switzerland. And he stroked

Peregrin's soft leather seat for two and comforted her.

Leah finished her second set. This time she talked a bit more in between the songs and smiled every now and then at the audience. She replaced a couple of her own songs with an up-tempo version of Taj Mahal's "Annie's Lover" and a jazz version of "It Ain't Me, Babe," that Kari had arranged for her. When she finished singing there was more applause than the first time, but still no great ovation. This time Arnold J. Saks said nothing. But Athena was waiting for her in the back room.

"How did it go?" said Athena.

Leah replied that it was a little shaky, but that it would improve.

"Saks thinks you have talent," said Athena.

She said it in a strangely provocative way, and peered intensely at Leah for some response. Leah smiled politely and said that meant a lot.

"To *some* it means a lot," said Athena, "but to others . . ." and she laughed a raucous, strange laugh that Leah couldn't translate.

Leah noticed that Athena was standing with another heavy woman whose hair was cut very short. This woman was wearing an army fatigue T-shirt and dirty blue jeans and clogs. She wore a thick silver watch and had bitten fingernails. She stood silently with Athena, her eyes squinted, and smoked a cigarette, opening her mouth very wide when she blew out the smoke. Athena did not introduce the woman.

"Are you going to the barbecue?" asked Athena.

Her voice was affected and provocative. Leah apologized and said she had to go.

"But where would one go from here?" asked Athena. Her friend seemed entirely uninterested. Leah explained that her boyfriend was waiting for her and she had to meet him.

"There was no law said you couldn't bring him," said Athena.

Leah said she was clear about that but that he'd been working too. Leah explained that he was playing cocktail piano at the Saratoga Silver Spa. At this Athena guffawed and her friend (whose hair looked greased in the light) grinned while keeping her lips together.

"You're an original," said Athena.

Leah didn't know whether to feel humiliated or encouraged by this remark. Athena left the room with no farewell.

When Leah arrived at the motel she could see from the outside that the room was entirely dark. At first she was fearful that Kari had met another woman and gone off. She knew she was careless and demanding. He had always been quiet and fragile and since his accident his gratitude for her humor and her spirit, even her body, was at times very moving to her and at times made her very cruel. Always she felt guilty. And then always she felt stupid because his response to her meanness was gentle and vague. His lightness made her feel brittle in comparison. His recorder, his soft voice, his light hands.

Peregrin was parked at a weird distance from the room, but Leah was glad to see it. She opened the door with her key and saw the profile of his body lying silent on the bed, the shadow of the shades flashing on and off in the rhythm of the traffic lights of the strip.

"Hello hello," he said in his soft voice. She flicked on the light and he put his arm over his eyes.

"Kari?" said Leah. "Acid flash, baby? Acid flash? Want some Valium?"

"Dunno, Madam," said Kari. But when she pulled his arm down from his eyes she became afraid. Both eyeballs were filmy and where the whites of the eyes usually were, there were red blisters. His eyelids were swollen and covered with mucus; the pupils were all one faded color.

Leah pushed her panic behind a layer of calm and forget-
fulness. Gentleness and grief took over.

"Kari baby, did you do something weird? Did you put
nose drops in your eyes? Were you fixing Peregrin with some
shit? Did you rub it by mistake in your eyes?"

"No, darling one," said Kari. "This is nature's own
fixin's."

Leah felt his head and knew he was burning a terrible
fever.

"You stay here, fella," she said. "I'm going to the front
desk to get some aspirin."

She slid out the door as quietly as she could. Little
screaming sounds were in her throat when she reached the
parking lot.

As they waited for the ambulance to arrive they held each
other's thin fingers. And she told him about weird Athena
and the fabulous Arnold J. Saks and he told her about the
grandmother with her sidestepping three-year-old escort.
And they laughed and touched lightly until they heard the
distant siren honking closer toward their door.

Leah spent the night with Kari in the hospital. After the
emergency doctor had put white gauze patches over his eyes
and given him a sleeping pill, the nurse called Kari's rich
parents. They told the doctor to give Kari the best private
room and that they'd drive all night to get there. Leah imagined Kari's dignified Pilgrim heritage and admired his parents for their pioneer spirit. She took her sleeping bag and
camped out next to his bed, playing him campfire songs,
though he was sound asleep.

When the mountain dawn came through the milky glass
of Kari's hospital window, Leah packed up her guitar, rolled
up her sleeping bag and began the walk back toward the
motel. She didn't want to meet anyone's parents and have
them invade her summer. She tried to sleep back at the
motel room, but she kept looking at the fat old-fashioned

phone on the bureau. Finally, at 9:00 A.M. she could wait no longer and called the hospital. The doctor told her Kari had been flown back to his home for an operation on his eyes.

Leah put her guitar in Que Fortuna de Los Angeles and drove away from Saratoga to a small village in Fleishmanns, New York, in the Catskills. There was a summer camp in the area for underprivileged children. She volunteered to teach singing and conduct the choir. They told her she had to buy herself all whites for their Sunday Vespers. She got back in the MGB and headed on Route 28 toward Kingston, where they had shopping malls. She kept driving.

21

Lazar, Esquire

Everything was going exactly according to plan. The social worker with the cute ass and beehive hairdo had righteously defended him all the way on the subway. And with her proper administration letters, a few monetary apologies from the government and Father's redemption fee (his monthly religious punitive damages), Lazar secured himself a dream storefront on Seventh Street between Avenues A and B. Of course curtains had to be hung to cover all the glass for several areas of insulation. One—the heat. Two—spiritual. Three—chemical. There was a doctor who helped him do that; he was young with fuzzy Afro-Jewish hair and beard and administered the likely Thorazine for inner thermostat control—not too much heat, Mr. Lazar, but certainly we can't let it go out. No no no. Life was too unbelievably good. Never had there been such clear proximity to the Hispanic population of America, nor a fine health food restaurant with a sexy Polynesian waitress, nor—of course, but of course—the Bowery bums. Lazar could not wait to get near these people who looked like photographs and quote the great poets with them. He imagined Yeats and Auden were particular favorites. He, Lazar, master of fate, could not drink—the young doctor had assured him a foul and bloated death if he did—but he certainly had his stories to tell, his own crutches, his artificial limbs and he welcomed many an hour on the street living out his version of prodigiousness victorious over sorrow.

These were the plans. Lists had to be made. Hung from

cork bulletin boards. In their proper color. In India ink. He had to find an accompanist for his new nightclub act. He had to find a publisher for his novel. He had certain political ideas on how the city should handle the disabled and he had to get the proper person in charge at City Hall. He wanted to go back to college and he felt it was essential to take up some sort of menial labor to discover the blue-collar essence. Here was why: given that a journey in madness is of course painful, we all know that nonetheless it is privileged. That certain privilege having expired, perhaps it was time to take tickets at Madison Square Garden or work in the shipping room of a post office. "We need not worry about friends," Lazar decided. This was a time of intellectual and practical rehabilitation. The human race could wait. It is a long and full day and who knows who's on the doorstep after a day out in the field?

My dear Sir,
    I have written a rather bold new novel. Don't put this letter in your young-men-who-think-they-have-written-bold-new-novel piles. If you want to remain that sort of editor—I am not the one to judge you—I would ask only that you consider the advice I give you on page two.

Page 2
    When a person finds a routine for himself, he is usually fending off a miracle. Your piles and files are safeguards against miracles. St. Francis of Assisi had no organized plan when he dealt with lepers and cripples. I offer this only as gentle advice since I am certain to be published anyway.
                        Thank you.
                        Sincerely,
                        Lazar, Esquire

P.S. If you find the time to read, however, pages 6–10 might lean toward the sentimental. I would be interested to

know your opinion on such matters. I am not sure if
sentimentality has any place in this culture.

Lazar insisted on having a pay phone installed in the
storefront. He convinced his bouncy social worker that this
would limit his outgoing calls and impose on him the absolute silence needed for productivity and clarity. As for the
incoming calls, only the doctor and the social worker were to
have the number. Certainly not Father, not Mother, not
Leah. And if by chance on a hot night in Harlem a jazz band
wanted him to sit in and croon, he'd list this number in the
Manhattan phone book under his uptown stage name—Ter-
rence McSham. And no one would know that. Perhaps he
would even forget it. Perhaps he would have already
changed names six or seven times when the big break came.

My dear Esther,
    You can remember a night at a lawn wedding when you
were playing medleys of old songs. I told you I particularly
liked your rendition of "Call Me Irresponsible." They'd im-
ported you from New York because you were a dear friend
of the Aunt of the Bride. (She by the way was my cousin—
which is no reflection on me one way or another.)
    The time has come for me to deal on some level with the
pressures of the coffeehouse circuit and I thought perhaps
you might be a very jolly companion. If nothing else I liked
your purple dress.
    I am in the process of working out some new material and
would appreciate piano arrangements and vocal coaching. I
might perhaps include a duet if the time befits.
    I have feelers from the Village Gate and the Bitter End.
At least to get into their open call night on Tuesdays. I have
some stunning ideas about the central character being a
fella in a bow tie with a tic.
    Please let me know about your availability and in no way
let our age difference deter you. I think there could be a

sexy edge to it full of Oedipal overtones and lascivious in-
nuendos.

Write to me care of the Wellington Rehabilitation Center
and I will check there daily for your reply. Thank you.

Sincerely,

Lazar, Esquire

P.S. I have included a self-addressed stamped envelope with
a list of choices that you might decide upon. A definite
yes, you should know, is very different from a yes for
the time being or a yes I'll meet you for lunch. I will
accept any of these positive answers without hostility.

If you check any of the negative answers I shall immediately look for another accompanist. Therefore
please keep this in mind during the time it takes you to
reply, because my career has been held up a bit and—
as you can imagine—I am anxious to get on the old
horse again.

L.E.

Rainy cloudy East Village. Bum-lined sticky streets—
soggy cardboard. It was tough going getting dinner. Thick
pea soup at the health food restaurant with water dripping
up his nose. Not that Mother had sent him a care package
mind you in a while. Once they weighed up to fifty pounds.
And the postage looked like Christmas seals wrapping paper.
Canned foods—squashed brownies—crackers—plastic rolls
of cheddar cheese. In the hospital they'd down it all in a
swallow. As if to leave any for the next day would be an in-
gratitude. Mother was picking up her life a bit now that
Lazar was better. That's what she said. She was talent scout-
ing for a local TV talk show. The M.C. was ugly; she'd do
her best. She loved loved loved him though. It came in
threes.

The Polynesian waitress gave him a chocolate-chip cookie
the size of a pie. When she went to wipe the drippy water

off his nose Lazar got violent. These areas of his helplessness or his "invalidness" were extremely complicated and
one had to learn the guidebook intricately. He'd pay for
the glass, he said. Of course, she said and her mother was
unconcerned. The political situation in their homeland
had left many young men distraught like Lazar. This was
never said; he figured it out. He would buy a globe and see
where they came from exactly. He must eat. That was crucial to his development. He could not walk fast. Men were
sleeping in hallways, half covered by cardboard. He remembered forts he'd made for Leah out of blankets and chairs. It
was there he'd intended to teach her basic values and funda-
mental morality. He made her a princess and taught her
how to rule. The rain against his legs sounded like a steel
drum. The Caribbean came to mind. Hadn't he won a
mambo contest?

Gentlemen—
   It has come to my attention that the young woman behind the bars who administers the subway tokens in your
fair city are not acquainted with the basic needs of the
handicapped in the city. Nor are your police officers.
   I have a certain handicap—which at this time it is more
diplomatic to keep confidential—and found that I was told
to "hurry along" by one of your tellers—a Miss Helena Gar-
cia Ignatales, to be precise. Then, gentlemen, as I was making my way through the turnstile, one of your officers—Sgt.
P. Anderson—told me to "*move* it, fella." Not only does this
kind of language reflect the inferior quality of the education
of your civil employees, but it is harassing to any citizen.
Therefore, I would expect a typed apology, personally
signed by the administration of transportation and no less
than the deputy mayor. Otherwise, alas, I will have to sue
for punitive damages and given my name and stature, the
publicity as well as the legal fuss could get ugly for you.
   I look forward to hearing from you. And please send a

carbon copy of your letter of reprimand to Ms. Ignatales and Sgt. Anderson. Thank you.

> Sincerely,
> Lazar, Esquire.

He was so busy these hours. Day and night were all the same. Negation and proof of the same photograph, gloriously interchangeable. There was so much to plan. Lazar was writing songs on the F A O Schwarz organ with the colored keys. He was writing his novel. He was writing poems again. Different poems in different colored notebooks, color-coded for emotion:

Yellow: Sunny
Blue: Ocean/depth
Green: Peace/nature
Black and White: Darky/home
Red: Rage

He had applications for Columbia, NYU, City College, Hunter, Fordham and The New School. He had each brochure. Every pamphlet describing every activity. He measured them, pondered, and finally decided to go slow. After all, just three days out of the hospital and the productivity in these days and nights had been prodigious.

This was definitely Father's speed. Father was on many committees and often spoke of them. Father said life was defined by overwork and just as Father would finish an enormous deal, packaging and boxing all the football shirts for the Minnesota Vikings, he would clinch another incredible honor—leading the citizens' committee to build the first superdome in upstate New York. Lazar was becoming industrious. It was also a bright flag to Mother. Here I am. Another way of signaling her on the tracks. She moved so slowly by. He was afraid she didn't see him. Wouldn't. Not that she was industrious. She was faded in.

The nights in lower Manhattan were inspiring for the soul. The man who beat the Bowery at Great Jones Street with drumsticks seemed like a natural for a Sounds of the City All-Rehabilitated Band. Lazar would teach them, book them into Radio City Music Hall . . . slow down, he'd think. Introduce yourself first. Here was the thing. The guy wouldn't talk to him. He just banged on the street.

"All right," thought Lazar. "I shall be tolerant of his rudeness."

An artist is an artist. So he sat listening to the Bowery and Great Jones while the cars screeched by. Other bums begged for coffee. Lazar pulled out a pitch pipe and played along. The drummer growled like a Doberman pinscher. Lazar went back to his storefront and locked himself in.

> To the Manager of the Village Gate:
> You may not of heard of me. (I know this is a typical letter—but read further, it gets better.) My name is Lazar and my approach to the nightclub act is one which may inspire you. (And many others, but I'll be modest yet.) It is a sort of act within an act, if you will. I do not perform as myself—but as a man with a tic who can barely achieve contact with his audience and then who, miraculously or not so miraculously, does—through song (perhaps a bit of dance) and medodica playing. If this sounds maudlin to you let me assure you it is comic in its intent. Though I also want to get something deeper—though I promise not preachy.
>
> I am accompanied by the very well known Esther Cohen on piano and we also do duets for a change of pace. Mrs. Cohen, if you recall, was audition accompanist for many Broadway stars. But ours is not to drop names—ours is just to write a friendly note and let you know I'm in town. Please drop your audition info (dates, times, personas) in the mail. I do not enclose a resume and photo because I just got into town and am having new pictures taken.

If I do not hear from you I will drop by on your open call nights and take it for granted that that is what you think is the best route for me.

Well, thank you.

Sincerely,
Lazar, Esquire

During these days Leah was coming in and out of New York. She wasn't sure whether to let Lazar know or not. He had said that this was his busiest time of the recent decade. Leah herself was being industrious. She lived in the country with a soft folk-rock group she'd started. They were located in a log cabin in Garrison, New York. Garrison was a Hudson River town (they'd filmed *Hello, Dolly* there). The log cabin was rented out by an alcoholic cocktail-jazz singer who was doing a summer at the Regency Room in New York. Her name was Biddle or Flora—Leah hardly could remember. The cabin had a lake and Leah and her band (they were all guys) and their girl friends smoked dope a lot, swam naked, and rehearsed through the night. The main bummer was that their pianist, Kari, was blind and he was going through a bitter period about it. He slept most days and refused to play anyone's music but his own. The other guys wanted to send him home, but Leah said no. He was an old pal and it was mainly her money that was renting the cabin.

Dear Lazar,

The lake here is beautiful. We think we've seen a turtle in it, but don't know for sure. Sometimes when the frogs are mating it can get pretty wild sounding. You would love to make sounds because they echo everywhere. You could whisper from one side of the lake to the other and anyone could hear. I hope your spiritual industry is booming.

Love,
Leah

Weird censorship. She didn't tell him she had a band. She didn't tell him they were going into New York for record auditions. She didn't tell him they were studying various styles of music and reading poetry and carrying on. She didn't tell him one of her lovers had gone blind and she didn't tell him she had lovers. She seemed to want to preserve for him his corner on being the artist in the family. Yet with the band—Stanley the lead guitar player and Jacob the bass and Alan the flute—she was vicious, absolutely. She ran it like her farm. She ran them like her Hitler youth camp. She could be very loving to them, but if she didn't get what she wanted her temper frightened her. Once she put her fist right through her classical guitar and shadows of Lazar came and circled all around her like a violent kaleidoscope. A Lazar carousel out of control. She'd gotten freaked out at the bass player because he wanted to sing a line she wanted to sing. So she cut her hand to bits and destroyed a five-hundred-dollar guitar. The boys came by her room all day knocking and trying to make peace out of the matter, but she was too haunted. Some preview of violence had her paralyzed. Only Kari finally made contact. He had his hokey white cane and he tapped it all over as if feeling for vertical sidewalks. Then he came and felt his way onto her bed with his all. He was blond and thin and dirty and nearly asleep.

"You and I are two dreamcakes," he said.

"Music is demanding," she said, "I can't be democratic about it."

"That's Bennington convent shit," said Kari; "that's not Leah talking."

"I don't like Jacob," said Leah.

"You don't like that he can sing rock better'n you," said Kari.

"And you don't like that everybody can *see,*" said Leah.

"Yes, but it seems I'm going to have to live with it. Otherwise people'll just have to keep lyin' to me, sayin', Hi, I'm David, I'm *blind.* Hello there, Kari, I'm Edgar and I have two

holes where my *eyes* used to be. Then I'll always feel safe."
Leah was starting to cry.

"Why're you so *awful,* Kari?" she asked.

"Because I can't see anything," he said very quietly, "and I'm not quite used to it yet."

"Good reason," said Leah, and she was getting sleepy on his smelly chest.

"Please," she said to him, "come to rehearsal and play decently."

"You've got a bargain," said Kari, "only no more Bruce Lee."

Leah smiled—he felt it—and was dozing off.

She said, *"You two guys.* What a duo."

Kari didn't know who the other guy was. But she was asleep so he didn't ask.

Sir—

I acquired quite by accident recently a copy of your magazine *Poetry.* I can find in it no poem which has near the heart nor quality of the twenty I've sent you—much less the originality. I'm sure you think my opinion is highly subjective and I'm a scorned college student or whatnot. I assure you, you are arrogant in thinking such thoughts. Your magazine proves your arrogance and your rejection slips make a joke out of the humanistic spirit of literature. In the old days such rejections were written with *script pen* and contained lengthy explanations as to why a certain poem wasn't published, leaving the poet some room to debate his particular case.

Perhaps you will practice this in the future. Form letters are more in keeping with legal offices and traffic tickets. I will certainly keep this in mind before I consider sending you another one of my poems.

I'm sorry to appear difficult. But surely you can't live off your sycophants and elderly subscribers alone.

Sincerely,
Lazar, Esquire.

Walking in the city was not easy. Lazar often felt as though his legs were eggs in two egg cups. They popped in and out of his artificial legs. He remembered a story he told Leah about a sailor with a wooden leg who painted a dart board on it for the poor of his village to play with. Perhaps he needed a day off. Perhaps he would not go to rehabilitation. Perhaps he would stay in his neighborhood. A young man was hosing off his car right next door—he looked like an Ohio type. Lazar asked him if he wouldn't mind hosing off Lazar. The young man smiled in an embarrassed way while Lazar brought out his shampoo and sang sea chanties with the dogs and the children of Seventh Street.

Leah had often sat on the lawn as a baby and played the sprinkler as a harp.

"Look at that, Mother," Lazar would say, "Leah is trying to get music out of the water."

Mother would look up and smile, but go back to her reading and her deck chair. The poetry would be lost. Once in the hospital when Mother very quietly whispered—hardly moving her mouth—asking Lazar what might've gone wrong between them, Lazar couldn't be specific. He said it was in the realm of poetry. Mother sent him volumes of Emily Dickinson and Carl Sandburg the next day. But as in *Through the Looking Glass* her visits "lessened and lessened," and every day Mother became less—until she was no more.

Kari had sold his motorcycle and got a Ford van that Leah could drive. They piled in all the equipment and drove south on the Taconic. Kari played blues harmonica and Stanley picked hard on the guitar. Jacob made bass noises through his nose. The others passed a joint around. They were going in for a record audition that Hermie's uncle— Hermie was their twelve-string player—had set up. They always broke down—usually the radiator hose—but the van was making Leah very nervous. It was jerking and sputting.

"Not *today*," she screamed at it. Hers was not a kind of screaming that brought laughter. There had been another confrontation at their cabin. Leah had found out—through some old West Virginia connections—that there was an underground coffeehouse circuit starting in Fort Dix, New Jersey, and moving south. Lots of young folksingers were being asked to go into army bases and sing antiwar songs to the GIs to encourage them to pull out. The backers of the movement even paid gas and a small per diem for food. Leah was excited by this. She liked to keep moving. It would keep Kari in the fresh air. It was dangerous. And the beauty of the country was starting to depress her.

But the rest of the band had said absolutely not. Many of them were still in college or just out. They were on fragile 4-Fs they explained to her. They'd really had to research their allergies or psychiatric problems. If they got caught on these army bases they could get drafted. Jacob, especially, was Leah's adversary. Uniforms made him sick, he told her. Short hair made him dizzy. It was fine for her to be romantic but all she'd do was go to jail for trespassing. The rest of the guys faced a lot crueler punishment. Leah had then and there told them they were spoiled and spineless and to get out of the cabin. She was going to do the town with Kari alone. But Kari was suddenly feeling loyal to the "band." They'd begun to make some sweet arrangements of his tunes. So it was nine men against one woman.

Leah drove into New York making sure all the amplifiers dumped over on the guys. When they screamed at her to slow down she sped up. She didn't care if she died. Again she felt as if she were having Lazar flashes. No one could talk to her. And when the van broke down she left them at the gas station and hitched into New York. She told them she'd meet them at the recording station. But she didn't know if she would.

Father was trying to reach Lazar for three weeks to talk about money. The doctors had advised Father to lie back and work through an intermediary, but no one could get Lazar to answer Father's letters or calls. Money was a problem between Father and Lazar. Often Father would receive a letter from Lazar asking for two thousand dollars for immediate emergency "mystery" medical problems. Father would want to know the name of the mystery. Lazar refused to give it. Father told Lazar that he would not deal in secondhand abstractions.

In truth Lazar had many debts. He had bought himself a new watch, a three-piece suit for office job interviews, a new desk for his poems, a one-hundred-and-fifty-color Magic Marker set for his writing and he owed a big sailor-type guy named Alex twenty-five dollars a week for bringing him chicken when he was too tired to go out for a day. Lazar had meant to make up all this debt business when he got a job; but it was taking longer than he thought. Lazar knew Father owed him the money anyway. It was a debt of blood and went back to the Bible. The only reason he couched his request in mystery was because of Father's violent psyche. Lazar saw no reason to get rattled at this delicate and historic point of his artistic career.

> Father—
> It is hardly within our boundaries for you to suddenly want domain over my medical problems. It seems that doctors know best what to do with the parts of the body they are assigned and it would do you well to learn from them, i.e., a brain surgeon does not set an injured toe. Must I be more blunt? Stay away from my affairs until I am ready to deal with your interference.
>
> Lazar

When Leah arrived at the recording studio the band was all set up. She had got an easy ride with some professor in a

Peugeot, but took her time getting to the studio. By now she couldn't remember the emotional source for her anger and was truly sorry to see her friends frantic. They were to do four songs for this record producer guy from Hollywood—two of hers, one of Kari's, and one of Jacob's. The setup seemed truly bizarre. The producer (he hadn't arrived yet) was going to sit in the control room and they were going to sing to him through microphones. He'd speak to them over the intercom. Leah felt this was inhuman but Jacob said it was common practice. The guys were in joking high spirits but Leah felt defeated. Somehow she knew her voice wouldn't carry in this ordeal and that Jacob was going to shine.

The producer was a cartoon. He walked into the control room twenty minutes late. He wore a light green summer suit and his hair was totally dyed and pushed over in the way bald people cover their bald spots. He wore sunglasses the whole time. He never said hello. The engineer instructed the band to begin. The studio was air-conditioned and Leah was freezing. No one played very well. They were nervous and uncomfortable. At first the producer leaned forward in his seat. By the middle of the second song he was on the phone and stayed on the phone for the rest of the audition. By the middle of the fourth song the whole band including Leah was giggling uncontrollably—relieved that the nightmare hadn't killed them—and relieved that, at this juncture, this particular humiliation was not very important to them. Even Jacob and Leah were rolling over on each other laughing by the end of the last song. In an unspoken way they all knew then they had no chance of making it together and their summer became an experiment again and each one of them looked forward to his or her summer pleasure with relief.

The producer left without their noticing. The engineer barked at them, told them they were fuck-ups and to pack

up. They decided to go to the Village and have a Chinese
dinner to celebrate. Leah noticed a stunning black man sitting quietly by the freight elevator. He was fortyish and wore
a black beret. He smiled and said he'd been through the
whole event himself a hundred times. His name was Brother
Simon and he was a jazz flute player who worked in the studio part-time. Yes, he agreed to eat with them and certainly
a weekend in the country jamming would be fine for the
soul. At first the other guys got their backs up in quiet ways
but Brother Simon was a very sweet peaceful fellow. He was
into Buddhism and jazz and Leah had decided it was time to
cool down. Kari called it Phase Two of ejection into her mu-
sical atmosphere.

Lazar was walking down Second Avenue. And it was his
avenue. He hadn't claimed full ownership of it yet but he
was drawing several sectors into his political arena. First
there were the gypsy children whom he gave money to and
told fables to in the late afternoon. Then there were the
freaks who hung out in front of the Fillmore East; of course
he was beautiful to them and he began to wear his arm in all
kinds of slings made of fabrics and macramé. Lazar would
not speak to the other poets on the block, the ones who sold
their poetry on scrolls or who recited, bobbing up and down
like hookers, on the street corners. He knew they were
phonies. He was the only one in the neighborhood who was
real and he expected the appropriate respect. If he did not
get it he hit people. He hit a boy in the health food restaurant just a day before because the boy would not stop speaking in rhyming couplets. Rhyming couplets were Lazar's ter-
ritory and no one else's. The boy hit him back and now
Lazar's glasses were broken and looked like avant-garde bifocals. It didn't matter. He had a great future ahead of him.
He'd written lots of letters, organized his apartment and,
although he hadn't gone to rehabilitation in several days or
purchased postage stamps, it was only a matter of time. The

main thing was that the world recognize its fragile leader—
that it make a simple path for him—not complicate this delicate fragment of his history.

As Lazar was walking slowly to his storefront (some days
he could recite two poems in the length of a stop), a large
van screeched up next to him and a girl's voice screeched his
name. "Lazar!" it screeched. It had an annoying adolescent
arrogant ring to it. "Lazar!" it screeched again. Lazar
laughed to himself and imagined a feather-headed teeny-
bopper at the Fillmore. He knew the sexuality of his nightclub act. He was well aware of the effect he had on people.
But he couldn't let the hysteria of this voice penetrate the
goodwill of his immediate meditation. The voice modulated
into a whine. He could see it, a face in his peripheral vision,
but that hardly mattered. All faces were distractions, especially whining faces. "Lazar," the voice whined and finally,
much to his dismay, Lazar turned full face to the wide-eyed
blond-haired hippie girl and said to her, "Not yet, my good
Madam."

With that remark the van pulled away. He felt the hum-
bleness of its motion. For some reason he was tired and
wanted to go home and sleep for a day or two. After all, life
was exceedingly full of errands. And a spiritual soul had to
protect itself from too much data.

He pulled down his shades, kicked the papers off his bed
and lay there—he didn't know how long or in what time
zone—until he heard the cute little social worker, with her
good ass and package of pills, clicking away at his window.

22

The Bird Inside Itself

Father thought that the four of them should go to an island for two weeks. Lazar had been ill with a double ear infection. Leah had wheezed from bronchitis during their last phone call and Mother hated spring in upstate New York. Father's business was picking up. He could afford to rent a three-room villa. He chose St. Croix for the scuba-diving facilities.

Lazar would only communicate through Father's secretary, Rosemary. He would not answer messages from Father. He sent little notes through Rosemary and called her "sweetie."

Sweetie—
    Please inform your employer (my father) that I have not yet received my check for February. Your voice sounded husky and petulant the last time we talked.
    My father knows the meaning of his actions—but only he can live with them. Until then I could not sit in a room with him, much less an island.
                                                Sincerely, Lazar.

Leah was living on the top floor of an experimental jazz school studio in New York. It was owned by a West Indian lady who specialized in orphans. Leah was now living with the forty-year-old black Buddhist flute player, Brother Simon. He was probably a junkie, though she never saw him shoot up. He taught her to play flute by telling her to smile on its hole. He smiled. He played saxophone solos on Third Street late into the night. Leah made money by teaching and taking tickets for the recitals. The school specialized in the music of Third World cultures. There was the Asian-American group, the Afro-American group, the Native American company, the Filipino company, an Israeli troupe and a visiting Korean martial arts expert. Brother Simon was the musician in residence for the Afro-American company. Leah felt at the heart of the world. The building was covered with posters. People dressed in ethnic costumes, toting exotic instruments, were always going in and out of the building. Everyone was poor. And there were rats. Leah wanted this to be a time of learning. There were strange moments when Brother Simon took her up onto the school roof and made love to her standing up. She'd wrap her legs around his waist and look over the smoking rooftops of the whole East Village. She loved the pigeons and flying papers. Simon would whisper obscenities at her and she'd laugh to herself.

But she was also ill. Brother Simon slept at odd hours. The room was extremely cold. Her body ached. She wheezed when they made love. Her throat was always sore. She listened to Brother Simon's records like "Music from the Morning of the World," which featured a bunch of Balinese men chanting in monkey voices in drum rhythms—but the music came through stuffed ears. She watched the Kala Kathi dance classes with the heavy stepping sideways head movements, but she had no energy to participate. She went to visit Kari, who lived down the block and was playing rock-and-roll piano. Kari said she had a total spiritual disorder. He told her she was one phase removed. He was playing Moog synthesizers now. He told her to get out of the city. She was getting like Japanese paper. Too thin. He could feel through her. She loved his greasy head and his bad haircut. She sometimes stayed with him when Brother Simon slept up in Harlem with his wife.

Hello Daughter,

After our last phone conversation, it occurred to me you might like a little sun. I've rented a villa (très bourgeois) in St. Croix and you'd have your own room, privacy, no interference and room service at your beck and call. What the hell. Let me know.

I love you,
Father

Leah figured she could get a tan. She knew there was voodoo on the islands. She planned to rent a car, find some natives—go to places where tourists didn't go. She knew she would have to eat some dinners with her parents, but she'd deal with it. Father could be asked to talk more quietly. Mother's silences were harder to ignore. Mother was very strange lately. Leah balanced these thoughts on her dawn walks on Second Avenue. There was less traffic, the air was cleaner. None of the street bums were playing music. She went to a pay phone. She'd call one of the guitar players she knew—an acid freak from Tennessee—and ask if he would cover her box office job if, by some chance, she had to go away for a while. He said he needed the money. Later Brother Simon said everything was fine. He was a bad mystic. He told her that when she wasn't there she was still there. In her brain she knew Brother Simon was stupidly stoned and probably a little evil, but his music thrilled her. As one day when he'd called her on the flute from across a pond in the country. Or when he'd taken her up on the city roof and told her to get naked and blasted his saxophone. She had to make her life from fragments. Kari said she had no chord progressions, just loose notes.

Father received a letter from Lazar. It said:

Dear Sir—

I am reconsidering your offer of late which I don't deny is generous but I suspect no doubt has ulterior motives. Therefore I must set down a list of rules with which you must accord absolutely or I cannot even begin to consider the pros and cons of time spent with you—either in business or leisure.

1) There shall be no talk of failure or success—in your business or mine.

2) All opinions on the arts will be kept private.

2a) Political discussion is open but it must be jovial and detached and not exceed a time limit of four to five minutes.

3) Any reminiscing about dead uncles, aunts or other ancestors shall be forbidden from mealtime (or other) discussion.

4) No references to my accident may be made—including how well I am doing.

5) I will be given an open return on my ticket so if any of my wishes are violated, I may be allowed to leave the island immediately.

6) My sister and I will not be forced to reunite if we do not wish to.

7) My mother and I will be allowed to find our way.

8) No special services for the handicapped will be waiting
    a) at the airport
    b) in the dining room
    c) at the bathing facilities
    d) in the rooms

9) After the vacation (if I do comply) you will not consider this a reconciliation. It is (if it is) an acceptance of a gift. We will resume negotiations through Rosemary and I will continue to owe you nothing in the way of money, gratitude or love.

Please reply specifically to each of my conditions as soon as possible so I can make the appropriate plans—if they need to be made.

Sincerely, Lazar.

Father drafted a letter through Rosemary. He put it on his business stationery. He was tempted to bicker with Lazar over several of the conditions. In fact, the whole letter infuriated him. But Mother had been so melancholy that if there was any hope of bringing the family together for any outing, Father would try. He numbered Lazar's statements one through nine and simply said, "Agreed." He had the letter sent express. Two days later Rosemary got a crackling call from Lazar. He was in a street corner phone booth in the middle of a Renaissance block party. He told Rosemary to listen to the lutes and madrigals. He reminded her that the music she was hearing was very close to Shakespeare. Shakespeare, he said, was very close to God, the high, the spirit, and Shakespeare was also totally acceptable to the man of the lowest common denominator. Lazar told Rosemary that he and she might meet over Shakespeare since he didn't know what her other interests were. Then he asked her to make out a ticket for St. Croix for one week later than when the rest of the family was arriving. He emphasized the open return. When Rosemary told her boss he became very happy and angry simultaneously, but Mr. Lazar was a brooding man, often given to several moods on any simple day.

Mother had hired a veteran of the Korean war to be her gardener. He was blond and muscular. He was very much like the character of Hal Carter in William Inge's *Picnic*— violent and boyish. She wanted a whole yard of flowers. A semi-circle of pansies, roses, tulips, daffodils. Lazar and Leah had given her a lilac bush years ago and she wanted it surrounded by an amphitheater of colors. She wanted her grass green. She wanted the weeds pulled out every day. She did not like crab grass. She wanted Bill, the gardener, to make elaborate watering systems out of hoses on wheels and sprinklers that moved in carousels and flowed back and forth. They looked like harps and moved like hair. She was very specific. But she did not want chrysanthemums. They reminded her of death. They made her think of weddings and corsages for holidays. Nor did she want lilies. She had many meetings with Bill. His eyes were evasive. He smoked many nonfiltered cigarettes and his blistered fingers were brown with nicotine. Mother knew a certain scene in *Picnic* very well. When the old maid schoolteacher rips off the shirt of the young man. She is enraged at him and she wants him. It occurred to Mother that Bill did not like flowers.

Mother often sat by the large bay window looking out over the garden. This year the spring would not come. The glass on the window was white with age and the pure outlines of the trees would not come through. There were no buds. She hated waiting for spring. It was the not knowing. In upstate New York it seemed to come very late. Perhaps by the end of the trip to St. Croix spring would have arrived. If not, the end of winter would wait for her at the airport, like a grim relative to escort her to a funeral. She sat by her window smoking cigarettes in slow measured moves. The clouds from her smoke colored the bay window more. Her thin garden was disappearing.

Brother Simon took Leah up to his home in Harlem the night before she was leaving. It was one floor of a duplex housing project. Leah thought it looked very dark. There was a simple mattress on the floor of the living room. Brother Simon told Leah to sleep there. He went into the bedroom to be with his wife. His wife, it turned out, was only about twenty-five or twenty-six years old. Her skin was light and her hair was conked. She showed no surprise at meeting Leah. Leah knew now Simon's wife was a hooker. She lay back on the mattress and smiled to herself. She did a little song. She sang, "Kari Kari, I'm an asshole." She fell into a sweet sleep—Brother Simon was playing an ascending line on his saxophone from the kitchenette.

Lazar had no beachwear. He sent a gypsy boy who lived in the back of the newspaper stand to buy him a rubber raft, an inflatable tube, goggles and snorkel gear from F A O Schwarz. Lazar himself went to Saks Fifth Avenue by taxi and walked slowly to the men's sportswear section. He bought swimming trunks and matching terry-cloth robes and color-coded sunglasses for his various costumes:
—mirrored goggles for his sporting man,
—thin black aviator-style for the undercover rock-and-roll star,
—silver-rimmed with strawberry-tinted lenses for the Hollywood executive,
—wire frames for the poet.
Lazar put his purchases on Father's charge and taxied back downtown. When he reached his storefront home, he found he'd left all the shopping bags in the taxi. He called Western Union and sent a telegram to the Yellow Cab Company—

EMERGENCY
VITAL CLOTHING FOR NEW WRITER ACCIDENTALLY LEFT IN
ONE OF YOUR TAXIS. PLEASE INFORM AT ONCE. CRUCIAL FOR
BUSINESS TRIP.

Lazar put his phone number at the bottom of the telegram. He waited several hours for the cab company to call and then fell asleep.

When Leah arrived at the Gentle Winds Resort Villas, Mother was asleep in a closed-off room. Father said she'd been fearful on the plane and had demanded to get off in the middle of the runway. Father was delighted to see Leah, although she looked very pale and did not look him in the eye. He asked if they might go for a walk on the beach and then he'd make no more demands of her. She changed into Indian sandals and a long faded purple antique skirt. Her feet were dirty and toenails raw. She wore a tank top with some rainbows and birds on it. Her neck was long like a bird's and gray from lack of washing. She and Father went out on the long beachfront. Father tried not to stare at her.

"How is your music?" asked Father. Leah replied she was getting into jazz.

Father was wearing plaid pants and a striped top. Leah remembered that he never knew how to match clothes. She told him he didn't match. He laughed and tried to strike a pose. "Hey I think I look jaunty," he said. Leah felt disgusted. She said nothing.

Just then the waves were pushing forward and back on the beach and running all the seashells hard onto the shore. They banged into Father's and Leah's feet and they both jumped. The other tourists were lying around on orange woven plastic resort chairs. Leah noticed how fat most of them were. One lady in a black one-piece bathing suit had a huge ball-shaped belly and a protruding ass. She looked as if she were built in two sections. One man was white as chalk and his stomach and chest were so fat and loose that he looked as though he were wearing his skin. The whole beach looked planted with fat bulbs of people. Some of them were greasy with suntan oil, some of them were beet red. One lady had her hair combed back like a nineteen-fifties hood; she had a nose job that pushed the tip of her nose into its bridge; she wore mirrored sunglasses and her tan was black-green.

"Isn't anyone here skinny?" Leah asked her father. Even Father was spreading—his plaid pants bulged and the zipper flap was open from the pressure of his stomach.

Father didn't answer. He got angry. He said, "Everyone around here is having a good time."

Leah wished Kari were with her and that he could see. For one thing, he was incredibly skinny, and for another he would've put the scene into a proper place for her. "These fat people are keeping this side of the earth balanced right in its rotation," he would've said. Or he would've collected different sized seashells and made a little skull orchestra by banging them. She didn't think about Simon.

Some black women were moving up and down the beachfront selling tie-dyed dresses and baskets. They had the clothes spread out across their arms to demonstrate the patterns. They looked like colorful sailboats, leaning into the tourists and making their sales pitches. Their teeth were sparse and orange when they smiled. One small lady with grayish hair and big eyes was after Father. Her West Indian accent was whining and provocative. She repeated half indecipherable phrases:

"You want some nice dress . . . tie . . . dress . . . basket . . . you take home?" or "You like the sun? Take pretty dress home from the sun!"

Father bought four dresses from her and two baskets.

"What do you need those for?" asked Leah.

"They might look very nice on you," said Father. He paused. "Maybe your mother would like one," he said. He was silent for a moment and then made a small growling sound in his throat.

"How is she?" asked Leah.

"The spring is late," said Father. "When the spring is late, it's like some cruel purposeful act I've inflicted upon her." He made the growling sound again.

"It is lovely here," he said, looking out over the sea. "Maybe she'll go for a walk or take a taxi into town and buy perfume."

Leah felt tiredness come over her. "I need to take a walk by myself," she said to her father. He looked angry.

"You promised," she said quickly.

"Yes yes," said Father, "but for godsakes at least take a swim."

Leah watched Father walk toward the villa. He waddled in his plaid pants. The bottom of him was shaped like a fat bowl. His feet were small in their white rubber beach shoes.

"It's nice here," she shouted after him. He turned around and waved. His hair was getting streaked with gray. Leah went to the edge of the ocean and pulled off her tank top. Then she took off her skirt. She went in with just her underpants on.

There was a young black boy floating in an inflated inner tube. He bobbed up and down and looked peaceful. The lids on his eyes were heavy and he smiled at her. He did not look at Leah's breasts. Leah kept herself respectfully covered by the soft ocean water. It felt soothing and private.

"Hey," she said to the boy.

"Hey," he said back.

"Where'd you get the tube?" she asked him.

"A friend of mine," he said. His accent was strong.

"You want to try?"

Leah refused. She was afraid to expose her body too much. She treaded water near the boy. She saw he was fifteen or sixteen year old.

"How long have you been out here?" Leah asked him.

"All day," said the boy and he smiled.

"What do you think about all day?" asked Leah.

"I float like this," said the boy and he giggled.

In a gentle burst it started to rain.

"The sea above and the sea below," said the boy. He laughed again. "Hey, lady," said the boy, "you want to buy this tube or what?"

"No," said Leah. She got embarrassed and swam toward the shore. The tide pushed her hard onto the beach and the shells got thrown up against her ankles and made little cuts. There was a black girl her age standing next to her when she stood up.

"You have to dance with it, you know," said the girl. "It has a way of chasing you if you don't pay attention." The girl was extremely tall and thin. She had an elegant face. She curled and uncurled herself in stretching standing positions. She looked like a black swan. She looked at Leah's ankles with amusement, but didn't say anything. Leah quickly put on her clothes.

"Wouldn't you like your hair plaited?" asked the girl.

Leah felt her long, thick sticky blond hair. She'd seen women in Simon's music group with twenty or thirty braids and it looked beautiful.

"I bring my own beads," said the girl.

Leah agreed and said she'd go to the villa, wash her hair, and meet the girl on the beach. The girl's name was Romita, but for some reason Leah was having trouble remembering it even as she was being told. The girl quoted her an extravagant price in American dollars and Leah agreed. She was sure Father was wanting to spend money. As she walked toward the pink stucco villa her chest tightened with fear. She was certain Mother would be awake. She had no greetings for her. She could not remember Mother in the same way Romita's name kept skipping from her consciousness. The air was wet from the rain and smelled of mint. Leah's chest was irritated from the swimming; she let herself into the villa and began coughing—a deep repeated cough. Mother was reading on the turquoise couch in the living room.

"What a greeting," said Mother.

Leah could not stop coughing.

Mother stood up slowly, came over and patted Leah on the back.

"Some cold you have there," said Mother. She seemed nervous and shy. She was thinner than Leah remembered her. Her face was sweeter. Leah gave her a small hug. Mother stood still in it.

"You ought to lie down," said Mother.

Leah lay down on the couch. It was hard foam rubber covered with motel upholstery. Leah saw the inside walls were all white stucco, but that the kitchen was decorated in bright enormous polka dots.

"Charming decor," said Mother.

She lay down opposite Leah so her feet were at Leah's

shoulders. Mother lit a cigarette and smoked slowly. She looked past Leah, through the big sliding doors of the porch, out to the sea.

"It was raining," said Mother.

"Yes," said Leah. "But it'll soon stop. It's amazing how it can rain at exactly the same time the sun is out. I don't understand that scientifically at all."

"It can rain on these islands," said Mother.

Leah was wheezing. She knew a shower would help her breathe. However she didn't want to interrupt this moment between herself and Mother.

"You can go on reading if you like," said Leah.

"No," said Mother. "It's nice just to look at you." Mother looked at Leah with a half-mocking–half-serious expression.

"You always have been very beautiful," said Mother. "And your body is developing into a woman's body." Mother took a long drag off her cigarette and looked out the window again.

"I don't suppose it will rain the whole time we're here," she said.

Leah told her mother she was going to take a shower to clear her chest. Mother picked up her book—an Agatha Christie mystery—and began to read. As Leah retreated to her room Mother said, "It was so kind of you to have joined us."

What was it Lazar had always said? Leah was trying to get the narration straight in her head. His monologue was always about Katharine Hepburn and Mother. How Mother was always moving lightly through dim rooms filled with antiques. How Mother was always setting herself up in angles so they'd see her profile. Mother's slight English accent. Her white handkerchiefs. Her changes of costume. How Mother's jaw was always set in a particular fashion so her words came out through her teeth. How Mother was as fragile as lace. Mother was Katharine Hepburn. Now she was doing a

movie about a tropical island. And she was waiting for a
ruddy yachtsman to find her. He would have come back
from deep-sea fishing. He would've caught a marlin, a bar-
racuda. They would drink on his yacht. He would tell her
how wasted and unappreciated she'd been until he'd found
her. He would run his boat full power and her rain hat
would blow off.

Leah ran out onto the beach. It was late afternoon, but
long before sunset. The wind was picking up on the island
and making rushing sounds in the palm trees. The tide was
bigger. Leah dashed up and down the beach breathing in
the clean air. She kicked up sand. She ran backwards, her
legs in front of her. She ran sideways. She was not sweating.
She went into a spin arms out to both sides. There were no
fat people on the beach. There was one mangy dog. His tail
wagged flap flap in a puzzled way. Then she jumped up and
down and did a soft shoe in the sand. When she was done
Romita was waiting for her. Romita did not say if she saw
Leah's dance. Leah did not care. She sat herself down on one
of the orange beach chairs and picked through Romita's box
of transparent plastic beads for some coherent colors. She
settled on red, white and yellow. Romita began pulling her
hair, section by section, and braiding it from top to bottom.
The pain was excruciating.

Leah and Father went diving together. Mother went
along, but she said she'd stay on the boat and read. They
went on a speedboat with two black guides named Howard
and Charles. The two young men were Leah's age and they
were muscled and beautiful. Leah was beginning to get color
on her face and her hair in its multitude of braids was
streaked blond and red. Mother was becoming a deep,
creased brown.

The speedboat went first to Buck Island, which was a kind
of underwater zoo. Tourist boats from all over were lined up

and people with snorkel masks swam in masses taking in the fish below the surface. Mother told Father that they may as well have gone to Fifth Avenue with all the people there but he said it was one of a kind in the world. Leah bobbed along with the masses and took in the angelfish, the fire coral, the fish with iridescent blue stripes. Mostly she looked at other people with their black fins, their bright orange life preservers, their wide eyes behind their masks. She felt as if she were in a pile of bodies after some kind of disaster. She couldn't see where Father was. There were little brown wooden signs with white lettering in three languages identifying all the fish. Leah didn't know how the fish knew to stay near their markers without floating accidentally into the next realm. By the time she finished the tour route she was very chilled and her chest was filling up again.

On deck Mother was still reading. She had a drink beside her. She'd hardly lifted her head. She did not ask how it had been. Father was enumerating each fish he'd seen to Howard and Charles. The next stop their boat made was on an isolated white beach. There were rocks up the hill and dense shiny foliage. The water was completely clear. Charles and Howard explained that this was where they would have a picnic lunch after the dive. They would dive only a few hundred yards from the shore.

Leah and Father and the boys put on the scuba gear and fell into the sea. Mother stayed on the boat. Leah watched her father as he fell downward toward the coral, his gray hair standing up straight, his eyes looking surprised behind the mask. He had a camera and he flashed it at her, at Howard and Charles, at the long fish that hovered near them; but the camera looked as if it were flashing on Father. Leah was not interested anymore in the coral or the huge schools of fish. She was watching Howard and Charles as they dived down, picked up shells, chased after little turtles, did somersaults, took their mouthpieces away—dived free-form. They seemed as much a part of the landscape as the waving black sea urchins and scooting tiny red fish. Father was trying to show Leah something—he kept signaling her to look at what he was seeing. She nodded in agreement and kept her eyes on Charles and Howard.

On the beach Father talked rapidly to Mother about the diving. Mother had drunk many glasses of whiskey and was staring quizzically at Father as if she were trying to remember where she'd met him. Leah was too frightened of Mother to say anything to her. She excused herself and took a walk. She climbed up the sandy hillside to the rocks. There were orange and green flowers with heads like birds. Behind the rocks she saw Charles and Howard, collecting shells dry and white from the sun. They explained to her that they could sell them for a lot of money to the duty-free shops in the ports. She followed them farther away from the beach and when the white sand and ocean were completely out of sight, she took the bottom of her bathing suit off and let each one of them make love to her while the other watched. She comforted them and said she wouldn't tell the Tourist Office— she said she wanted it. She stood with her back against a tall rock and let them be with her while they stood. Their legs were hairless like Simon's and they moved on her the way they swam—easy and experienced. When it was over they gathered up the shells, and went back to the beach. Mother was sitting very still with her back to Leah. Father had gone in some direction to find Leah. When he returned his face was very red and he was winded. Also his shoulder was blotched and a purple color. He'd been stung while swimming by a jellyfish with a green stripe. The boys gave him some antiseptic ointment. Nothing was said. They rode back to the resort dock silently. Leah was interested in the features of the island. It looked like a jungle with volcanoes. At one point Mother lowered the book and looked Leah straight in the eyes. Leah noticed Mother's eyes were getting yellowish around the pupils, but she couldn't decipher Mother's expression. It brought a chill to Leah and she began to cough violently.

"You ought to watch that cold," said Mother. She went back to her book.

There was a cross-island road which went through the rain forest in St. Croix. It was a steep and narrow drive. For miles there was nothing but sandy jungle and every now and then the ruins of a sugar plantation. Leah rented a white car and set out by herself. She hoped to run into Romita or Charles or Howard. But the solitary drive was good for her. She could pull up to the side of the road, step into an expanse of jungle, see a lizard or a dark bird. She could clear her mind. At one moment she stuck her fingers down her throat and made herself vomit. The hot air made her want to purify herself. She did some yoga breathing, some dancing, some calls, some of Brother Simon's African bird sounds and click noises. She missed New York. She missed Kari. But she was healing her body on this trip. And she was gathering information. Little bugs whizzed into her legs and stuck into her. She tried not to mind.

It was said in the local papers that this road was prey to wild island robbers, young men who attacked tourists both for their money and because the racial climate on the island was getting strained. It was said that they raped women. One of the white women who ran the diving shop had been raped and robbed. There had also been twelve murders in the last months in the town. Black youths raging at white merchants. Leah could understand this rage. She didn't want to be afraid. She was taking the afternoon to think about her brother Lazar—who would be arriving the next day. How should she greet him? They had so many ritual hellos and goodbyes. Each contained its own set of rules.

Leah heard footsteps all around her. She looked about and saw a group of six or seven black young men walking through the jungle. They were young and they were laughing. Leah figured they might be drunk. She knew she couldn't hide so she stood where she was in tight blue-jean shorts, her tank top, and a head full of braids.

The young men spotted her and spoke to each other in patois. Their voices were gruff and mocking. Leah was waiting for the worst. One of the voices called out to her, "You ought to go home, you know. This is a dangerous jungle—lions and bears eat you." The voice translated its message into patois for its friends and there was more laughter and then the fading of their presence.

Leah walked back to the car and locked herself in—all four doors. She lay her head on the steering wheel and began to cry. She cried with long moaning sounds and the wheeze in her chest made it deep and full of chords. She didn't know why she was crying. When she finished she started up the car and drove toward an isolated riding stable on a cliff at the end of the jungle road. Her eyes were blurred and it made the jungle seem soft and wet as if just covered by a rain.

Lazar arrived in St. Croix dressed as a Vietnam war veteran. He wore a green private's shirt, camouflage-patterned pants. He had a green scarf tied around his long hair as if he were a renegade Green Beret. He had two aluminum nametags strung around his neck, both with the customary indentations on their edges used to shove them between the teeth of the dead. Lazar had both his artificial legs off and zoomed down a ramp in a new electric wheelchair. He had leather bracelets around his wrists and beads around his neck. He'd sent his prostheses through baggage in a leather stand-up bass case. He was wheeled through air customs by a sympathetic American Airlines representative. He asked her to stop at one of the tourist shops before depositing him and his luggage in a cab. There he bought a digital-style radio clock so he could be sure always to be in his own time.

The taxi drivers, who usually were hostile to tourists,

treated Lazar with respect. His driver's name was Willie. Willie asked Lazar how he had become injured, if he didn't mind his asking. Willie wore thick glasses and had enormous buck teeth. Lazar said it was "from a war, my good man. A definite war."

Willie said, "I never had to fight no war, you know, man. It must be hell." Lazar replied that it was hell but that it had its high points too. Lazar asked Willie if he could imagine that a war could be actually sexy. Willie said, "You know, man—deep-sea fishing can be that way. When the boat gets tipping back and forth and you don't know is the fish going to get caught or catch you."

Lazar thought this was a fine conversation and that Willie had real poetry in him. When he arrived at the villa the first thing he said to Mother and Father was, "I've brought a gentleman here whose name is Willie. I think we should invite him in. He will give us some perspective on our grief. Also, I've hired him to be my guide and bodyguard for my time spent here."

Mother looked at the incredibly ugly man pushing Lazar's wheelchair and her expression looked as if she were wondering if he was clean. The man had a slight stoop and smiled stupidly as Lazar talked, as though he were trying to tell Father that this had not been his idea at all. Willie kept nodding his head up and down, but it had no connection to what Lazar was saying.

Mother offered to get Willie some coffee. Willie brought in Lazar's luggage as well as his legs in the bass case. Father looked over Lazar's outfit and said, "What is this attire? Are you planning to go to battle?" Lazar replied that it was the proper jungle wear and none of Father's business. Father replied that it was his business what his son wore in a vacation spot with civilized humanity present. Leah heard this from her room and decided to come out. This was her usual cue. Time to rescue Lazar. She was wearing one of the island tie-dyed dresses and Romita had embroidered her hair with more beads.

When Lazar saw her he genuinely smiled. She took the tips of her fingers and brushed them gently over his straggling beard.

"A native princess," Lazar said. Lazar called Willie from the kitchenette area and introduced him to Leah.

"Your sister is very beautiful," said Willie. Mother stood behind him, expressionless, looking at Leah and Lazar. Then she said something that had been on her mind all week.

"She'd look better without the antlers and a map of the countryside woven all over her head," said Mother. "What a waste of beautiful hair."

"Nonsense," said Father.

Lazar said he wanted to go see some sights. Leah said she would go with him. Willie gratefully accepted the large tip from Father and disappeared.

Mother, Father, Leah and Lazar all went together around the winding roads of the resort area. Lazar whistled a calypso tune between his teeth. Mother kept at his side. Father was nervously naming different aspects of the foliage in the area when Lazar asked him to "cease from *National Geographic.*" They stopped at the resort pool and bar. It had round wooden tables covered by thatched umbrellas. Mother and Father ordered a drink, Lazar a milk shake, Leah ordered nothing. The pool area was crowded with the tourist clientele. Leah noticed that many of them would sneak glances at her brother.

Lazar announced he wanted to take a swim. He deftly unzipped his camouflage pants and revealed a pair of bright Hawaiian-patterned boxer shorts. He asked Leah to pull his pants the rest of the way off and she complied. Lazar pulled his skateboard from a side pocket in the wheelchair and, in an athletic gesture, dumped himself from the wheelchair onto the skateboard. Then with his one arm he pulled off his

T-shirt. Now all he wore were the boxer shorts. Mother smiled a frozen smile at him and held on to her drink. Father turned toward the bar. Leah watched as Lazar whistled a calypso tune happily through his teeth, pushed himself on the skateboard to the pool and tipped himself into the deep end. Once in the water he could not hold himself up with only the one arm. Leah watched Lazar bob up and down, gasping, trying to get to the shallow end. She jumped in after him and put her arm around his neck and dragged him to the blue-tiled steps. A fat man in a red bathing suit helped her by holding up Lazar's torso. He asked Leah if the "fella" was all right. She glared at him and then regretted doing so. Water was dripping off Lazar's beard. His glasses, which he hadn't bothered to take off, were fogged. He was smiling dreamily, leaning back, breathing heavily up and down. Leah looked at him, but did not let herself focus.

Father came around with the wheelchair and told Lazar to get in it. Lazar had no way of getting back into the wheelchair. Father asked the fat man in the red bathing suit to help lift him. The two of them were bungling it terribly, nearly dropping him. Leah hissed at them to be careful. Lazar was still smiling, eyes closed, seemingly in a trance. Leah asked Father where Mother had gone. He said back to the house. As Father and Lazar and Leah started back, Father told Leah he was sorry, that he never should have included Lazar in this vacation. Leah looked anxiously at her brother, whom her father was pushing along absentmindedly, and saw that he was sound asleep in his wheelchair, his chin tucked to his chest.

At night the ocean was very loud. It comforted Leah's sleep. The wind in the palm trees also soothed. Usually she fell into a deep state of rest, filled with epic dreams and moments of wakefulness, where her body felt comfortable against the soft bed and large pillows. Mother often walked the house at night, as she had when Leah was a child. Leah could hear her fumbling with the glass cabinets, pouring herself a drink. Or she would hear her opening and closing the screen door to the porch. One night, early in the vacation, Leah had ventured to join Mother as she looked at the huge sky, so quiet that she had hardly acknowledged Leah. Mother seemed indifferent to the night. Still the stars were magnificent. Their huge expanse and brightness made Leah want to roll somersaults on the beach and run with the wind slamming on the back of her legs. She could not any more imagine what Mother was thinking.

There was a knock on Leah's door. She recognized it.

"Pumpkin?" came the voice "Native princess?"

"Yes, Lazar," whispered Leah.

"Let me sneak into bed with you," said Lazar. "I want to discuss our grief."

"No, Lazar," said Leah. "I'm very tired. I need to sleep."

"I learned many songs to sing you, pumpkin. And you can sing some of your songs for me," said Lazar.

"Tomorrow," said Leah. "It'll be a date on the cliffs."

"We can't ignore our grief," said Lazar.

"Go to sleep, Lazar," said Leah and she rolled over on her side and listened to the pull of his heavy metal legs against the hall rug and the sound faded into the ocean and wind.

The next day Father got up very early to go deep-sea fishing. Mother and Lazar were still sleeping when Leah went outside. The sun was bright and hot. The fat people were distributed between the pool and the beach. Leah caught a glimpse of Romita and two boys sitting on a rock at the far end of the shore. She joined them. They were looking at something. A little brown bird lay puffed up in the brush around the rock. It looked like a blowfish Leah had seen pursued by a diver with his stick. One of the boys lifted the bird up scornfully and held it like a rag. He tossed it toward the ocean's sky. The bird flew level, but did not soar. It skidded midway into the mossy grass. And then it sat there, still. Its wings were humped to its eyes. The black boy called to the other in patois; his voice sounded half concerned and half angry. He was genturing toward the lump of bird. The other boy came along and lifted the bird up like a handful of dripping sand. Leah got concerned. She said, "What happened to the bird?"

Romita answered her in a tone that was not empty of sorrow. She said, "Oh they were playing and now there's trouble. That's a savage bird, you know. They caught him and it humiliated him, you know. He'd rather die than admit he's been touched by a human. He won't fly now. You know, he's vexed. He wants to die—in himself, you know. He's so vexed he got caught he'd rather die than fly. That's a savage stubbornness. That's a bird who's all inside itself."

The two black boys walked away arguing between the two of them. Leah asked what they intended to do with the bird. She felt fearful.

"Oh nothing much" said Romita. "They'll put him in a cage, feed him, let him be until his pride comes back. You know. Then they'll let him go."

Leah asked Romita if she would help undo the plaits she'd done the week before. Romita was unhappy to see her work so impermanent, but she agreed for the money. Leah's hair billowed straight out in frizzy waves. Her scalp felt looser and it felt good to have the softness all over her back and shoulders. She kicked along the sand, running again, jumping, glad to be accompanied by the wind from her hair. The tourists were blurs in her eyes, as was Romita, the hotel, the sea—all she saw was her own ring of yellow hair and the red from the sun. She knew she would go back to the villa, write an appropriate note, get a taxi and fly back to New York to Kari and Simon and her music and her own solitary dance. The black kids were laughing at her on the beach as she continued to romp and kick up shells. It didn't matter. She was not happy, but she was moving.

23

Ending

Though it had been several months since St. Croix, and her life had moved off into a totally separate sphere, it was still Leah they came for. The lady who owned the Bowery music school and whose floor she slept on, came to her late in the night and sat her up by grabbing both her shoulders. She'd heard the lady's bracelets jangling in the empty loft first and went into a dream of a camel caravan. Then the lady sat her up. "The police are here," the lady said. Her West Indian voice sounded afraid. The lady was black so it was only her eyes she saw and the lady always smelled of musk. Leah mumbled something about not having done any drugs for years, but the lady didn't say anything because she already knew why the police had come and she was fretful and sorry and didn't want to say anything herself. Leah always slept in a T-shirt and jeans because she never knew who would be coming into the space to practice or at what time and didn't want her students to see her without clothes. But she couldn't find her shoes under her sleeping bag so the lady gave her a pair of Indian sandals. They walked down to the office together and Leah saw two policemen—both in their mid-forties, one bald, the other with red hair—looking out a window that had bars on it because there were so many robberies. She was very sleepy from playing for dance classes all day long and giving conga lessons. The lady turned on the lights to her office and Leah saw the drums from all over the world and the diplomas and the pictures of famous people who had come to visit the school and give the poor kids en-

couragement. The policemen didn't turn around when the
lights went on and they didn't turn around when Leah was
almost right next to them and then she knew why they had
come too and she squeezed the hand of the lady, who said,
"You'll tell me if you need anything—*anything.*"

Then the redheaded policeman who had a little mustache
asked Leah if her name was Leah Lazar and did she have a
brother whose name was such and such Lazar and was he a
crippled man who lived around the same neighborhood.
Leah asked the lady for a cigarette and she got a long Benson
& Hedges and the bald policeman lit it and she answered
them and said yes she had a brother and was he in trouble or
was he hurt though she knew the answer as if she'd been
born with it in her and it had been waiting for years to explode in front of her just like this at this moment in a small
dark room full of strangers. Then the redheaded policeman
told her to sit down or asked her why didn't she sit down because moments like these were difficult and Leah thought
that this moment was more difficult for him than her because she knew the outcome of the story, had always known
it and he was just starting it, just a poor character dropped
in by chance. But she knew she had to hear him out because
only then would she know for sure, and it was then that she
became terrified because she had only wanted this truth to
be a fear, an imagining, and it was about to become fully
real. The red-haired policeman said that a man had been
found dead in an alley they didn't know what of, probably of
bad drugs, maybe some poison, maybe starvation, perhaps a
heart attack—there was no evidence of violence. The man
had no identification on him but word around had it that
this young man in his twenties was this such and such Lazar
and his sister taught in the music school nearby. And now
came the tough part, said the red-haired policeman. They
wanted to know if she would identify the body, although
there was a phone right there and she could certainly

call her parents and have them fly down and do the identifying if it would be too much for her.

Leah instantly said she would do the identifying because she wanted this first and last moment with Lazar, needed it, deserved it and knew it was a show at which he would want her to officiate. It was late October so the lady gave her a Guatemalan poncho and the lady herself put on a mohair cape though both of them still wore sandals without socks. The bald-headed policeman who hadn't said anything said they had a car waiting outside and they would take her right away. It was almost dawn. Markets and delis were getting their deliveries and the bums were awake from the cold. She and the lady walked the block to the police car with everyone greeting the lady and the lady sweetly giving everyone a good morning and no one able to look Leah in the eyes. There had been a light, early snow and it got onto Leah's toes and in between her toes and the cold felt good and it was the pain on her feet that almost made her cry, but she did not cry, not yet. The garbage trucks were moving around the neighborhood like white monsters and the people who owned delicatessens were unloading big dead fishes and piles of vegetables.

The two policemen got into the front of their car and Leah and the lady got in the back. The streetlights were still on and the sky was becoming gray. The tires of the car pressed patterns onto the thin snow and the bald-headed policeman drove too slowly, uncomfortable like a man told to walk quietly. The lady sat beside Leah and did not touch her or say anything because she knew exactly how to be since this was hardly new to her, being who she was, living where she did, having gone through this sort of thing many times in her life, what with the jazz musicians and troubled kids and heartbroken artists who frequented her school. So they arrived at the morgue, which had a front like a big public high school and two tall front doors, and Leah asked the lady to

please stay in the car and not come with her. And she went
into the building walking between the two men in uniform,
small with her head bowed like a child about to light a private candle in an old empty church, full of dread, full of responsibility, unable to turn around; and the lady in the back
of the police car pulled her cape around her, closed her eyes
and wondered what light would be gone from or given to the
girl's face when she walked back through the two enormous
doors.

24

A Music Lesson

The next day Leah was taken on an excursion. The West Indian lady was pulling her down Second Avenue toward a loft building. The West Indian lady had a ring with so many keys that they jammed each other around the whole circle. She was dressed in a long skirt from the bedouin tribes of Lebanon. Her top was purple lace from an antique shop in Paris. On her head she wore a beaded cap that half covered her massive gray Afro. The West Indian lady had so many holes pierced in each ear that some of them were cut right through the lobes and couldn't hold the circles and studs and bangles she wore. Her eyes were large and Indian and dark and full and she stared at Leah with such intensity that often Leah had no response. Now the West Indian lady was opening the metal door to a loft off the avenue and Leah was apprehensive about spending time alone with this woman who employed her. But the woman had said they *had* to go, and these kinds of orders were never met with denial. No one ever could refuse. In the time that Leah had taught at the West Indian lady's music school she had never learned anything really about her employer—everything was sensed, implied, as if the music itself were an astrology made of sounds that one moved to and lived by.

The loft was a clear empty factory floor redone with shiny wooden floors and only one small couch in the middle. Leah didn't know whose loft it was but there were instruments lying around everywhere, instruments such as she had never seen. She had dreamed of such instruments, and read about them, but she had never thought she would see them. On one wall there was a gong and the gong covered the wall. Its mallet was as tall as Leah and its head was the size of a human head.

"It's from Tibet. Hit it," said the West Indian lady, "and you will . . ." Her arms made a circular motion that implied moving through moons, Saturn's rings, down caverns, into souls, and her arms kept going around and around as if once Leah heard this gong she would never stop hearing it.

Leah turned abruptly and saw a line of drums. Some had faces of lions carved on them, some had bald-headed, pointy breasted women; there were snakes and birds, and one drum had words written on it in letters that looked like pictures— the drum was bright red and the size of an enormous caldron.

"Japan," said the West Indian lady and she walked along the row of drums as if introducing a line of eager well-behaved children.

"Mali." She touched each head. "India, Navajo, Java, New Guinea—*hit* one, baby," said the West Indian lady.

But Leah was uncertain. Because it was clear to both of them that a kind of deafness had set in. Whereas she had arrived at the school full of energy, alive with games for the students, brilliant in the ways she taught guitar, long before Lazar's death she had come to flounder. The dance instructors who had so eagerly requested her to play drums or chant or invent sounds for their classes now requested other accompanists. And Leah's guitar students were falling off—they either played better than she did or were no longer inspired by her. When Leah thought about it, she imagined she'd been dying along with Lazar; giving up with him in unison. Instead of fighting, as she'd wanted to and wanted him to.

Leah smiled at the West Indian lady, but her eyes were frozen with fear. She practiced rhythms in her head—clave, samba, Indian tala, even rudimentary rock and roll—but the beats crashed together in her consciousness and there was no underlying downbeat. It kept speeding up. It did not keep, like a heartbeat.

"This man," said the West Indian lady, "went somewhere collecting these instruments. Often, you know, he has people over and they make an orchestra. Oh it would not be acceptable to the New York Philharmonic, but it is *your* kind of orchestra."

Leah looked at the medieval wind instruments hung from the ceiling like royal statues. There was a great bass recorder and a wooden contrabassoon; there was an English hunting horn, an antique viola da gamba. She thought she heard what they sounded like together but her mistakes of the last weeks washed over her imaginings and left her blank. She heard the little dancers shrieking, "We can't *dance* to her beat." She heard her saxophone partner whispering at her, "Leah, where are you?"

"Try one, baby," said the West Indian lady, "any one— get yourself started. These sounds—they have a kind of magic, you know. Once they get inside you they'll . . ." Again she finished her sentence with a gesture that showed waves and a kind of churning flame. Her hands moved up and down.

They didn't talk about the death of Lazar because they did not communicate directly. They talked with objects, jobs and sounds. So many jazz musicians and young actors and hopeful rock singers had overdosed lately, or been killed in violent careless accidents, that Leah knew that Lazar was a vague statistic to this lady who had seen everything and lived many lives before (she said). It was Leah's gradual loss of music that seemed to disturb the lady profoundly. Leah couldn't explain out loud her sudden fall from grace. She wanted to tell the lady, "I've been busy dying with my brother," but she thought it sounded insane. The West Indian lady had planned a tour for Leah through Indonesia, Korea and Africa to collect instruments and learn music to teach at her school. The West Indian lady had no money but had a method of getting plane tickets and free places to stay for her protégés all around the world. Every time she brought the trip up Leah found herself thinking that Lazar wouldn't see the world. He would never even get to San Francisco, as he had planned, to do a stand-up comic act and eat steamed dumplings in Chinatown. These facts moved dumbly through Leah's thoughts without feeling or voice. She and the West Indian lady were standing silently and uncomfortably in the middle of the loft. And Leah knew if she didn't respond soon—in some active way—the West Indian lady would have to move on, because her generosity couldn't linger; she had too many needy people hovering around her like clouds around the sun.

"This place is a little overwhelming," said Leah.

"Overwhelming?" said the West Indian lady. "But all these sounds are inside you. I heard them the first time I saw you play your little guitar. And when you picked up my old drum, you remember, from India? It was as if you'd been born there." Leah tried to remember one pattern she'd played on that drum. Or why the deep sound that came from the black spot in the middle had moved her so. When you put talcum powder on it and hit it in a certain way it bounced—it sounded like a hippopotamus. She'd laughed and kept that sound going while her other hand made a forest of animals that accompanied it. Now the impulse was cut off. She hit drums—they sounded flat. The thought of drums was empty. She was cut off; she didn't have a clue as to why.

Then the West Indian lady began to do something Leah had never seen before. Like a jester she began hitting the drums herself, making wide eyes and showing Leah the beats with her head. Everyone knew the West Indian lady was no musician. She danced beautifully with no form or training, but she had no feel for the music she had given to so many people in her life. Her drumming was comical and awkward, but she pretended to be possessed by the sounds she was making. She was like an African goddess out of sync, her bracelets jangling, her long nails clicking on the wrong beats. And this incredibly generous gesture toward Leah—which seemed motherly and sexual and helpless all at once—this concert given by this mysterious powerful lady pounded in Leah's ears and built up in her an unbearable tension. She put her fists to her ears and began to cry.

"I can't, I can't, I just can't. I'm sorry," cried Leah. She swayed back and forth in pain as if she were dancing to the terrible music.

The West Indian lady stopped playing and gathered the sobbing girl into her arms. Leah felt all the layers of muslin and silk. The amber beads pressed against her chest as the West Indian lady held her and she felt the bracelets on her head as her hair got stroked and she smelled the odor of the African musk and the woman put her smooth, cool black face against Leah's tears.

"Shh, shh," said her teacher.

Leah cried there for a while. But she knew she couldn't cry long. The West Indian lady required pride. So Leah pulled herself away and looked around the loft. Her eyes settled on the Tibetan gong, the size of one wall.

"I want to hit that," said Leah and the lady smiled at her and told her to go ahead. Leah stood still for a moment, afraid she was going to be left alone. She was tired of empty rooms and concerts for herself, but had no words to ask her teacher to stay. As if reading Leah's mind, the West Indian lady sat herself on the floor, her long skirts making hoops around her, and clapped her long black hands. "Now where's *my* concert?" asked Leah's teacher. She was clapping impatiently and her numerous bracelets added to her noise. Leah felt shy, but encouraged. She went over to the gong and took its big, fuzzy mallet and began swinging with both hands. The pulsing sound of the gong was low and vibrating. It had overtones that made full chords. Leah kept hitting at it, hearing more and more every time the mallet banged the metal. She kept looking over at her teacher to see if she was still there, and she was. Leah's whole body was into it, half music, half baseball. She felt energized. She ran over to a couple of hand-carved, long ceremonial drums and began pounding them with her palms and fingers. Now the West Indian lady was very still, just smiling and nodding her head up and down as if Leah were making a statement and she was agreeing. Leah ran over to the antique contrabassoon and blew hard on it, her cheeks bulging and her ears crackling from the strain. It squawked like a duck and Leah laughed. Her teacher laughed with her. She kept blowing on it until she got a pure long tone. Leah was racing around the loft. She tried the metal bowls of the gamelan, the wood-block from Mexico. She pounded on the large round drum from Japan. She had two mallets and pounded on both sides as if she were leading a parade. Seated on the floor, the West Indian lady had lit a cigarette and was rummaging through her cluttered, beaded handbag for phone numbers and her appointment book. After a while she said, "Well, Miss Thing could stay here all night, but her mama's got to run a school." Leah had worked up a sweat and the West Indian lady gave her a Kleenex which smelled of powder and was covered with lipstick. She wiped Leah's face, then opened the door in a grand gesture as if ushering out an honored guest.

All the sounds were still pounding in Leah's ears and now she heard the jangle of her teacher's large key ring as she locked the door to the loft. "It's there anytime you want it," said the West Indian lady to Leah. "We just have to keep living, that's all." Leah gave her teacher one last hug as they stood at the top of the loft building's steep stairs. Her long messy hair got caught in the woman's hoop earring. They laughed and cried for help as they carefully disentangled themselves.

25

Reincarnation

Leah walked east on Seventh Street past the occult book-store and Indian restaurant. She was wearing a pair of blue jeans and her hand was in one pocket, checking for a little key with a grubby string tied around it. She turned the key over and over, feeling its lumpy shape, making sure it didn't fall out. Lazar had been dead two weeks and this key had just arrived in the mail. There was a note with it; the paper was ripped from a lined spiral notebook.

"Please clean out some of his things," said the note and Leah had waited a few days before making the walk to the storefront which Lazar had used as his hideout during the last part of his life. Leah counted. She was now nineteen. Lazar had died at twenty-four. He'd been bumming around this neighborhood for at least a year.

Leah had never been inside Lazar's storefront and she dreaded the trip. She was also curious. All his homes repre-sented poetry to her. They were messy and full of metaphors. She wondered who had sent her the note. The East Village as usual was filled with gypsies, bums, merchants, and art-ists. A couple of street musicians hung out on a doorstep playing incoherent blues—one with an electric guitar plugged into a cheap amplifier, another with an out-of-tune harmonica. They were junkies and they were not listening to what they were playing. The guitarist looked up and ac-knowledged her as she walked by. "Hey," he said. "Long live Lazar." Leah wondered how this guy knew she was Lazar's sister. She cringed at the thought that Lazar had a community who knew him and knew what she looked like. Perhaps they disapproved of her because she'd lived so near by and had never come to visit. She wanted to tell the guitarist that she'd had to take some distance because she needed to rest, but she looked at the stoned hippie and told herself she was insane for worrying. A couple of fat women were slapping the dust off a rug. They wore flowered scarves around their bleached hair and their cotton dresses were soaked in sweat. They spoke to each other in Ukrainian and as Leah passed them, they nodded solemnly and talked in low tones. Leah wanted to ask who'd sent her the key and the note, but again she was afraid someone would want to know why she hadn't been to her brother's house even once, or why no one had come to tell Lazar's neighbors what had happened to him. "Why he was buried with full civilian middle-class honors," Leah said to herself. "There were wreaths and flowers and gefilte fish, a rabbi, a sermon, and each cousin put a rose on his coffin. Then he was lowered down as if off a ship. You would have been proud." Leah tried to convince herself that nobody would care; but she knew better. Lazar made a village wherever he went.

She arrived at the door of the storefront and saw that there was a gypsy boy of about nine sitting on the stoop. He seemed quite at home and not at all surprised to see her. How romantic, thought Leah. And how typical.

"I'm Lazar's janitor," said the child. "The landlord wouldn't let me use the key after Lazar kicked so I sent for you. Loretta's probably dead by now; you sure took your time answering."

"I was out of town," said Leah. She struggled with the padlock on the gate and couldn't get it to budge. The gypsy kid got the whole contraption free in one movement. He started to open the main door and inexplicably Leah became enraged. "Get out of here," she shouted at the child. "I want to go through the door first."

The boy got sulky. He threw the key at her. "What the fuck, lady," he said, "Loretta's probably dead anyway."

Leah didn't want to befriend the gypsy boy. She didn't want to pay debts or hear stories. She didn't want to be generous and offer him her brother's clothes. She didn't ask him who Loretta was. She told him just to go away and to leave her alone.

"I'm the only one Loretta will come to besides Lazar," whined the boy.

"What the fuck, kiddo," said Leah. "She's probably dead anyway—whoever she is." Leah was shocked at her own nastiness but she was feeling a surge of enjoyment. The grubby gypsy boy seemed capable of taking all kinds of abuse.

"Move your ass," said Leah, "or I'll call the cops."

Leah slammed herself into her brother's apartment and was immediately sorry she'd done so. It was absolutely dark; Lazar had hung black velours across the large storefront windows. Leah couldn't find a light switch. The anxiety brought about by death took over her thinking. Who else had a key and was living there? One of Lazar's junkie friends, a tribe of murderous child delinquents? Leah found herself breathless. She'd seen Lazar buried, but now she was having a fearful hallucination. She imagined his neglected corpse lying somwhere in the room. She was afraid she'd step on it if she walked through the room to look for a lamp. She imagined the mutilated body, soft and moaning. To calm herself she opened the front door again, let in a bit of daylight. The gypsy kid was sitting calmly on the stoop, as if there had never been any exchange. "Light's on the left-hand wall," he said. Leah slammed the door again. "Goddamned mind-reading Lazar mystical bullshit," she said out loud and had no idea where her fury was coming from.

She felt her way over to the opposite wall, trembling about what she would encounter on the way and was relieved that the space seemed empty. She felt as if she were in the basement of a tomb; her unfamiliarity with the space made height and depth seem interminable. When her hands found the light switch she was both relieved and in an agony of suspense. She closed her eyes as she switched on the light. She had a picture of a frightening clutter, piles of mess, the contents of which would be full of the mystery and pain of her brother's last years. She opened her eyes slowly and was surprised to see that the room was spotlessly clean. There were cartons packed with Lazar's things, there was a mattress on the floor, but it had been stripped. The walls were bare except for the marks where posters had been Scotch-taped. There was a mop and bucket in one corner, a broom in another. Leah felt at that moment shame for the way she'd treated the gypsy boy, the Ukrainian women, the junkies. She was sure they'd done all this. She was shamed for the way they'd taken care of the real Lazar while she and her family had been burying an imaginary Lazar in a small-town cemetery that looked like a phony park. The softness passed, however, and she felt no inclination to thank anyone. "I'm allowed to be here by myself," she said aloud and then remarked to herself how often she'd been talking out loud. "Shut up," she said and rapped herself on her head.

Leah sat down on the mattress because she had no energy to examine the contents of the cartons. She examined the space with her eyes. It felt oddly like the inside of a cardboard box. The room had been cleaned almost antiseptically and Leah was glad to not have to deal with her brother's complicated atmosphere. He had been a poet, a prophet, a madman. He was a song to her. "Let's leave it that way," she said. "No more trouble. Enough with reality." She sat biting her nails, trying to figure how to get the cartons past the gypsy boy, when she heard a sound from the opposite end of the room. It was a rustling. A kind of swimming without water. "Rats," Leah said to herself. The sound became louder and more violent. It was definitely coming from the closet. Leah did not want to let a huge rat into the room, but she went toward the closet door with the broom in her hand. She heard a voice from behind the door. It was a weak voice; it creaked; it was wheezing. "My good sir," "My good Madam," it was saying. "My good sir," "My good Madam," it repeated. It was Lazar's voice being imitated. Leah opened the door and saw an enormous parrot nestled in a pile of Lazar's hats and underwear. These hadn't been removed, obviously for the parrot's comfort. The parrot was a bright forest green with orange markings. And when Leah went to look at its eyes, they blazed at her in fury. The eyes were yellow and seemed demonic. "You must be Loretta," said Leah. "Loretta," repeated the parrot and then she took off over Leah's head with incredible strength and speed. Her wingspan was vast and she blasted the bleak apartment with a flash of green before disappearing into the ceiling.

"Loretta," Leah called out. "I'm Leah, Lazar's sister."

The bird let out a throaty Oriental-sounding shriek and dive-bombed for Leah's head. Leah threw herself to the floor while Loretta took her place in the top of Lazar's closet—just out of reach.

"Call me irresponsible," sang Loretta.

Leah stayed prone on the floor, her head tucked in her arms. She was sorry now the gypsy boy hadn't come with her, and she understood why he waited so patiently outside. Obviously he'd been living there, taking care of the parrot. Maybe he was being thrown out. Once again Leah was angry. She felt no sympathy for the urchin sitting outside. She wanted to tame Loretta and take her back to her own apartment. She knew exactly after whom Loretta was named—the actress, Loretta Young. Lazar had always been fond of Loretta Young. He said she reminded him of their mother with her "'pre-death, somewhat consumptive" style of acting. Leah lifted her head cautiously from the floor. Loretta, the parrot, was strutting arrogantly on the top shelf of the closet. "Embraceable you," she said. "Embraceable you." Loretta didn't sing these phrases, but squawked them. Leah could hear her brother crooning. Leah moved very slowly toward the closet, her forearm protecting her eyes. "Is Loretta hungry?" she asked the parrot and felt stupid for her sickeningly sweet tones. "Loretta Loretta," answered the parrot and stood still for a moment staring quizzically at Leah. The yellow eyes were strange, like the crossed eyes of a Jewish zealot. They were suspicious and sad. Leah rummaged through her handbag and found an old pack of wild cherry Life Savers. She cracked one in half and put it in her palm. She held it out tentatively. "Unleavened bread," squawked Loretta and Leah snorted with laughter. Of course that would be Lazar's way of teaching a creature to identify a cracker. Meanwhile Loretta had tipped herself so her beak was centimeters from Leah's palm. Leah was excited. Then Loretta nipped hard and viciously on Leah's forefinger, making a huge gash and began dive-bombing all over the room. Leah fell to her position on the floor, felt frustrated and humiliated. "You stupid bird!" she screamed at the parrot.

"Give me your tired, your poor," recited Loretta and in the midst of raging and worrying, Leah couldn't help but admire the extent of the bird's vocabulary. Leah stayed absolutely still while her finger throbbed and her head ached. She was physically strong but she was worn out. Eventually she dozed.

She dreamed she was a drummer at a macumba ceremony in Brazil. She was drumming in a small room and there were parrots all around. There was Lazar in front of her doing a flamenco tap-dance ballet. She herself was drumming fantastically on a pair of bongos made of driftwood. "You're really getting it, sweetie," Lazar was saying. And his arms were flailing around as if he were finally doing a nightclub floor show without censorship. "Let's levitate me a bit," said Lazar, "so I can stay up in the air." But as she was watching him, Lazar began to lose his balance and fall and he seemed to be free-falling through sand and through sea and although he was still kicking and shuffling a wild kind of soft-shoe, he was also drowning and choking. Leah drummed harder and harder in the dream but that seemed to make Lazar sink deeper into a blackness. And suddenly he exploded like a show of firecrackers, into a kaleidoscope of fire and rain. And particles of him began to fall to earth like pebbles and she could hear the click click click as the pebbles fell onto the earth. Leah awoke hearing the click click click. Loretta was walking on the floor next to Leah's ear. Leah watched her suspiciously. Loretta jive-walked like a pompous black teenager in a bright green cap. "Call me irresponsible," said Loretta. "My good Madam, My good sir" said the parrot. Leah was sweated up and fearless and she threw her arm out violently to catch the bird, who screeched furiously and flew back to her nest on Lazar's underwear. Loretta seemed genuinely hurt by Leah's display of violence and curled up in the back of the closet where Leah couldn't reach, stared out with her yellow eyes and said nothing.

"Demented demented demented." Leah stood up and began screaming. She threw her arms around as if there were papers to rip or curtains to tear down. She was wanting to destroy objects in the empty, stuffy vacuum. "Everything about you is demented!" she yelled. "Everything about you has always been demented!" Loretta kept silent and her eerie yellow eyes glared out at Leah with pity and scorn.

Leah left Lazar's apartment in an angry storm. The gypsy child was still sitting on the stoop, calm and expressionless. Leah squatted down to him and talked through clenched teeth. "Listen, you," she said. "That parrot is *mine*. You understand? You are not to steal it. You are not to feed it. You are not to set foot in this apartment until I say so. You understand, you little liar?"

The gypsy child looked at Leah indifferently. "Whatever you say, lady," he replied. "Loretta won't leave the apartment anyways. Don't think we haven't tried."

"Well she'll leave with me," said Leah, and again she couldn't understand her own nastiness and yet did not stop herself.

"Good luck with that," said the gypsy boy. He showed her a huge scar on his arm. "Inside she's okay, but try to get her out the door, man—she'll eat you."

"That's because you were taking what isn't yours," said Leah and she felt like an odd proper matron and couldn't stand herself. "Did she walk around on Lazar's shoulder or what?" asked Leah.

"They was like a pirate and his lady," said the boy.

"And what does she eat?" asked Leah.

"Matzos and granola," said the boy.

Leah felt embarrassed going into the Second Avenue deli getting matzos way out of season. She ordered some apricots with the granola and some yogurt for herself to make the purchases seem more normal. The Hispanic man at the counter smiled at Leah, counted up her order and said, "Loretta likes the onion matzos better."

"Everyone knows what Loretta likes but me," said Leah and refused to exchange the box.

"Loosen up," said the clerk with a friendly smile.

"Fuck yourself," said Leah, and she was shocked, felt possessed by rage, ran out of the deli without waiting for her change.

Leah walked around the neighborhood for a while, trying to cool down, imagining herself with a beautiful green parrot perched on her shoulder. She daydreamed about taking Loretta to her music classes, to parties. She thought about buying long Indian skirts and patterned scarves that would match the pattern on the parrot's back. The East Village was noisy with the late afternoon—rock music was blaring from record stores, sirens howled, deals and laughter came and went in different languages. Leah felt despondent and left out. She felt guilty for her violent behavior. She went into a pawn shop and asked the storekeeper for a butterfly net. "A what?" sneered the old man. He was bald and wore the thick bifocals of one who is always examining jewelry. Leah mumbled again that she wanted a butterfly net.

"Lady," said the storekeeper, "I don't have a butterfly net. I got a fishing net. I don't have a butterfly net."

Leah stood at his glass counter thinking for a long time. It seemed only a butterfly net would do, but she accepted the bulky, shapeless brown fishing net as her only alternative. She paid for it, and exhausted, returned to Lazar's apartment.

She was relieved to find the gypsy boy was gone. She let herself in and easily found the light. She went straight to the closet and found that Loretta was not there. *"Damn,"* she cursed. She was positive the gypsy boy had not obeyed her and in a manic newsreel she saw herself having him arrested, taken to court, put on trial, sent to a juvenile camp. Her foul temper infected her whole body. She checked herself for dust, for bugs—she thought her blood was diseased. She lay down on the middle of the plywood floor, used the grubby fishing net as a pillow, and fell asleep.

In her dream Lazar ran a pet shop. "A fine vocation for a poet," he said to her. He took her around his store. The store was like his apartment. It was filled with tropical fish tanks, large full banana plants with parrots and mynah birds, glass cages with snakes and turtles. The turtles all had pastel maps painted on their backs like the kind Father had sent them from San Francisco when they were kids. The store smelled and it was clear Lazar wasn't cleaning up after his animals. There were raw meat and vegetables rotting in tin plates. The water in the fish tanks had a soft brown coating as if the filters were out of order. The feathers on the birds were thin and covered with mold. Leah tried to behave as if she saw nothing. "Who are your customers?" she asked Lazar. "I sell to laboratories," said Lazar, "and to Chinese restaurants." Leah couldn't find the courage to tell her brother to take better care of his animals. Even as she was sleeping she was telling herself this was a needlessly cruel dream. She was trying to wake herself. She went over to one large square fish tank and saw an enormous goldfish the size of a very large angelfish. She knew the fish was Lazar. It became lighter and lighter. "Oh no," she said in the dream and a dread came over as when she'd seen her own little pets begin to fail. The softness of the turtles' shells, the tiny sores around her parakeet's eyes. The large goldfish began to float to one side and its eyes became gray and filmy. It struggled on the bottom and kept tilting. Finally it floated to the top and became a large orange-black mass in the dirty water. Leah still couldn't wake herself. Now she was swimming in the same tank, trying to get air, trying to reach the light on the surface. The orange mass had grown and covered the whole top of the tank. It was sticky and gummy—she couldn't get through. She yelled and woke up.

Loretta was back in the closet. She was perched way forward and had herself tilted on an angle, peering curiously at Leah. "What a pal," Leah said to her. "Where've you been hiding?"

"Cry me a river," said Loretta. "Cry me a river."

Leah unpacked the granola and matzos and tried to hide the fishing net. She felt tired from her dreams. She looked at the beautiful parrot whose green feathers and wild heart-shaped head were in magnificent condition. Leah marveled at how Lazar, full of demons and hardly able to move himself, had kept Loretta so alive. She felt jealous of the parrot.

"Unleavened bread," Leah called out to the parrot. "Unleavened bread."

Loretta did not answer Leah, but began to climb cautiously down toward the pile of crumbs Leah made in the center of the floor. Leah moved away and squatted in a corner, holding the net behind her back. Loretta was starving and walked stiffly. She looked like an old lady made innocent and childlike by need. Her gestures reminded Leah of her brother who at times had been a real song-and-dance

man and who had lived out his last years as a dignified but
stiff broken doll. She let Loretta eat the food, watched the
parrot sift through the pile with her claws and pop the grain
and crackers into her mouth. When Loretta was completely
hunched over and no longer aware of Leah in the corner,
Leah sprang out and threw the net over everything. The
clumsiness of her gesture caused the food to spread everywhere and Leah was sorry for the mess but elated that she'd
caught the parrot.

Loretta struggled violently under the net and the spaces
between the ropes were wide enough that she could poke her
head through. Loretta was raging and flapping so wildly
that Leah was sure she'd strangle herself. Loretta was making awful choking sounds and screaming with such intensity
that Leah was worried a neighbor would hear. She went over
to the net, though she was terrified and guilty, and began
punching Loretta in the head. The bird went for Leah's
hands like a killer. Leah kept punching, ignoring the gashes
she was receiving and not caring if she murdered the bird.
Finally, Loretta quieted down. She seemed to give up. Leah
prayed she hadn't hurt her. Leah's hands were sore and
bleeding. Tears of rage fell over them, over the spilled food
and over the parrot, who had tucked her head into her feathers and was mumbling little squeaky sounds. "I'm sorry,
Loretta," Leah said to the parrot, and she stroked its green
back gently with her forefinger and thumb. "This really has
nothing to do with you. I'm angry at Lazar."

"Lazar Lazar," repeated the parrot.

Leah became fearful that she might have broken some of
Loretta's delicate bones. The day had been a nightmare for
her. She no longer understood what she was doing alone in
her brother's cardboard-box apartment, being rude to his
friends and tormenting his pet bird. She left the net on
Loretta and opened the door to the street. The gypsy boy
was back on the stoop. He was crying. He reminded her of a
war orphan in the streets of Beirut, his complexion was so

dark, and he wiped his runny nose on his arm. "What'd you do to Loretta?" he sobbed. "What's the matter with you, lady?" Leah sat next to the boy on the stoop and put her arm around him. She was surprised he didn't push her away, but rather leaned into her. "Lazar Lazar," he cried.

"I didn't hurt Loretta," said Leah. "I just put her in a net so you can take her home."

"Lazar'd kill you if he found out," said the boy. "Go in there and get Loretta," said Leah. "Take her home and forget I was here."

The gypsy boy ran into the storefront and appeared soon after beside Leah with the green parrot cradled between his two dirty hands. He seethed at her.

"You broke one of her wings," he cried. Leah felt chilled. The boy sat down next to her and examined Loretta tenderly. Except for the wing, which was shaking like a leaf under rain, she seemed alive and furious. She was nipping at both of them.

"Impossible bird," said Leah and she laughed with relief.

"She'll be all right though," said the gypsy boy. "Can I have her for good?"

"I said you can take her," said Leah. "Why don't you get moving?"

Leah watched the boy run down the street toward his home. Loretta looked like a green flag he was waving. Leah lit a cigarette and then went back inside the apartment and swept up the mess of matzos and granola. Then she piled the four heavy cartons of clothes and books and notebooks one on top of each other and with a heave, struggled her way out to the street. She hailed a taxi and got in, gave the address to her home around the corner and was nearly there when she remembered she'd forgotten to close Lazar's door.

About the Author

Elizabeth Swados, at thirty-one an internationally known writer, composer, and theater director, grew up in Buffalo, New York, and attended Bennington College. Her musical and theatrical career has taken her to Europe, the Middle East, and Africa and has included more than a dozen plays and musicals, an equal number of television specials, concerts, films, and four books based on the films. Her 1978 hit Broadway musical *Runaways* received five Tony nominations. Ms. Swados has received numerous other honors including a Guggenheim Fellowship, three Obie Awards, and the Outer Critics Circle Award. Her first opera, *Lullabye and Goodnight,* premiered at the Public Theater this year. *Leah and Lazar* is her first novel.